DOUBLE VISION

L.M. HALLORAN

COPYRIGHT

Cover photography from Shutterstock.com

Editing by Chelsea Kuhel

Proofreading by Judy's Proofreading

lmhalloran.com

Níl aon chinniúint ann
ach cad a dhéanaimid.

*There is no fate but what
we make for ourselves.*

PART ONE

EVERYTHING HAS A PRICE

1

NOW

ON MY EIGHTEENTH BIRTHDAY, my parents told me I was adopted. I already knew, having found the paperwork four years before. Rather than admit to picking the lock on my dad's filing cabinet, I pretended shock. Convincingly, I might add.

I told them it didn't matter, that I couldn't have asked for better parents. That yes, I forgave them for not telling me sooner, and that no, I wasn't interested in learning about my birth parents. All of which was true.

My mom was so relieved she burst into tears and tackled me on the couch, squeezing me against her ample chest like I was five years old again. That moment —smothered by her love while my stoic dad looked on with a small, satisfied smile—was perfect.

Do I think being adopted led me to this moment in time?

Not really.

Although if I'm being honest, none of what's happened would have been possible otherwise.

I sometimes wonder what my life might have been like had a different couple adopted me. A couple less loving, less honest, less good. Say, a mother who taught me to be ashamed of my body, or, conversely, to use it like currency to get what I wanted. Or a father who ruled by the fist, or drank and cheated, or taught me that I shouldn't-couldn't-can't instead of what my dad had actually taught me—that with hard work, perseverance, and an attitude of gratitude, I could do anything.

Anything.

Here in the dark, to avoid thinking about the pain, I often reminisce about that day on my parents' couch. The moment my life forever changed course. I remember the tickle of hair on my neck as a breeze moved through a nearby window. The smell of my mom's lavender perfume. The scratchy fabric of the couch cushions against my bare skin.

I remember what it felt like to be eighteen and fearless, with a belly full of dreams. The expansive feeling of possibility. The hunger for work and accomplishment.

I should have listened to their warnings.

When my mom stopped crying that day, I told them my plans. I wasn't staying in our backwoods Oregon town where my dad was an electrician and my mom a preschool teacher. Nor was I going to an in-state university, two of which had offered me hefty incentives.

Just like they'd taught me, I'd gone for what I wanted. Worked my ass off and earned it. Bursting with pride, I told them that with a combination of student loans and partial scholarships, I was going to UCLA. The first, biggest step on my road to medical school.

I mistook their silence for stunned joy, the fear in their eyes and words of caution for parental worry.

After all, how could I have known?

What were the chances?

In a world of billions, and a city of millions, the probability of finding Alexis Sharpe was next to nil.

We found each other anyway.

Alexis said it was kismet—that destiny brought us together. And despite my worship of science and logic, I believed her. I still do. There's simply no other explanation.

Meeting her was sheer magic.

And the beginning of my end.

2

THEN

THERE'S nothing glamorous about working the graveyard shift at a diner in West Hollywood. Every hour between midnight and 6 a.m. is a test of endurance, as every tourist and wannabe actor-model-director stumbles out of the nearby bars and clubs and straight into Al's Diner.

They come here because it's convenient and the food's cheap, but they also like the retro atmosphere, which makes them feel younger, hipper, and more relevant than they actually are.

Most of all, they come for the novelty of being abused

by the costumed servers. Yes, Al's Diner is one of those places—we're paid to be mean to our customers. It's not that hard, honestly. Most of them are assholes.

"Order up!"

I dodge a tray-wielding arm and pop up at the kitchen window. Raul frowns at me, his face glistening with sweat, eyes racooned by melted mascara—a look I think he cultivates on purpose.

"Girl, you look one wrong step from the grave." Fishnet encased forearms thump onto the counter between us. Lowering his voice, he murmurs, "Insomnia shit bothering you again? You need something to help you relax?"

I roll my eyes. "Yeah, a vacation."

Raul smirks, lifting his hands in surrender. Him offering me drugs to help me sleep is an ongoing theme in our unlikely, two-year friendship.

A plate breaks somewhere in the kitchen, and a line cook shouts angrily. With a final wink for me, Raul spins toward the chaos, his voice ringing out in fluid Spanish. Macho he is not, but the man has a voice that demands obedience. His weekday work is doing voiceovers for telenovelas and porn. But oddly, what he loves most is the insanity of running the diner's kitchen.

As I load up a tray with my table's order, Sammy sidles up next to me. Nosy in the worst way, she whispers, "What did Raul say to you? Did he offer you weed?

Alice says he sells weed, but when I asked him, he ignored me."

That's because you can't keep your trap shut.

I keep the thought to myself. "Nope."

"Aren't you guys friends, though?"

I heft the tray to my shoulder and give her a flat look. "Yes, we are. Any other questions, or can I deliver food to the bratty coeds at table twelve now?"

Her cherry-red lower lip juts out. "Fine, be rude."

I grin tightly. "That's what I'm paid for," I say, and I beeline for the table of sorority girls.

As I move closer to the table, I see that Stacy 1.0, 2.0, and 3.0 have been joined by Brad 1.0, 2.0, and 3.0. The booth is now a swirling vortex of drunk, barely legal hormones.

"Hey, weren't you my Biology TA?" slurs Brad 2.0, squinting as he examines my face.

I ignore him and begin slamming food onto their table. When the plates are down, I tuck the empty tray under my arm and point at the Brads.

"If you assholes want to order, now's the time. I'm not coming back unless you promise me a fat tip."

Stacy 3.0 waves me away with a haughty, "Bye, Dorothy. We'll share."

"Suit yourselves," I snap, and hustle back to the window where another order is waiting.

"Did that bimbo call you *Dorothy*?"

I glance over at Karina, whose fingers are slamming buttons on our antique, piece-of-shit cash register. "Yeah," I answer with a shrug. "Whatever. Dorothy was badass. Survived a tornado, killed a witch, wore great shoes—"

Karina's laugh interrupts me. "Okay, okay. Clearly you've heard that before." She tilts her head, studying me like one of her unfinished paintings. "I can see it, actually. The freckles, the wholesome, girl-next-door vibe. Personally, I see you more as a cross between Mary Poppins and Dita Von Teese."

I make a face. "Dita Von Teese, really? Her waist is probably the circumference of my arm."

"Bullshit," Karina retorts. "Anyway, it's more an attitude thing. Like, you *look* all innocent, and even though we all know it's an act, we still can't help believing it."

I roll my eyes and finish loading my tray.

As I walk away, Karina calls, "You coming to Frank's with me after our shift?"

I throw over my shoulder, "I'm still thinking about it."

Her loud groan makes me smile, until I see a table of newly seated customers glaring at me with bleary, entitled eyes. One of them summons me with a slowly twitching finger.

I salute him with a finger in return—my middle one

—before walking in the opposite direction to deliver table four's food.

I'M NOT the same anxious, starry-eyed girl who hightailed it out of her tiny town at eighteen. Four years later, with a BA in Biology from UCLA under my belt, I don't even recognize that girl—her smile too wide, her hair in a perpetual braid down her back, her clothes ill-fitting and drab.

That girl, and every last pair of unflattering jeans, all the multicolored skirts, clunky sandals, and boxy flannel shirts, all of it, all of her, is gone.

Los Angeles has a way of changing you. There's black magic in the sour air. Magic generated by millions of minds focused on a singular greed—*to make it* and damn the cost.

That magic seeps into you whether you want it to or not. Stay in the city a while and it begins to mold you. Stay long enough, and it will push you to breaking points you never knew existed. Push you until you shatter. Or triumph.

More than any challenge before in my life, living in Los Angeles has stripped away who I thought I was. Left behind is someone sharper and harder. Less forgiving.

More calculating. Not broken, but rearranged by disappointments and heartache.

The new version of me still believes I can do anything, but has a much better understanding of what anything costs.

I hate this city and yet, I'm grateful to it. Los Angeles taught me the difference between dreaming and doing. And I've *done*, graduating a semester ahead of schedule in the top 2% of my class.

The happiest result of all is that in three months, on August 1st, my time in the City of Angels will be over. When my lease ends on my studio apartment in Westwood Village, I'm moving. I didn't even bother applying to UCLA Medical School. By the middle of my sophomore year, I knew I wasn't staying.

The University of Washington in Seattle is my new destination. Great med school, not too far from my parents. Most importantly, there's less poison in the air of the Pacific Northwest.

A different, softer magic.

Exactly what I need.

3

KARINA GUIDES me up a winding driveway with a python-tight grip around my waist. The gate at the bottom was open, cars stacked against curbs to either side. Despite the evidence of a gathering, we're the only ones moving in the night. Not that the night is over in Los Angeles at 3 a.m.—far from it.

This isn't Karina's boyfriend, Frank's, house, where she promised we'd do a mellow night of beer, pizza, and a movie. Ohhhh no, my terminally impulsive friend decided we needed to crash a party in the Hollywood Hills. Wearing jeans and tank tops, with lank hair and skin that smells faintly of grease.

That we're going to stick out like sore thumbs doesn't bother Karina one bit. And though I wish it didn't, it does bother me. I don't like attention. Especially the kind that comes from men and women whose pets wear nicer clothes than I do.

"Why can't I ever say no to you?" I mutter.

She laughs. "Because I know what's good for you. Besides, when are we ever off early enough on a Saturday to hit a party?" She squeezes me hard and plants a kiss on my cheek. "And we haven't celebrated your graduation yet, or the fact you got into med school. I'm so freaking proud of you."

"Buy me ice cream or something," I say dryly.

She snickers. "How about some free booze instead?" Another squeeze. "We don't have to stay long. It'll be fun. Prime people-watching."

I sigh and squeeze her back. "Okay. Sorry I'm being a brat. I had some rough tables tonight."

She just nods, knowing exactly what I mean. When you spend hours on end playing a foul-mouthed, ornery woman for money, sometimes it takes a few hours to remember you're actually a nice person.

I peer at the house ahead of us. Two stories and well-lit, it's done in the Spanish style popular among Southern California's wealthy, cream stucco with ornamental ironwork over the lower windows and vines covering the arched entryway. The front door is closed, but a seductive, electronic bassline comes from inside.

"Who lives here?" I ask.

"Someone rich. Mitchell or Malcolm or something. Raul said he's in the business."

"And which of his businesses was Raul referring to?"

She laughs. "Good point. Well, given the size of this house, the fact the guy is white, and the Ferrari parked next to a Bentley over there, I'm pretty sure it's not telenovelas. So, that leaves porn or drugs."

I sigh.

I can't wait to get out of this city.

THE PARTY ISN'T AS bad as I feared, and ten times worse in other ways. Oddly enough, Karina and I don't stick out at all. The crowd is a strange mix of glazed-eyed artsy types, bohemian-chic twenty-somethings, and a small contingent of men wearing the remains of business attire.

Unsurprisingly, within minutes of arriving Karina sees someone she knows. After depositing me near a tropical fish tank with a bottle of Corona and promises to return, she disappears.

The abandonment is standard behavior for her, but I don't really mind. She's a social butterfly and I'm a loner, but it works for us—I rein her in when necessary, and she forces me out of my shell. Perfect symbiosis. And I know she'd never leave me if she thought I wasn't safe.

She's one of the few people I'll miss.

"Are you here alone?" asks a voice to my left.

I lower the bottle from my lips and glance at the speaker. Male. Mid-twenties. Too much hair gel and not enough sunblock. Still using textbook pick-up lines.

"Nope."

"Cool, cool. I'm John."

"Hi, John," I say with the bare minimum of politeness.

He clears his throat. "Can I get you another drink?"

A masculine snort draws my gaze to a nearby wall, where I discover blue eyes watching me. Or rather, watching poor John trying to flirt with me.

When the voyeur notices my regard, a dark eyebrow rises and his lips twitch behind a tumbler of liquor. His gaze narrows, cataloguing me head to toe without shame.

I return the favor.

He's older than me, late twenties or early thirties, and still in work attire. White dress shirt open at the collar, loose tie. Dark slacks and shiny black shoes. A suit and tie on a Saturday makes him a... real estate broker? Lawyer?

Short, messy brown hair. If he uses gel, it's the expensive kind. His face—now that it isn't half-covered by his glass—is all rugged symmetry and potent masculinity. He has that special scruff only certain men can master, the kind that tells the world he's too busy doing important things to shave, and his job doesn't care because he's *just that good.*

He's 100% my type. Two years ago, I would have convinced him to take me home for the night.

Two years is a lifetime ago.

I stare at him until white teeth flash in a knowing smile. The suggestion in his curved lips snaps me out of my daze. I turn back to John, who's waiting for my reply.

"Thank you, but no. I need to find my friend."

His hopeful expression crashes and burns. "Oh, okay. Maybe I'll see you later?"

"Sure," I say noncommittally, and go in search of Karina.

I don't see Blue Eyes again, or John, and it takes me an hour and three more beers to find Karina.

No one else talks to me. No one invites me into one of the back rooms, where I see people periodically disappearing, then emerging wearing newly acquired euphoric expressions.

Given the eclectic crowd, I've already surmised it's not a porn party. After watching the conveyer belt of anxious people IN, euphoric people OUT, I now know it's drugs. And definitely not pot.

Mitchell, or Malcolm, or whoever is a drug dealer. A white-collar one, from the ambiance and what looks like free party favors. A supplier, maybe.

I couldn't care less.

I'm tired, and buzzed, and need sleep. Whatever everyone is on is making for a frantic upswing of noise, so I search for a quiet corner to text Karina. Spying empty chairs out on the back patio, I head for the sliding doors.

Halfway there, someone collides with my back. A small, feminine elbow hits my ribs and a fist finds my kidney. The force rocks me forward. If not for the back of a nearby sofa, my face would've become personally acquainted with expensive Spanish tile.

Oh, *hell no.*

Ready to break a fucking nose, I whip upright and spin around.

4

"I KNOW WHAT I SAW."

My shoulders tight with defensiveness, I jam a spoonful of cereal in my mouth and aggressively chew.

"I'm not calling you a liar," Karina says as she butters a piece of toast. "All I'm saying is that you were four Coronas deep."

Raul drops into the third and final chair at the tiny kitchen table. He's freshly showered and in pajamas, ready to sleep the day away. After getting off work at the diner, he'd done God-Only-Knows-What until strolling in around ten just as Karina and I were waking up.

Cradling a cup of tea, he squints at me through the steam. "No offense, chica, but white girls like you are a dime a dozen in this city."

Karina chortles. I throw a cereal O at Raul, who dodges it easily. "Ugh, you guys are probably right."

I maneuver out of my chair and take my bowl to the sink, rinsing it quickly. As much as I want to deny their words, doubt is chipping away at my certainty.

Karina's right—I'd been pounding Coronas and things had been a bit fuzzy by the time the woman knocked into me. Plus, she'd looked right at me and hadn't even blinked. Maybe my eyes *had* been playing tricks on me.

"Thanks for letting me crash here," I say, fishing in my purse for my car keys. "And feeding me cereal. And letting me shower and borrow clean clothes."

"No problem," replies Karina through a yawn. "Call me later? Raul wants to go to that art-rave thingy out in the valley tonight. Let me know if you want to go."

I grimace internally. "I will. Have a good day off."

Karina waves and Raul pauses rolling his breakfast joint to blow me a kiss. "Go sell the rich bitches their lotions and potions."

I give him a mocking salute and let myself out of their apartment, heading down the outdoor hallway to the cement stairs at the end.

As I tromp toward the parking lot and my car, the midmorning sun hits me full force. Dense and hot, it prickles through the hair on my scalp, which makes me think of the woman's blonde hair. I try to remember if her roots had been darker, closer to my medium brown.

On the congested drive to Santa Monica, I do my best

to stop thinking about it. About her. But it's too little effort too late. She's inside my mind; I see her in every blonde on the street and in every car I pass.

I'm fixated.

Almost three years ago, when I started working at Al's Diner and hanging out with Raul and Karina, I told them I didn't do drugs, didn't even smoke pot, because I tended toward obsessive behavior. It was the truth, but it wasn't until they got to know me—particularly during exams and the months leading to the MCATs—that they realized just how obsessive I could be.

My mom calls it perfectionism. My dad calls it work ethic. Neither of them know how much worse it's become in Los Angeles, the land of *betterstrongerfaster*.

Only one thing has ever managed to subdue the monster coiled in my psyche, but it brings with it another set of dangers and repercussions. Two years ago, I learned that the hard way.

Since then, I've kept the monster at bay, distracting it with school and working two jobs.

Until last night.

Until her.

5

THE SAME DAY I graduated college, I called my second job and told the manager my new availability. She promptly started scheduling me twenty to thirty hours a week. Sunday through Wednesday I work retail, and Thursday through Saturday I work nights at Al's.

It's hell, but it keeps me busy. I like busy. I *need* busy. Besides, my student loans aren't going to pay themselves.

At least my retail gig smells a lot better than Al's. I sell vegan products for the body, face, and home at a tiny boutique on Santa Monica's famous Third Street Promenade. Sandwiched between two retail giants, Veritas is a narrow, closet-like space that becomes claustrophobic if more than five customers come in at the same time.

Sundays usually start off slow, and today is no exception. My manager, Lucille, is taking advantage of the lull by doing next month's schedule in her cramped office. I spend the first hour and a half of my shift cleaning the glass shelves with our signature vegan multipurpose cleaner—that leaves streaks if I'm not careful—and humming along to mellow indie music.

I still study every blonde woman I see walking outside, but the multitasking helps me stay focused on the present.

When there's nothing left to clean or dust, I stand near the front door and smile at passersby. Another distraction is in order, and customers will fit the bill nicely.

I discovered early on that friendliness goes a long way in sales. If I talk to people like they're more than just wallets, they pretty much buy whatever I tell them to. Which means I win employee contests and take home free products. Not a bad arrangement, all told.

Around twelve thirty, two repeat customers are browsing the store while I linger in the doorway chatting with an elderly couple. Joy and Marvin walk the promenade every day around lunchtime with their two Pomeranians, all four of them dressed in matching Hawaiian shirts. They're always good for a laugh and are currently arguing about which of them guessed last night's Wheel of Fortune final puzzle first.

While they bicker, I tune them out and feed vegan treats to the dogs. I'm cooing and scratching the chin of Twinkles—or is it Chuckles?—when Joy's age-spotted fingers snap in front of my nose. Looking up, I see her head twitching back and to the right. She's blinking oddly, fast and unsynchronized.

I straighten, eyeing her worriedly. "Are you okay?" I ask, glancing at Marv, who merely rolls his eyes.

Out of the corner of his mouth, he whispers, "She can't wink."

I bite my lips on a smile.

"Oh, Jesus," mutters Joy. With an aggravated huff, she stops twitching and points sharply over her shoulder. "Two o'clock. There's a boy who's been staring at you and he's quite a looker."

I glance in the direction she indicated. There's a kiosk selling cellphone cases, but no one standing around it besides Franco, the owner. Franco and I are friendly, and he's married with six kids, so I highly doubt Joy's referring to him.

"I don't see anyone," I say, then glance into Veritas to check on my customers.

The two women are chatting near a display of essential oils. I stick my head inside and ask if they have any questions even though I know they don't. Between the two of them, they own every product in the store.

They wave me off with smiles.

"Oh, there he is again!"

At Joy's words, the back of my neck crawls with the sensation of being watched. My head jerks toward the kiosk. A family crosses before it, angling toward a nearby coffee stand. When they pass, I see Franco again.

This time, he's talking to someone.

I let my gaze wander down from the stranger's reddish-brown hair, over a face that needs a shave in all the best ways, and along a jaw that could cut glass. Broad shoulders and a trim torso fill the jacket of a charcoal suit so perfectly it has to be custom made. His shoes are dark and shiny, reeking of labels like Handcrafted and Made in Italy.

He's way out of my league.

And looks oddly familiar.

When I look back at Joy, her smile is smug. "Told you."

"That's definitely not a *boy*."

She giggles. "At my age, they all look like boys. You should wave him over. Tell him he can buy you a drink."

"Uhh—"

Marvin clears his throat. "Time for us to scoot. Twinkle and Chuckles need to potty, and I need lunch. Eden, wonderful as always to see you."

I smile at him in gratitude. He winks—properly, with only one eye—and touches the brim of his cowboy hat.

Joy, already on to the next adventure, waves over her shoulder.

I watch them depart in a flurry of yipping dogs and lime-green Hawaiian print. As I turn to reenter the store, I can't help another glance toward the kiosk.

The stranger is gone.

6

A HALF HOUR LATER, the store is empty and I'm bored again. Crouched behind the counter, I attempt to restock our recycled-material bags. They're slippery as hell, and just when I have the last stack tucked away, they avalanche onto the floor for the third time.

"Damnit."

A shadow falls over me as someone leans across the counter. "Everything all right down there?"

Deep, amused voice.

I shove fruitlessly at the bags. "Hi! Yes, just a stocking mishap. Be right with you!"

Finally admitting defeat, I stand up to greet my customer. "Welcome to Veritas. What brings you—" My chest deflates, taking the rest of my words on an exhale.

The stranger from the kiosk stands in front of me. Only he isn't exactly a stranger.

Hands tucked in the pockets of his slacks, he wears the same smirk he had last night while watching me reject Greasy John's advances. In the light of day, the blue of his eyes is startlingly vivid. Almost turquoise.

He stands absolutely still and relaxed, exuding the easy confidence of a man who's sure of his place in the world. Not arrogance—deeper. Born not of external trappings like wealth or a handsome face, but of inner discipline. There's something else, too. Something powerful behind his eyes that I'm unused to seeing directed at me. It makes me flush. Makes my lips part on a shaky breath.

The stranger blinks. His mouth curls the tiniest bit, and I suddenly know what that something is. A predatory intent simmers behind his amused blue eyes. His approach, his confidence—they are the alpha tendencies of a virile male.

This man *dominates* the world around him.

"Do you carry soap?" he asks, the mirth in his eyes flaring.

Does he not recognize me?

What does my hair look like right now?

I pull together my frayed edges, gluing them into place with my years of customer service experience.

"Yes, absolutely," I say, walking quickly around the counter.

I gesture for him to follow me the paltry six steps to our soap display, while out of the corner of my eye, I study his face for flaws. I find none. Even the little laugh lines beside his eyes are sexy.

Though he wears a suit like a second skin, I decide he'd look more at home in jeans and a t-shirt bent over a car engine. Or even khaki shorts and an unbuttoned white shirt, standing on a yacht somewhere being all rich and famous.

Is he famous? I don't recognize him, but it's not like I follow the revolving door of celebrities in the city.

"Hello?" His concerned voice brings a hot wave of mortification to my face.

Clearing my throat, I do my best to pretend I wasn't just ogling him. "Is the soap for body or home?"

His shoulder touches mine as he leans toward the display, the heavier fabric of his suit whispering against my cotton t-shirt. The contact makes my stomach clench.

"Body," he answers, glancing at me with a small smile.

Did he touch me on purpose?

Is he flirting with me?

Oceanic eyes travel my face, no doubt delighting in my schoolgirl blush. *How old is this guy?* He doesn't look that much older than me, but there's something about him... a stillness, a depth that speaks to maturity.

I want to tell him to stop staring.

I want to tear his pants off.

Focus, Eden.

I stare pointedly at our soap display. "Sorry. I, uhh… didn't get much sleep last night. Do you have a preference for fragrance or treatment? Our bestseller for men is this bar, Tuxedo. It's a mix of clary sage, cedar, bergamot—"

"Sounds great, I'll take it."

Reaching past me, he grabs two bars of soap. His chest grazes my bare arm; driven by primal instinct, I take a greedy pull of his scent. Freshness with an underlay of earth and spice. In that aroma I imagine the hard heat of his body, the pressure of his fingers on my hips.

My spine tingles. My knees go weak.

On a biological level, I realize my visceral reaction to him simply means my pheromones like his pheromones. As in really, *really* like. Unfortunately for me, my life experience thus far has proven that trusting those instincts is tantamount to self-destruction. Men like this are my weakness.

Men like this are my downfall.

An unwelcome thought floats up from the recesses of my mind, from the prison it's festered in the past two years. My former professor's face, stern and flushed. Lean, corded arms braced to either side of my head. He'd told me I was special. Beautiful. The smartest, most promising student to grace his classroom in a decade. He'd said a lot of things—like he was leaving his wife. That we had a future. That he loved me.

As repugnant as the reminder is, it's the impetus I need to resist the threat of this stranger. Because my professor's magnetism doesn't hold a candle to that possessed by this man.

I want what this man offers with the very air he breathes, and I'm terrified of what that means.

7

I RING his purchase as quickly as possible. I don't even look at the name on his credit card or ask for ID, just swipe it and hand it back. Seconds later, I pass him an eco-friendly bag with his soaps and a few free samples inside.

I flash a bright, fake smile. "Thanks so much, have a great day!" Without waiting for a reply, I drop behind the counter to deal with the bags.

Leaveleaveleave.

A few moments later, I realize with dismay that his shadow hasn't moved.

I swallow hard and look up.

Long, elegant fingers swipe over the stubble on his cheeks and jaw. He's staring at the ceiling, frowning like there's an answer to a riddle up there.

"You know," he says suddenly, his eyes lowering to mine, "when I saw you standing outside earlier, I thought you couldn't possibly be the same woman from the party. For one, you were smiling, and I didn't see you smile once last night."

My heart kicks into gear, stampeding against my ribs. Memory fractures, dissolves under the weight of his gaze. A familiar urge takes hold of me, stirring the dark, coiled monster at the root of my obsessive tendencies. It's what my professor saw in me, the need he drew to the surface and—for a brief time—fulfilled. My craving for the threat of pain. For pain itself.

Caught in the jaws of my baser self, I stand up, grabbing the counter for support. "I didn't think you recognized me."

His eyebrows lift. "That makes two of us."

A smile tugs at my mouth. His gaze narrows briefly on my lips before meandering across my face. His perusal is lazy and thorough. I feel catalogued—every freckle, imperfection, and flyaway hair. But when his eyes drift back to mine, all I see in them is interest.

"What's your name?" he asks.

"Eden Sumner."

He chews on his lower lip, a line forming between his brows as he mulls on thoughts. Finally, he says, "I'd like to take you out, Eden."

Effervescent wings tickle and clash in my belly, while

my heart simultaneously squeezes in warning. Thump—*not again.* Thump—*not again.* Before I even know I'm doing it, my head shakes.

Testing the waters is one thing—lighting them on fire is another. I have the scars to prove it.

"Thank you for the offer, um…"

"Liam Rourke."

"Liam," I echo. "I'm flattered, really, but I'm moving out of state in a few months. I'm not looking to date anyone before I leave."

His head tilts, eyes churning with curiosity. "Why not?"

My expression goes incredulous, which makes him laugh—a deep, dark sound that shimmers down my spine like a touch.

"I'm not asking you to marry me," he says, a smile lingering on his lips. "I want to take you out. Have a meal. Some drinks. Ask you questions and see if you're as interesting as you look. Say yes."

Thump. Thump.

I'm standing on quicksand. Fighting a losing battle. I know it—he knows it. The darkness behind his eyes captivates me, slowly leeching my will to resist. I'm a butterfly under his pin.

I think of the woman at the party. My doppelgänger. *What would she say to him?* She'd been wearing high heels, expertly applied makeup, and a short, sassy red dress.

I know what she'd say.

So I say it.

"Yes."

God help me.

8

NOW

THERE ARE moments in my life that, when I look back, are mile-high walls between my past and future. Once erected, there's no longer any question of going back. There is *before,* and there is *after.* We all have them. You just have to look hard enough.

These walls cut us off forever from who we thought we were, forcing us to write new stories about our lives. To mold our thoughts in new ways. They alter how we feel in our skin. Change the shape of our smiles. Extend the depths to which we love, grieve, and regret.

The conversation on my parents' couch before I left

for college was one such wall. Another was erected when I met Liam Rourke.

And one more wall, the highest of all—Alexis.

The first time I saw her, I thought I was hallucinating. Karina loved LSD, and that night in the Hollywood Hills when I saw Alexis for the first time, I seriously thought my so-called friend had somehow dosed me with a hallucinogen.

But the truth crashed into me. Literally. Five-feet-eight-inches of truth, with eyes my dad calls cracked marbles. Blue and yellow and green with drips of brown.

My eyes.

Seeing my eyes in someone else's face was weird enough. But then she grabbed my shoulder to steady herself and apologized distractedly for bumping into me. And I saw her lips—rose colored, the top thinner and bowed, the bottom slightly fuller. The tiny cleft in her chin. The shape of her nose, long and just slightly upturned. Her freckles, almost invisible beneath tanned skin and makeup.

She was me.

A bleached, tanned, glamorous *me*.

In that moment, a wall—miles upon miles upon miles high—shot up between my past and my future.

Everything changed.

9

THEN

WHEN I SLIP into the creamy leather passenger seat of Liam's black Mercedes S-Class that evening, I almost jump right back out. It's not the $100k car that has me reeling, but the fact he's wearing jeans and a black t-shirt with a faded band logo on it.

I, on the other hand, expecting to have dinner at a nice restaurant, am wearing a short red dress I found on clearance at Nordstrom, my tiny diamond solitaire necklace and matching earrings, and strappy sandals I borrowed from Karina.

I look amazing.

My date looks like he just rolled out of bed. And as much as my primal brain purrs at his dishevelment and wants to drag him back into my apartment, my modern sensibilities are annoyed as fuck.

"When you said dinner, I wasn't expecting a taqueria."

A smile twitches his lips. "Hello, Eden. You look lovely this evening. And we're not going to a taqueria."

"Where are we going, then?"

He nods at my legs, one of which is still outside the car, my foot braced on the curb in readiness to bolt. "Close the door and you'll find out."

My eyes narrow. "You're enjoying my discomfort, aren't you?"

"Very much." A grin finally breaks free, sparkling in his bright eyes. "Now close the damn door. I'm taking you out."

"Oh," I say flatly, "you're one of those."

An eyebrow twitches. "One of what?"

"A Neanderthal who thinks women like being bossed around."

Less than a second after the words leave my mouth, I regret them—and the shot of booze I'd downed to quiet my nerves.

Liam's smile softens as his gaze narrows with glittering intent. The car suddenly feels smaller, the space between us paltry. He hasn't moved, but his presence seems to swallow me. Cocoon me. Inside my belly and between my legs, a need I haven't felt in a long, long time ignites.

Liam's eyes are crystal clear and oddly knowing, like he has a window into my mind and can see exactly what he does to me.

Maybe he can.

He makes a soft noise in his throat, close to a growl. "I was teasing, which you know. But as for your assumption, there's a time and a place for that, don't you think?"

Impossible to ignore the subtext—this man wants to take me to bed. I honestly don't know if the prospect excites or terrifies me more.

I keep my composure. Barely. Thank God that when Karina found out I was letting a strange man pick me up, she insisted I share my location for the evening. If I don't check in by ten, she and Raul are going to hunt me down. They may not look that tough on the outside, but I know better.

"How about we start with dinner?" I ask, closing the door and buckling my seatbelt.

"Excellent idea." He flashes me another grin, then puts the car in gear and accelerates away from the curb.

I take advantage of his distraction, shifting in my seat to study him. I was right, he looks even more at home in jeans and a t-shirt than he does in a suit.

Who is *this guy?*

"So, Liam, what makes you the big bucks?"

His eyes flicker to me and back to the road. "I'm in acquisitions."

I wait for more, but there's nothing. "Well that's vague."

He laughs. Loudly. Weaving confidently through the light traffic on the I-10 toward Santa Monica, he laughs like I'm a comedian here for his amusement.

Am I?

It occurs to me that perhaps he's purposefully playing with me—that he enjoys finding and pushing my buttons. Maybe it's his specific brand of emotional kink. Maybe he prefers me combative, pushing back and challenging him.

I like it too. The push and pull. It's as familiar as my grandmother's apple pie.

Let's play, Liam Rourke.

"What kind of acquisitions?" I demand.

His answer comes fast. "Anything important enough to warrant acquiring."

"Are we talking companies, art, artifacts, drugs, guns, or humans?"

He shoots me a look of disbelief. "Are you joking?"

My expression stays blank. "I don't know, am I?"

Something flashes in his eyes. I wouldn't call it anger, exactly, but it's close. Eyes back on the road, he murmurs, "Just as I hoped."

"What is?"

"You. You're exactly how I hoped you'd be."

No longer in control—playing right into his game—I tense. "What's that supposed to mean?"

He glances my way, a smile spreading as he sees how irked I am. "It means only that I'm very glad you said yes."

My retort dies on my next breath. Shaking my head, I release a little laugh. "There's something seriously wrong with you."

"Yes, there is," he says pleasantly. Turquoise eyes slant to me. "Go ahead and ask."

"Ask what?"

"The question burning a hole in your head."

I blurt, "What do you want from me?"

All traces of humor leave his face. He doesn't look at me when he says, "More than I should."

That makes two of us.

I don't say it, but it's there. The flavor of my silence, my sudden arousal. *Will you be cruel, Liam Rourke?*

I study his mouth, firm now. His eyes, so vivid. Unnaturally blue, like the waters of a postcard paradise. The thick, muscled arms. Broad shoulders testing the confines of his shirt.

I am afraid.

I am electrified.

10

LIAM TAKES me to Pacific Park at the Santa Monica Pier, like we're tourists checking off an item on our Los Angeles Bucket List. We eat hotdogs and funnel cake. He wins me a horribly cheap stuffed alligator from a ring-toss game, which much to his delight, I pass off to a wide-eyed toddler.

When he's not trying to rile me up, he has a knack for making me laugh. For making the world go hazy and bright at the edges. I've never met anyone with such expressive eyes. Like the mood rings we wore in grade school, they shift hue based on his expression. Teasing. Testing. Surprised. Amused. And so focused on me, it's impossible not to feel like I'm worth his notice. Fascinating and worldly. Sexy and confident.

It doesn't take long for me to peg Liam as one of those people who sees humor in everything. He smiles a *lot.* Not in the slimy way that men smile at women they want to screw, but in a way that feels authentic and rare—like he actually believes in half-full glasses and bright sides.

It's alarmingly seductive. Especially in contrast to the darker current that lurks in his eyes. The speculation and cunning I glimpse when he thinks I'm not looking.

When my feet begin to hurt from my impractical heels, I don't say anything. But he knows. Threading warm, strong fingers through mine, he guides me onto the pier. We lean on the railing side by side and stare down at the dark waters.

"Did you know there used to be five amusement piers in Santa Monica?" he asks lightly, breaking the thick, vibrating silence of the last minutes.

I shake my head.

"It's true. Back in the day—early twentieth century—developers went a little nuts and decided to build amusement parks on the ocean. Not enough action on land, I guess."

"What happened to the other four piers?"

He shrugs. "Storms. Bankruptcy. Who knows."

"Interesting," I say, eyeing him with a smile.

Liam lifts his gaze from the water to my face. "Are you having a good time, Eden?"

Not a simple question, not a simple answer. I know it

for what it is—a jumping-off point. An admission. A concession. The first of what I know would be many.

But I cannot resist.

"Yes," I answer.

Thump. Thump.

Waves crash below, mirroring the pulsing rush of blood in my ears. His smile is slow and full of purpose. I don't resist as he draws me against his chest. One hand lifts to cup the back of my head while the other grips my waist.

"Who are you?" he whispers, but doesn't wait for an answer.

The second our lips touch, the fetters binding his own inner beast drop away. His grip moves from my waist to my hip, and he yanks me hard against him. The fingers in my hair tighten, sending warm sparks of pain through my scalp.

Surrender isn't a choice. It's instinct. A biological and psychological imperative.

I'm a goner.

Liam feasts on my lips and tongue, effortlessly manipulating the angle of my head to his whim. He tastes like funnel cake and sunshine and man. My body is putty in his arms. For a time, the world around me ceases to exist.

When he finally draws back, his teeth give my lower

lip a playful tug goodbye. I stare up at him dazedly; I feel like I'm floating.

I want more.

I want *all of it*.

No one has ever looked at me the way he does now, with unguarded wonder. Like I'm a treasure he's waited his entire life to discover. It's flooring, totally baffling, and it takes a few more moments for my brain to come back online.

His eyes scan mine, full of need. "You're leaving?"

"Yes," I admit. "August first."

His thumb strokes my cheek. "I want to see you again, Eden, as many times as you'll allow before you leave."

My answer is a foregone conclusion, but I say it anyway. "Okay."

11

THREE WEEKS to the day after our first date, I park in Liam's driveway, grab the small, wrapped present from the passenger seat, then walk up the stone pathway to the front door. Today is his twenty-ninth birthday, though he doesn't know I know. One of his favorite games is making me guess his age. Too bad he hasn't figured out that I play dirty.

The second time I slept over at his place, I rummaged through his pants for his wallet when he was in the bathroom. The wallet wasn't the only thing I found, but I'm not sure yet how to handle the other item.

A switchblade.

Definitely not the legal California maximum of two inches long—I looked it up—and definitely not a standard accessory for a businessman. But definitely his. The embedded-ivory handle bore the engraved initials LMR.

Liam Mathias Rourke.

Somehow, I've managed to put it out of my mind and focus on other things. Like what to get him for his birthday. I'm pretty sure I nailed the perfect gift, though to be honest, it's more of a gift for me.

I press the doorbell and wait for the sound of his footsteps down the hall. A minute passes, then another, before I ring again. This time, I pull out my phone and send him a text telling him I'm here.

He's probably in the shower. Or listening to music in his study. Or asleep. He has a remarkable talent for napping whenever and wherever. Once, he fell asleep on top of me. Not during sex, thankfully. I would have flipped.

I'd been lounging on the grass in his backyard listening to music while he finished up a work call. When he came outside, he stretched out beside me, gradually maneuvering until half his body was sprawled over mine. It took a cramp in my arm for me to realize he was fast asleep. Frankly, I didn't care about the pain in my arm.

Nothing in my life has ever felt quite as right as Liam Rourke's weight atop me.

A part of my brain knows that what's happening between us is dangerous. Not just because it threatens my resolve to leave Los Angeles, but because of the man himself.

Liam is the sun. Vivid and warming. He makes me forget. He blots out the past and future and recolors my entire world. With him, I'm stuck in the present. Each moment feels inexplicably precious. A gift that can be taken away at any time.

Liam doesn't trigger my monster.

He replaces it.

WHEN A THIRD RING of the doorbell elicits no response, I take a few steps back and peer at the second story. I don't see any lights on, but that's not uncommon.

As I pull up his contact on my phone to call him, a car engine growls behind me. Relieved, I turn to see his Mercedes pulling up the driveway. He parks beside my used Corolla and opens his door.

Before I see him, I hear his angry voice on the phone.

"Give Maddoc the message, or I'll cut off your dick and shove it down your wife's throat."

I freeze in shock.

I've never heard him raise his voice before. I've never seen him anything but amused and affable. Except in bed. I've had to explain more than a few bruises and bite marks to Karina and Raul.

"That's some Fifty Shades shit right there," Raul had said

once, eyes narrowed on the red marks on my throat. *"Always knew you were a freak. Get it, girl."*

Karina wasn't so dismissive. I had to talk her down from calling the police by swearing that I give him consent. That I want what he does to me. That we have a safe word.

She wasn't convinced until I told her the real truth one night after three shots of tequila. The truth that haunts me, that I avoid, but that constantly wavers in my peripheral vision like a phantom.

"There's something wrong with me, K. You know it. I know it. And the part that's wrong with me—he takes it away. Being with Liam is the only place I've felt freedom from myself."

The concern in her eyes didn't dim, but she didn't question anymore when I showed up to work limping a little or wearing a scarf around my neck.

12

LIAM WON'T TELL me who was on the phone, only that it's nothing to worry about. The answer doesn't surprise me. The balance of power between us is already skewed —he charmed my life story out of me on our second date, but I've yet to learn anything about his past save the most general narrative.

Born in Ireland. Moved to the U.S. when he was eight to live with his aunt and uncle in Los Angeles. Went to Cal State L.A. and graduated with an MBA in business economics. Made his fortune in… *acquisitions.*

I still don't know exactly what he does. It bothers me sometimes. Mostly when I'm not with him, standing warm and adored in his sunlight.

For all his joie de vivre, Liam is extremely private about his work. And though I might be just a moon in his orbit, I'm not without wits. The fancy car, the private, uber-modern Hollywood Hills home, the fact that he works from home and most of his work is done at night… I'm starting to think his casual mention of working for a financial conglomerate was pure fiction.

Despite his easy dismissal of the phone call, it sticks with me. *I'll cut off your dick and shove it down your wife's throat.* Who *says* that? Maybe I'm being irrational. Maybe it's just normal male posturing in the business world. I don't know, but I can't let this one go. One way or another, I'm going to find out who Maddoc is.

Late that night, as I lie in bed listening to his deep, even breathing, I finally allow myself to consider whether Liam is a criminal. If maybe my joking guess on our first date was true—what he acquires and sells are illegal goods. Drugs would certainly explain his presence at the party that first night.

After several sleepless hours, I slip from beneath the sheets and tiptoe out of the bedroom. I know his home well enough by now that I can navigate it easily in the near-dark.

In the kitchen, I pour myself a glass of water, grab my phone off a nearby charge cord, and hop onto a stool at the white granite island.

A voice inside me whispers, *Do you really want to know?* But another, louder voice rebels against the emotional ties Liam has so easily woven around my neck. I don't wear a collar—never have—but sometimes I think I might as well. The bond is there, even if it's invisible.

I PROCRASTINATE A WHILE. Check Facebook and Instagram, neither of which I actively participate in. I clear my email inbox of junk. I check tomorrow's weather and confirm my work schedule this weekend. I play a game of solitaire.

When the threat of being discovered missing from bed is high enough to make my skin prickle, I open my browser and search with the keywords *Maddoc, Los Angeles,* and *Crime.*

The first result hits my eyes and mind with a chill that radiates down my back. Goose bumps spread across my body. My heart pounds as I look toward the shadowed hallway. Expecting a tall shadow there. Expecting him to stop me.

He doesn't come.

Maddoc Donnelly, Businessman with Suspected Ties to Organized Crime, Escapes Justice Again.

I don't read the article. What would be the point? I'm not shocked, or disappointed, or horrified. I feel nothing —or something if numbness counts. I have my answer, and now I have to decide what it means.

Leaving my phone on the island, I walk over to the

floor-to-ceiling windows that showcase a glittering view of the city. Standing close enough that my breath lightly fogs the cool surface, I look for answers when I should be looking for questions. The questions come anyway, teasing through my mind.

Why am I here?

Is the bond I feel real or am I just obsessed?

Is there something wrong with me?

Do I need professional help?

From my vantage point, Los Angeles is beautiful. Though few stars shine above, night camouflages the ever-present blanket of smog. Spread below, the city looks like a cosmic circuit board of currents and purpose. Majestic and mysterious. A veritable Oz.

I hear his soft footsteps. Warm hands cup my bare shoulders and lips graze the hair over my ear.

"What are you doing up, dove?"

His dove. Innocent, according to him. A symbol of peace in his life. He's never disguised his need for me. Not once since the moment we met. It scares me, the look in his eyes that I'm seeing with increasing frequency.

What I feel in return.

I turn, pressing my camisole-clad chest to his. Muscled arms move around me, hands flowing confidently down my back to my ass. He gives me a light squeeze.

I press my mouth to the pulse at his throat. "Just getting a glass of water," I lie.

"Mmm," he replies, dipping his head to drag his lips across my cheekbone. "Couldn't sleep again?"

I shrug, allowing him to provide a reason. An answer to a question he doesn't know to ask. Cuddled against him, blanketed in his heat, I can almost forget what I just discovered.

What business do you have with Maddoc Donnelly?

I don't speak. Can't.

And when he spins me around, grabbing my hands and pressing my palms to the cold glass, I do forget. I forget everything but him. The scrape of bristle on my neck as his lips find purchase. The rough tug on my hips as my panties disappear.

I gasp as he yanks up my camisole and pushes me forward, forcing my breasts against the glass. My nipples harden at the contact. At his contact.

"Liam," I breathe.

Fingers dip between my legs, and he growls approvingly when he finds me soaking wet.

"Spread your legs, dove," he says.

I do.

He kicks them out further, but gently, murmuring appreciation as I bare myself to him.

"Arch your back. Ass up."

I obey, and am deeply pleased by his muttered expletive. The hint of his childhood accent, which only appears when he's tired or aroused.

A warm hand smooths down my spine. That's all the warning I have before he pushes inside me. Bare, because he paid for blood tests for both of us and a birth control shot for me.

My eyes flutter closed, my teeth catching a whimper before it releases. It doesn't hurt—not truly. In fact this is one of my favorite ways. No foreplay. Just his insatiable desire to claim me. Mark me as his.

I feel his need. I revel in it. I match it with mine by surrendering.

I always surrender to him.

13

NOW

"HE'S NOT COMING," says a voice in the dark.

I keep my mouth shut. I'm not sure I could speak if I tried, my throat painfully raw from screaming and lack of moisture. I haven't had water in… hours? Days?

I have no idea how long I've been here. In the musty, damp darkness, time is measured in the drips of a leaky ceiling pipe.

Drip. Drip. Drip.

On and on for eternity.

I've been here forever.

"Just tell me where they are."

I close my eyes, wishing I could close my ears, too.

"If you tell me, I'll give you some water."

Not set me free, but give me water. There's a difference, I know. Still, the temptation is so strong it burns, a pain both psychological and physical.

Every cell in my body roars, visions of oceans and rivers and waterfalls taunting me. I bite my tongue until I taste the coppery tang of blood.

My parents believe there are some things—some people—worth dying for. I really hope this is one of those things. One of those people.

A sigh punctures the silence, not so much impatient as disappointed. It's unnerving, how easily I can differentiate between their sighs.

Then again, they sigh a fucking lot.

"Your loyalty is misplaced," says the voice softly. "And it always has been. What a shame."

Footsteps move up wooden stairs. I count seven creaks, then two softer steps across what I assume is a landing. More steps follow, maybe ten, before the groan of a distant door opening and closing. Then silence again.

Darkness.

14

THEN

ON THE EVE of June 14th, my twenty-third birthday, Karina and I stand on the curb outside my apartment building. We're dressed to the nines but have no idea what the night has in store. I'd been told to dress for a party and bring a friend. That was it. Every time I'd pressed Liam for details, I'd received a slap on the ass. And not the teasing variety, either.

A few minutes till eight, a limo rounds the corner and pulls to a stop before us. I gawk at the sleek giant, and Karina gives a soft whistle.

"I'm so glad I took the night off work," she says

fervently. Her heavily made-up eyes glisten with excitement. "Are we going to Vegas or something?"

I shake my head. "No clue."

When the back door opens and Liam emerges, I suck in a breath. Not since the day he came to my work have I seen him in a suit. Slacks and freshly pressed shirts, yes, but this is different.

He looks like a different man. Sharper. Older. Sophisticated beyond my understanding. The trappings of wealth magnify his natural power. Make it dizzying. This is the version of him that intimidates me the most. The one who seems so far out of my league.

"Happy birthday, Eden," he says with a secretive smile, bending to kiss my cheek. "You look incredible."

"Thank you." This close, his familiar scent invades my nose. *Liam. Still Liam.* As my nerves settle, I run the tips of my fingers along his smooth jaw. "You shaved. Is this my present?"

"Not even close, dove." His eyes flicker away from me for the first time since he exited the limo. "Hello, Karina."

"Hey, Mr. Fancy. Nice ride."

Though they've met several times, Karina has yet to call him by his name. Mr. Fancy is new. It's normally Mr. Hollywood, Mr. Moneybags, or Liam the Dom (though the last she only uses in my company).

Liam laughs good-naturedly and takes my arm,

guiding me into the limo. Once Karina and I are settled, he slips in beside me and nods at the driver. As the limo pulls away from the curb, he pours Karina and me glasses of champagne.

"I could get used to this," Karina says, smirking as she sips her drink.

I've never been a fan of champagne—it gives me a nasty hangover—but one sip tells me this isn't a grocery-store purchase. It's light and dry, with the barest hint of fruit.

"Do you like it?" Liam murmurs.

I nod and force a smile, taking another sip. Liam has never flaunted his wealth; for all his material comforts, he doesn't live lavishly. The reminder is making my head spin. I feel ill at ease, my skin too tight. Out of my element and out of touch.

Maybe it's as simple as the flashy silver mini-dress Karina cajoled me into wearing. But I think it has more to do with the man beside me in a tailored suit, his eyes simmering with easy confidence and worldliness.

This doesn't feel like us. Not the us I'm used to, anyway. The us that fights over the bedcovers, that eats sushi out of takeout containers on the beach. That laughs at reruns of *Seinfeld* at three in the morning because I can't sleep and sex didn't help.

Liam leans close to me, his mouth near my ear. "Stop it," he whispers.

I stiffen. "Stop what?"

He draws back, eyes intent on mine. "Stop thinking that because our surroundings have changed, we're different people."

His thumb slides across the back of my neck, caressing a pressure point. A sycophant for his touch, I feel my anxiety melting away.

"You're mine, Eden. And I'm yours. Limos don't change that."

Yes, but for how long?

HE TAKES us to Providence on Melrose, a Michelin star-rated restaurant I'd never heard of until this past Sunday. There was a review for the restaurant in the morning paper—Liam refuses to cancel the subscription even though he can just as easily read the contents online.

Over Belgian waffles, coffee, and fresh fruit, I'd read the review aloud. Now, staring at the sign over the restaurant's door, I also distinctly remember sighing over the fact that we could never eat there, as reservations had to be booked at least three months in advance. We have just under a month left together.

When the host greets Liam as Mr. Rourke with an air of recognition if not familiarity, I have part of my answer. The rest, I'm not sure I want to know. Call me willfully ignorant, but I haven't found the motivation yet to ask him about Maddoc Donnelly.

Our meal is exquisite. We don't actually order food; instead, a seemingly endless array of tasting dishes and paired wines come and go on the white linen surface. By the third serving, I've forgotten my earlier stress. And it's not the copious alcohol.

It's Liam.

Knowing that neither Karina nor I could ever afford to eat at a place like this, he keeps us from feeling like lambs among wolves by laughing louder than we do, stabbing food off both of our plates, and generally being himself.

Men glare from surrounding tables, disguising their envy with disapproval, while women watch Liam surreptitiously with hunger in their eyes. I can't blame them. In the mellow lighting, he looks every inch a leader among men. His hair gleams darkly with auburn accents, perfectly tousled. I happen to know he never brushes it. Broad shoulders at ease, their angle and strength apparent. The long legs, the trim, fit build. He's the definition of eye-candy.

Apparently our table makes an impression, because after dinner the chef comes out of the kitchen and sits with us for a while. He and Liam trade fishing stories from their youth—the chef's in the Northeast and Liam's in Galway, Ireland. With a handshake and an invitation to return whenever we wish, the chef leaves us to finish our desserts.

Karina and I trade a wide-eyed glance, then hide laughter behind our hands.

Liam leans back in his chair, smug and amused. "Finish your desserts, ladies. The night has just begun."

Around a mouthful of truffle, Karina asks, "What? You're going to have to roll me out of here."

"Oh no," he chides, "you're not getting off that easily. We have places to go, parties to crash."

I almost choke on my chocolate. "As long as there are no Ferris Wheels involved."

He smirks. "Would I do that do you?"

"Yes. Yes, you would."

He laughs and signals for the check.

The limo appears like magic when we walk outside. It's not quite ten o'clock and the sidewalks are still bustling with people—tourists, hipsters, and dinner-goers blending together.

A young woman squeals and aims her cellphone at us, snapping pictures, while her friend hisses furiously in her ear. Locals look us over, then roll their eyes at the antics of out-of-towners. Across the street, two men scream at each other outside a store, and an old homeless woman is weaving her shopping cart through traffic.

Just another night in Los Angeles.

15

THE LIMO STOPS outside a mansion in Malibu. Knowing that if I ask where we are I'll be spanked later, I hold my tongue. It takes some effort, especially when Liam releases the driver from his duties.

As he guides us toward the front doors, we pass cars stacked tightly together in the curved driveway. A Lamborghini. A Bentley. BMWs and Mercedes. Four Teslas.

Screw the spankings.

I grab Liam's hand. "What is this?"

With a wicked glint in his eye that promises a sting, he replies, "You keep asking to meet my friends, so here we are."

My anxiety returns in a rush. I plant my feet, yanking him to a stop. Karina pauses nearby, staring at the mansion with a mixture of eagerness and envy.

Liam touches my face. "Little dove, why are you nervous?"

"Because... fuck, I don't know. Tell me I'm being stupid."

Because it's my birthday, you ass, and you know I'd rather spend it naked with you than at a party of strangers.

He tugs on my hand until I'm in his arms. Smiling softly down at me, he murmurs, "Don't ever call yourself stupid. If you do it again, I'll add it to your punishments."

The word ignites the usual need, but it simmers beneath the thick border of my fear. "You know I'm no good at shit like this. Remember? We met at a party like this one."

Like this one...

The party had revolved around drugs, that much I knew. My palms grow clammy as I wonder if the answer to my question has been staring me in the face all along, only I've been too scared to face it.

Liam knows Maddoc Donnelly because he works for him as a drug dealer.

I don't know what Liam sees in my eyes as I have the thought, but his own darken. "Not quite like this one. Besides, I dropped my car off earlier. We can leave at any time."

He sounds completely normal. At ease and in his element. I want so badly to believe him.

And I want so badly to know.

A small voice inside me whispers, *What will you do? Will you leave him?*

Yes.

I don't know.

"Come on, live a little," cajoles Karina.

I look between them and finally nod, bolstering myself with the knowledge that I can leave whenever I want.

Liam kisses me swiftly and we resume our trek to the front doors. They're unlocked, and open onto a scene I'll never forget as long as I live.

At least twenty people scream, "SURPRISE!"

Familiar faces fill the spacious entryway and adjoining rooms. Raul, wearing a rainbow party hat above a shit-eating grin. More coworkers from both Al's and Veritas. Jen Campbell and Lucy Yang, my roommates for the first two years at UCLA, and a host of other friends from college who I've been horrible at keeping in touch with.

When I see my parents grinning and waving in the front row, I almost pass out.

Soft lips press against my temple. "Happy birthday, dove."

LIAM RENTED ALL the cars in the driveway as party favors for the guests. Over the next few hours, I hear numerous stories from awed coworkers and friends about cruising town in the luxury automobiles.

The gesture was completely over-the-top, and I see my own discomfort reflected in my parents' faces. Driving a Benz in an unfamiliar city was more intimidating than enjoyable for them.

"I'm grateful, don't get me wrong." My fingers clench on the sleeve of his white dress shirt. He discarded his jacket and now looks more like himself, top button undone and hair an absolute mess.

"But?" he murmurs.

We're alone in one of the bedrooms. Music filters to our ears from the party, and I hear Raul and Karina's loud laughter. My parents left twenty minutes ago for their hotel. They were by far the oldest people at the party, and I know the late hour was taxing for them.

I force myself to meet his eyes, almost indigo in the low light. "It makes me uncomfortable."

His brows lift. "That I'm wealthy?"

"No." I pause, looking down. "Maybe."

His fingers on my chin lift my face. "Look at me."

The command is spoken in a tone I have no willpower to resist. When my gaze meets his, he gently palms my face. His soft expression, and the adoration in his eyes, make his next words all the more shocking.

"I won't spout the usual drivel about how money is useless unless I can spend it on the ones I care about. The truth is much more simple and not nearly as self-flattering." His fingers move into my hair, releasing several pins to the floor. "I want to keep you, Eden. I want to *own* you. And if that makes me a brute, so be it."

Desire and satisfaction shimmer in my veins. That primal, unstoppable, *fucked-up* core of me rises and twists and blooms.

I don't pretend to misunderstand him. He wants me to give up medical school. He wants me to stay. To be *his*. And Liam knows exactly what he's asking. He knows how much my future means to me. That, before him, it was my primary focus in life.

I'm sickened by how tempting his offer is. Sickened by myself.

Anger straightens my spine even as tears well in my eyes. "You had to do this—to say this—today? On my birthday?"

He shrugs one shoulder. "Would you rather I'd done it the night before you left me?" His fingertip catches a tear. "I'll do whatever it takes. Do you want me to pay off the mortgage on your parents' house? Set them up so they can retire?"

The words stab and slice, leaving bloody pieces behind. My adoration—and dare I admit, love—for him suffers what feels like a death-wound. In this moment, I hate him. His power over me. His unfailing equability. His conceit.

With an intelligible yell of fury, I put both palms on his chest and shove as hard as I can. He barely moves, but we both freeze. Him in surprise. Me in dismay.

Liam's eyes soften with worry. He reaches for me, but I turn and flee. I don't glance at the bed, where just ten minutes ago his mouth brought me hard and fast to climax.

I tear open the bedroom door and run into the living room. I ignore everyone except my two real friends. They see me at the same time and jump to their feet.

"Get me out of here."

And like real friends, Karina and Raul don't question. They get me out of there.

16

MY PARENTS' flight is mid-afternoon the following day. I spend the morning with them, putting on a brave front and studiously ignoring their concerned looks. They know I'll tell them the reason for my puffy eyes when I'm ready. They won't push me for details or judge. And they love me enough that they don't once mention him, the party, or the Mercedes we returned this morning.

Instead, we talk about my plans for the future. The room near campus I'm subletting until I can find a job and get a place of my own. The long drive from Los Angeles to Oregon and where I'll stop halfway for the night. Things I want to do while I'm at home before my final move date of August 15th.

By the time I drop them off at the airport, I'm exhausted, and by the time I get home, I can barely keep my eyes open. Stumbling into my bedroom, I fall onto my bed and bury my face in a pillow with lumps that only remind me of the perfect pillows in Liam's bed. And Liam.

He hasn't tried to contact me since the party. A few texts from people who were there informed me of what happened after I left.

Nothing.

Liam had walked out of the bedroom a few minutes later, told everyone to enjoy the property until dawn and the cars until the following day, then left. No tires had squealed. No bottles had been thrown. He was, as always, in control of himself and his surroundings.

I think of the traces of me left in his home. Flowers on the kitchen island. Clean underwear in the corner of a dresser drawer. A toothbrush sharing a cup with his.

What will he do with the pieces of me? Better yet, what will I do with the pieces I have left?

Tears come, hot and silent. Knowing that this moment was inevitable doesn't lessen my pain. In fact, it's magnified from what it might have been.

We'd never explicitly discussed our relationship past August first, and I'd allowed myself to hope that he would want to try long-distance. The flight from Seattle to L.A. was a short one; we could spend weekends together here and there. I'd fly down on every break. Spend the summers with him.

I'm a fucking idiot.

None of this would have happened if I'd said no. If I hadn't in that pivotal moment thought of the woman who, in my inebriated state, I'd decided looked like me. If I hadn't wanted the fearlessness I'd ascribed to her.

She's a stranger I'll never see again.

And so is he.

KARINA AND RAUL show up at five with Thai food, a bottle of rum, and a beauty case with contents that remain a mystery until I'm drunk.

Among Karina's many artistic talents is hairstyling; she'd gone to cosmetology school right out of high school, worked for a year in a salon, then decided she'd rather stab herself with shears than cut hair.

I tell her to do whatever she wants.

To my surprise, she only gives my long hair a trim and some flattering layers. The actual shock comes when she mixes a bowl of dye, applies it with a color-brush and foils, and washes it out fifty minutes later.

"Parting gift from the land of plastic tits," she says, our eyes meeting in the bathroom mirror as she finishes blow-drying my hair.

"I'm blonde," I say, hiccuping.

Raul pops his head in, grinning when he sees me. "Oh shit, we're not in Kansas anymore."

Karina rolls her eyes. "Do you like it, Eden?"

I nod. I actually do like it—she didn't bleach me so much as brighten my existing color. But I still look different. Me but not me.

A new me.

"It's perfect."

Raul checks his watch. "Ready to roll, K? We've got twenty minutes to get to work."

They leave me with the rum, leftovers, and promises to check in on me tomorrow.

I fall asleep on the couch watching *Seinfeld*. I dream of hands in my hair and a kiss on my forehead. The sensations are so real, I even smell his cologne.

I wake the next morning to a hangover from hell, blonde hair, and a postcard of the Santa Monica Pier resting in my lap.

With shaking fingers, I lift the postcard and turn it over. Three words. His slanted handwriting.

I found her.

WHEN LIAM OPENS his front door, I storm past him and spin around, my index finger aimed at his face. I've never been so furious in my life.

"You've known where she is all along, haven't you? Talking me down, telling me I just imagined her... all of that was a lie. You were saving the truth for now—your final move to stop me from leaving this cancerous city. You're a piece of shit, Liam Rourke." I suck in a deep breath, winded from my tirade.

Expression unreadable, Liam crosses his arms and leans against the closed door. "Does any of that really matter, dove?"

"Don't call me that," I snap. "Whatever this was—we were—was over the second you tried to buy me."

His brows lift with incredulity. "That's what you think I was doing? Trying to *buy* you? Eden, if I wanted to buy a girlfriend, I would. Easily. There are plenty of women who are actual submissives—formally trained—who wouldn't cost me nearly as much as you do."

My heart stutters and drops, stealing all color from my face. Liam's jaw clenches. He takes two swift steps and before I can jerk back, his hands are on my throat. Not tightly enough to cut off my air, but enough to assert control. To demand my obedience.

Instead of lowering my gaze, I stare into his glittering eyes. My defiance proves his point, but I don't care anymore. I'm not his toy, his pet, his dove. I'm *me*. And I thought—I really believed—that was who he wanted.

"Fuck you," I snarl.

His lips compress, nostrils flaring. "All in due time. But right now you need to shut up and listen. Two months ago, you walked into the wrong party. You have no earthly idea how dangerous it was for you to be there."

I blink in shock, my mouth dropping. "What are you talking about?"

His hands give a warning squeeze. "Listen, damnit. That house belongs to a man named Maddoc Donnelly." He sees the comprehension on my face and sucks in a breath, gaze narrowing. "Ah, I see you know the name. Googled him, did you? That night I found you in the kitchen?"

His accent is noticeable now, a sign of him losing control. My pulse fluttering, I nod.

"Do you want to know why I was there that night?" he asks stonily.

"Yes," I breathe.

"I was *working*."

My head shakes; tears gather in my eyes. "I don't understand."

His fingers loosen, thumbs now stroking my skin. "I know you've tried your hardest to *not* understand, Eden. But I think you do."

I blink rapidly, struggling for breath even though his fingers are gentle now. Words stutter from my lips. "Do—do you… k-kill people?"

He sighs, shaking his head. "Of course you would think the worst. No. I find them."

The edges of my vision darken, the awful truth closing in.

"Who?" I whisper.

"Eden Elizabeth Donnelly. Born July 23, 1994 to Maddoc Donnelly and Elizabeth Sharpe. Disappeared July 31st of the same year with her mother. Her twin sister, Alexis, was left behind with their father."

A tremble moves through me, crown to feet. A seismic eruption of self. I sway and Liam catches me, lifts me against his chest.

Everything goes black.

I COME to on Liam's bed. He's lying beside me propped on an elbow, his free hand stroking my hair. Sunlight streams through the windows behind him. In his white shirt and black slacks, he looks like an angel. Or a devil disguised as one.

He smiles a little. "Welcome back."

Before I do something stupid like curl into his warmth, I wrench away and swing my legs off the bed. Head in my hands, I fight a surge of nausea. Through the confusing jumble of thoughts in my head comes a singular one.

"Alexis," I croak, looking over my shoulder.

Liam hasn't moved. His ease, his stillness, I now know are merely products of his formidable control. His inhuman discipline. How had I not noticed this before? The man even makes relaxing look predatory.

"That's her name, yes. The woman who crashed into you at the party was your identical twin."

I stare at the sheets between us. "Oh my God. This is insane."

"I had your DNA tested against Donnelly's. There's no doubt you're his daughter."

My biological father is Maddoc Donnelly.

The criminal.

I meet his eyes. "What is he, a drug kingpin or something?"

"Among other things, yes. Never been caught, though I'm sure the Feds have a mile-long dossier on him. He's slippery as an eel and smart as a fox. If I didn't loathe the man, I'd respect him."

Puzzle pieces connect in my mind, forming a picture I can barely make sense of. Maddoc Donnelly. Liam Rourke. Both Irish names. My skin, pale and freckled.

Watching Liam's face carefully, I say, "I thought the Irish mob didn't really exist in the U.S. anymore."

He remains still and silent, expression placid. But I know him. I see the infinitesimal tightening around his eyes.

"Holy shit," I choke out. "He's a freaking mob boss."

"Not a boss, Eden. *The* Boss." He shifts, sitting up and letting his feet fall to the floor. His shirt stretches over the muscles of his back as he props elbows on his knees and stares out the nearby window.

I don't ask him to tell me the rest. I feel it coming like a missile straight for me. He begins to speak, voice muted and even.

"Before you ask, I'm an independent contractor. Much to Maddoc's endless frustration. I only took this job because I owed him a favor. A rather large one, I'm afraid." His back rises and falls with a heavy breath. "I'd already found you, the night of the party. I paid one of Karina's acquaintances to invite her. I didn't actually know you'd be there."

"You stalked me?"

"I *found* you," he corrects. "And I've been hiding you ever since."

18

"HIDING ME?" I echo in bafflement. "Why, Liam? Tell me what the hell is going on!"

He pivots to face me, one leg coming onto the bed. A rare show of temper flashes in his eyes. "I will, goddamnit. I'm trying to find the words. Jesus H. Christ, Eden, this isn't exactly easy for me."

Sheets bunch in my fingers. "Easy for *you*? Asshole!" Unhinged by rage, I launch myself at him, raining punches on his chest and arms. He doesn't try to stop me, sitting immobile beneath my abuse.

When I've exhausted my meager energy reserves, I collapse sobbing against him. Only then does he move, encasing me in his strong arms.

"I'm sorry, dove."

"Don't call me that," I say without bite. Lifting my

tearstained face, I search his eyes. Looking for answers. Finding only mysteries. "Why?"

"The simple answer is I don't want him to have you."

"And the complicated one?"

"He thinks you know where your mother is. From what I gather, her disappearance with you was unexpected." Before I can ask what the fuck he means, he continues, "I don't know why he wants to find her, but I can guess it isn't for a happy reunion."

"But I don't know my mother," I protest. "I was adopted when I was a year old—"

"I know, but Maddoc believes otherwise."

I shudder and he holds me tighter. "You haven't told him? About me?"

"I didn't tell him, but he knows. He's got rats in every gutter in this city." He pauses. "Let's just say we're at an impasse in our negotiations. He isn't allowed to come near you unless it's on my terms."

Fear runs like ice in my veins but despite it, I don't pull away. "Who *are* you, Liam?" I whisper into his shoulder.

"Someone who wants to protect you," he murmurs. "Who's willing to go to great lengths to keep you safe. Trust me, you don't want the life your sister has."

The word *sister* blows every other thought from my mind. My head whips up, narrowly avoiding his chin. "Tell me where she is."

"I'll tell you—with conditions."

The trap is set, and regardless of knowing how much it will hurt, I walk willingly into it.

"What are they?"

"The first one is that you stay."

LIAM PRESENTS his terms in a voice that brooks no argument. Sitting a safe three feet from him on the bed, I listen, my heart shriveling a little more with each pronouncement.

I move in with him immediately and for the foreseeable future.

I tell my parents I've decided to postpone medical school for a year.

I tell Karina and Raul nothing. Or anyone else, for that matter.

I quit my jobs.

I allow him to track my phone and car.

"You want me to be your prisoner."

"I want to keep you safe."

We've been going in the same circle for more than fifteen minutes. Either he can't understand my perspective, or he simply doesn't care.

"Safe from *who*? Maddoc Donnelly? Do you think he wants to hurt me?"

"I doubt it," he says. "But there are worse fates. Once he has you, he won't let you go."

My eyes narrow. "How is that any different from what you're doing to me?"

Liam throws up his hands. "You're impossible to reason with."

I stand and pace to the bedroom doorway and back. When I stop, I square my shoulders with newfound conviction. "I'll disappear. I'll get in my car and drive out of town, and neither of you will ever see me again."

"This isn't the bloody movies, Eden," he growls. "There's no escape from men like your father."

"You mean men like *you!*"

He's unaffected by my accusation. "And you'd leave your sister behind? Your parents? What would you do when you run out of money? Because you will, and I'm sure as fuck not giving you any. Will you sell that sweet pussy on the streets?"

As I weigh the odds of whether or not I can strangle him, he leaps from the bed. Faster, stronger, so controlled, he pushes me backward with one hand cupping my shoulder and a forearm on my neck.

My spine meets the wall beside the bedroom door. Chest heaving against his, I dig fingernails into his forearm. He doesn't even flinch. Once again, he's not cutting off my air, just subduing me.

An image pops into my mind of a cat being immobilized by the scruff of their neck.

I laugh. Hysterically. Then I spit in his face.

A grievous error.

Seconds later, I'm flat on my back on the bed with him on top of me. My legs are wrenched apart, my wrists captured in one hand and held against the headboard.

I scream and writhe beneath him, shouting profanities and trying to slam my head against his. When my thrashing heels find one of his kidneys, he sucks in a sharp breath of pain.

"God forgive me," he says right before slapping me across the face. Fiery pain blooms in my cheek and jaw, the shock of it stunning me silent and still. Tears of rage and helplessness cloud my eyes.

"I hate you," I sob.

His forehead drops to mine, his panting breaths warm on my stinging cheek. "If only that were true, dove. You might stand a chance in this world."

"Let me go," I beg him. "Please, don't do this to me."

He's gone a moment later, striding to the door and pausing briefly on the threshold.

"You have twenty-four hours to decide. Option A, you let me keep you safe. Option B, you run. If you decide on the latter, you have my word that I won't try to stop you. But you'd better hope I find you before Maddoc does. Choose wisely."

The door closes.

When I finally muster the courage to venture from the bedroom, the house is quiet and Liam's car is missing from the driveway. I don't hesitate, grabbing my keys from the floor just inside the front door and racing to my car. For all I know, there's already a tracking device on it, but I don't give a shit if he knows where I'm going.

Fifteen minutes later, I pull into the parking lot of the nearest police precinct.

THE DETECTIVE I speak to is a balding man in his fifties with a bulky physique and steady eyes. He hears me out, taking occasional notes on a yellow pad of paper.

He doesn't say it outright, but by the end of the interview, it's clear he thinks I'm batshit crazy. Not an hour after I arrive, I leave, my stomach sour with disappointment and bad coffee.

In the parking lot, a niggling suspicion makes me call Veritas. An associate answers, and I ask to speak with our manager. Lucille picks up the line a few moments later.

"Eden?" she asks in surprise. "What's up?"

"I just wanted to make sure I'm still on the schedule this week."

There's a long pause. "I'm confused. Shouldn't you

be on your way to Oregon? How's your dad doing, by the way?"

My fingers clench on the phone. "Good. He's, uh… doing fine. So my shifts are all covered?"

"Ohh, I get it, you couldn't help being your responsible self. Seriously, Eden, don't worry about a thing back here. Focus on driving safely and being with your family. We're all so sorry about the accident."

"The accident," I echo.

She hums in sympathy. "Your final check should have gone through direct deposit today. Let me know if you don't see it. And if you ever decide to move back our way, please give us a ring. You'll always have a position here at Veritas."

"Thanks, Lucille," I force out. "Take care."

I hang up and toss my phone on the passenger seat, then pound the steering wheel with both hands. Not until the pain overcomes my misery do I let my arms fall to my sides.

When my former professor explained to me why I craved sexual submission, he told me foremost about the difference between surrender and defeat.

Surrender, he'd said, was an active choice; it didn't diminish an individual's power because the choice itself was a powerful one. At his hands and at Liam's, I've experienced the ecstatic sweetness of surrender.

And now I know the difference.

I know defeat.

I HEAD NORTH on the I-5, through Van Nuys and into the San Fernando Valley. I don't turn on the radio. I don't look at my phone when it buzzes repeatedly. I just drive. I'm not running; at least, not consciously. But I also can't seem to make myself turn around.

When the sky begins to darken, I take an exit in Bakersfield to fill my gas tank. I don't know what I'm doing. Where I'm going. I can't think straight. Can't even remember the last time I ate. Was it the Thai food yesterday?

Was that only yesterday?

At the gas station, I use my credit card at the pump, then head into the attached minimart for coffee and a snack I probably won't eat. While paying for my purchase, I glance outside just as a car pulls into the station and parks at the pump behind mine.

It's a black sedan. Middle-grade, no distinguishing features. A single figure occupies the driver's seat. I wait for the person to exit the car, but they don't.

"Miss, are you all right?"

I blink at the cashier, an older woman with tired eyes. Feet shuffle impatiently behind me.

"Yes, sorry." I scrawl my signature on the little screen,

press the green button, and grab my items. "Don't need a receipt, thanks."

When I push through the doors, hot, dense air pushes back. Wind whips my hair up and around my face.

The occupant of the sedan is now standing against the hood, arms crossed over his chest. My palms dampen with sweat as I realize that he isn't pumping gas, just standing there.

Waiting.

You'd better hope I find you before Maddoc does.

Liam's words ring in my ears like a prophecy. My heart races. He was right—this isn't the movies. This is real. This is my *life*.

And I'll be damned if I'm going to give it up without a fight.

I stalk toward the man, who turns his head as I approach. I don't recognize him. Blond hair, classically handsome, wearing a navy polo and jeans that fit his muscled form like a glove. Colorful tattoos run the length of both arms.

"Are you following me?" I demand.

He doesn't insult me by pretending surprise, merely uncrosses his arms and reaches up to remove dark sunglasses. His eyes are greenish brown and surprisingly warm.

That doesn't mean anything.

"Hello, Eden," he says, offering a hand. "My name is Chris Daley."

His voice is like his eyes—warm and deep—but I barely notice. What I do notice is his accent, it's lilting, musical cadence.

"Who are you? Who sent you?"

Chris lowers his hand. "Do you have a preference?"

"What?"

He shrugs, a smile playing on his lips. "A preference, lass. Would you be more relieved if I was a messenger of your father or Liam?"

Staring at him, I come to a profound conclusion.

"I'm losing my mind."

Chris merely nods. "I'm sure it feels that way. Been there once or twice myself. Why don't you gather what you need from the car and come with me. I'll answer your questions on our way home."

I laugh. "L.A. isn't my *home*, asshole."

"Ach. You've got a tongue, haven't ya?" He grins, but his eyes aren't warm anymore. They're dark and cold. "We can do this the hard way, if necessary."

Tires squeal behind me and a car door slams. I recognize the measured pace of expensive shoes on the asphalt, and I'm not ashamed of the relief that cascades through me.

"Get gone, Christopher," growls Liam.

"Allo, Liam. Been a while."

Liam scoffs and takes my arm. I don't resist as he pulls me to the passenger side of his car. When I'm inside, he hisses, "Don't move," and closes the door.

I watch him walk back toward Chris. Standing face-to-face, the two men are of equal height. Chris is a little bulkier. If I didn't know Liam, I might bet on the wrong man in a fight.

But I know Liam.

Whatever he says makes Chris laugh and bring his hands up. He backs away, his grin opposed by Liam's scowl, and gets into his car. Then, with a jaunty wave in my direction, he speeds out of the gas station.

Liam opens the driver's door of my car and bends inside. When he stands, he has my cellphone and purse. Whatever emotion he displayed in his conversation with Chris is gone. The man who walks toward me is control personified.

He gets in the car, tosses me my belongings, and turns the key in the ignition. All without looking at or speaking to me. The part of me that still loves him—or loves what he gives me—wants to apologize, but the rest of me is disgusted by the thought.

"This isn't fair," I say through clenched teeth.

He says nothing.

It's a long, silent drive back to Hollywood.

20

NOW

AFTER SEVERAL WEEKS IN CAPTIVITY, I stop caring about things like pissing myself or how long it's been since I bathed. The smell doesn't bother me. The pain in my raw wrists, my aching bones, and cramping stomach all cease to be a concern.

My humanity has been systematically stripped away. I am more animal than human now.

Drip. Drip… Rush.

Somewhere in the house above me, a toilet flushes or a faucet runs. Water churns through the pipes above my head. Taunting me with the sound of rivers and waves. I don't care about the pain anymore, but I need water.

The average human, without extreme circumstances like hot sun or snow, can last about a hundred hours without water. That's a little over four days.

I'm given water every three.

21

THEN

THREE DAYS HAVE PASSED since Liam pulled my ass from the fire. I'm grateful, but he'll never hear me say it.

I have yet to leave the guestroom on the opposite side of the house from the master. Holing myself up and refusing to speak might be juvenile of me, but what's the alternative? Sauntering out naked to make the bastard breakfast?

Not a chance. As far as I'm concerned, those days are done and buried. The only thing Liam Rourke will receive from now on is my resentment.

At 9 a.m. exactly, the bedroom door opens. I don't

turn from the window where I'm watching a hired gardener mow the grass.

I hear him move across the room and put a plate and mug on the nightstand. When his footsteps don't recede, I stiffen.

"I had no idea you were this stubborn."

My answer is a glare over my shoulder. I shouldn't have looked at all—Liam is shirtless, wearing gray cotton pants that I know are soft as butter. They're also thin, and do little to conceal his substantial endowment. I can't seem to tear my eyes away. Not until I see him begin to swell and harden.

"Ah," he says on a sigh. "I thought I'd lost you completely. But you're still in there. Still mine."

"Don't flatter yourself," I retort. "The only thing I miss about you is your cock."

Liam laughs. "Not as much as he misses you."

Aggravated at myself for breaking my silence, I turn back to the window. The gardener is gone, the lawn below cropped and iridescent in the sunlight.

When he speaks again, his voice is soft, threaded with rare emotion. Regret, maybe. If I thought him capable of it.

"When I came to your work that day, I came to seduce you. I won't deny it. What I didn't expect was how attracted I'd be to you."

I can't repress a flinch. "Sorry, no tan or fake tits here."

"That's not what I meant and you know it." His footsteps cross the room, stopping somewhere behind me. "You weren't as interesting as you looked—you were *more* interesting. I've often wondered if it wasn't me that found you but the other way around."

Romantic words. Too bad they're lies.

He's close now. Too close. I can feel the heat of him on my back, can smell his intoxicating skin. Unwanted desire blooms in my breasts and between my legs.

"I recognized the war inside you," he murmurs. "The struggle between innocence and depravity, between aggression and submission. Sweet Jesus, it was impossible to resist. And when I tasted you for the first time, I was lost."

Turning, I look into his stormy eyes. "How are you planning to finish this flowery little speech, Liam? With something even more trite, like I'm the first woman to reach your damaged heart? Spare me the bullshit. Like you said, this isn't the fucking mov—"

His mouth slams onto mine, swallowing the rest of my words. Fingers on my jaw force my lips to part and his tongue invades. I bite down hard.

He reels back, releasing me with a curse. My freedom, however, is short-lived. I try to dart past him but his arm snakes out, catching me in the stomach. Breath whooshes out of me. I'm airborne, spinning, until I land facedown on the edge of the bed.

I scream in abject fury, bucking against him as he yanks my pajama pants and underwear to my knees. My hands are pulled behind my back, trapped in one of his.

"Are you going to rape me, Liam?" I yell belligerently. "Are you?"

"Of course not," he snaps. "I'm merely proving a point."

Fingertips land on my tailbone, swirling up and down, teasing the swell of my ass. I renew my efforts to escape, but it's no use. I'm drowning, beyond saving, my body betraying me further with each second that passes. With every millimeter those fingers move south. An agonized moan escapes me. My hips jerk up, seeking him.

"There's nothing wrong with you," he says softly, reverently. "You're absolutely perfect. And even though you lie to yourself and to me, spewing hateful words you don't mean, we both know the truth. This isn't about what my hands and cock can do. This is about *us*."

"I hate you," I whisper.

"Maybe a little. I did conceal the truth from you, and loyalty runs strong in your lineage. I'm sure you can't help but feel angry and betrayed. But you also can't help this."

His fingers slip between my thighs. A heavy sigh

whispers across my skin. "See?" he murmurs. "Made for me."

He's merciless with those fingers.

And then he's merciful.

I come on his hand, crying out my love, my desire, my fear and confusion.

After, his knee hits the bed and he leans down beside me. Panting, mindless, I watch him lick me slowly from his fingers. The eroticism triggers aftershocks in my womb.

Those blue eyes flare with heat. "*Mine,*" he whispers, and gives me a gentle kiss on my cheek. When he draws back, his smile is radiant. "Get dressed, dove. I'm taking you to meet your sister."

22

OF ALL THE places I expected to meet my twin sister for the first time, Al's Diner didn't even make the list. As we walk toward the familiar entrance, I bite back questions. *How did you know Karina and Raul wouldn't be here? Did you know they only work nights?*

I'm not avoiding punishment, I'm avoiding asking questions I already know the answer to. And I'm avoiding conversation in general. I don't want his eyes on me, his proprietary stare that sees right through me. I don't want his smile or his sonorous voice in my ears.

I don't want him.

But mostly I don't want him thinking that what happened this morning means anything. Because it doesn't. It's exactly like I told him—I don't miss him, I miss what his body can do to mine.

"Here we are, dove." Liam opens the door and gestures me to proceed.

"Don't call me that," I mutter, stepping inside and scanning the familiar tables and booths. Eagerness tickles in my palms and the soles of my feet.

My sister.

Instead, I see the sole occupant of the last booth on the left. A blond man. Tattooed arms. A smile directed at me as he lowers a cup of coffee from his lips.

Liam curses beneath his breath.

Before I can respond, he grips my elbow and all but drags me to the booth. I slide into the vacant side, and Liam settles beside me, his body flush against mine, arm around my shoulders. I don't throw it off for a simple reason. The man across from us scares me more than Liam does.

Chris nods. "Fine morning, isn't it?"

Liam doesn't respond. I take my cue from him and stay silent, my hands clenched together in my lap.

Eventually, Chris takes another sip of coffee, then lowers the cup with an air of finality. "I do commend you. Both of you. It takes some brass balls to defy Maddoc's orders." Hazel eyes swing to me. "Eden, you're looking lovely today. And rather confused, if I might say. Our Liam does like his secrets, hmm?"

Liam's hand clenches in warning on my shoulder. *Don't speak.* I don't.

"Ah, I see how it's gonna be," Chris says. He lifts up, removing something from his back pocket and tossing it onto the table. It's a folded piece of lined paper. Watching me carefully, Chris says, "Maddoc isn't without a heart. This here is for you, Eden."

Chris slips from the booth and stands. With a mocking salute for Liam, he saunters toward the front door.

I unclench my hands and reach tentatively for the paper. Liam doesn't stop me. With cold, tingling fingers, I unfold it. It's a narrow sheet filled with glittery pink handwriting, one edge torn like it was pulled from a notebook or journal.

Eden -

I'm so bummed I didn't get to meet you today!! Can you believe how cool it is that we're twins? I'll let you in on a little secret—I always knew you were out there. I know, that sounds crazy, because Daddy didn't actually tell me about you until a few days ago, but I swear I've always known something was missing. Like a part of me. Like there was a hole, you know? Ugh. I'm not explaining myself well, am I? Sorry, I'm just so excited that you exist!! I can't wait to learn everything about you. Daddy says we can meet soon!! Here's my # in case you want to call or text me. 323-555-6831.

xoxo,

Alexis

"Eden? Are you all right?"

I fold the paper carefully on its creases. Looking at Liam, I shake my head. "I… don't know. I guess I expected to feel something different."

Or something at all.

Liam hears what I'm not saying. Expression grave, he says, "You've lived very different lives. Alexis is…" He mulls his thoughts. "Well, she's basically your opposite."

"How so?" I press. "Tell me, Liam."

He sighs in concession. "Not here. Let's go home."

Numb from the inside out, I don't correct his choice of words. Because right now, all I want is to feel safe, and deep down I know there's nowhere safer than with the man beside me.

LIAM DEPOSITS me on a padded teak lounge chair in the backyard. I close my eyes and let the sun warm my skin, wishing it could sink deeper and warm the cold core of me.

I've stepped into a parallel universe and no longer recognize the person I was before. Before my birthday.

Before Liam. Before Alexis and Maddoc Donnelly and veiled threats and traps and the vast, terrifying unknown.

Who was I? Who was the woman *before*? Not a woman, really—a girl. Young and innocent. Not naive, not sheltered from struggle, and yet totally clueless of essential truths about my life.

My mother took me—stole me—and put me up for private adoption. My ex-boyfriend and warden is somehow associated with the Irish mob. My biological father is an underworld kingpin. My twin sister is a stranger who writes in pink pen.

The lounge beside mine creaks as Liam sits. I open my eyes, and he hands me a glass of iced tea. I hold it between my hands, feeling the cool condensation on my palms. As though the physical sensation can keep me anchored while my identity fluctuates.

"Tell me, Liam."

He does.

And I learn how sometimes nurture wins over nature. How identical twins can grow in opposite worlds with opposite moral conditioning.

I thrived in school, the accumulation of knowledge symbolizing an escape from obscurity and boredom. Alexis barely graduated high school, more concerned with boys and nightlife than honing her intellect.

She grew up in a bubble of wealth. A princess who

acquired anything she desired with a snap of her fingers. Cars. Clothes. Boys… men.

"How do you know so much about her?" I ask when Liam pauses.

"I've known her a long time." His set jaw tells me that's all I'm going to get out of him.

When I finally take a sip of my tea, the ice has melted, diluting the flavor. I likewise feel watered down, diluted by this new information. Less myself. More someone I don't know—someone I'm not sure I want to know.

Our first date on the Santa Monica Pier seems like ages ago. As do the past two months I've spent with a man who I felt I'd known for years. With a man I didn't know at all.

Perhaps there's something to be said for nature, after all. I think of what kind of man Maddoc Donnelly must be. And I wonder what my mother was like, and why she ran from him.

Perhaps the part of me I've rejected and embraced in turn isn't necessarily wrong or sick. My craving for dominant men. Men who'd rather tie me up and fuck me than buy me flowers.

Maybe it's in my DNA.

23

LIAM MAKES DINNER THAT NIGHT. For the first time in days, I'm actually hungry. No longer petulant enough to hide in my room, I occupy a stool at the island while he tosses linguine and vegetables with lemon and butter.

The muscles beneath his white t-shirt bunch and relax as he works. From discreet speakers croons the likes of Ella Fitzgerald and Nina Simone.

Almost, it feels like stepping back in time.

I watch him suck a bit of buttery sauce off his thumb. He's not trying to seduce me, which makes the gesture all the more captivating.

My earlier thought floats hazily through my mind. *Maybe it's in my DNA.*

"You don't look hungry, dove. Not for food, at least."

My gaze jerks up from his mouth, now curled in a

smirk. "Nice try," I quip, but my voice is breathy, giving away my arousal.

Liam cocks his head. "My lady doth protest too much," he murmurs.

"Quoting Shakespeare isn't going to get you into my pants, Liam."

His gaze narrows, darkening to stormy indigo. My core clenches, knowing what's coming, thrilling in it even as my mind recoils.

"And what if I told you that tonight you'll eat dinner in the nude?"

That voice. So smooth. So controlled.

"Fuck off," I bite out.

Liam grunts, chest expanding on a heavy breath. His hand skates down the front of his slacks. I can't help but follow the movement, to see him thick and hard behind his zipper.

"Even your vitriol makes me hard, dove."

I open my mouth but no sound comes out. Liam doesn't move, watching me. Waiting. Electric want lifts the hair on my neck. A storm is coming—he is the storm.

"Take them off, Eden."

Lightness over steel. Desire cloaked in discipline.

Is this who I am?

Is this what I want?

Does anything fucking matter?

"One more chance before I make that ass as red as your cheeks."

I jerk to my feet. My breath comes in short pants. My fingers tremble as I lift my shirt over my head. Unclasp my bra and let it fall. Shimmy out of my jeans and underwear. Step to the side, away from the island. Exposed to him.

With slow, measured steps, Liam rounds the island. I know—even before he unbuckles his belt—what he wants. Only he doesn't realize it's more reward than punishment to me.

I am as he said—depraved.

"On your knees."

The wood is unforgiving. I embrace the small pain in my joints. Let it heighten my other senses. The sound of his zipper going down. Pants hitting the floor, belt buckle clacking on impact. The whisper of his boxers following.

The head of his cock drags over my lips. I open for him. Greedy for his taste. Unashamed in my surrender. He immediately thrusts to the back of my throat. I swallow, pulling him to my body's limit. My eyes water, lungs burning as I suck what air I can through my nose.

His fingers cradle my head, thumbs gathering the tears leaking from the corners of my eyes. When he draws back, I inhale swiftly—my only reprieve before he begins to move. Owning his pleasure. Owning me.

A pulse along his shaft warns me he's close. Sometimes he gives me a choice. Not tonight. He climaxes with a sigh, and I swallow his pleasure.

For brief moments, I own *him*.

I stay on my knees, my eyes closed as he pulls from my mouth. Boxers and pants slide up his legs. Zipper. Belt.

I'm aching, throbbing and wet.

My punishment.

His footsteps move away. "I'm famished. Come on, dove, time to eat."

AS MUCH AS I might resist the truth, Liam remains what he's been since the first touch of his lips on mine. My obsession. My fixation.

My escape.

For tonight, I relinquish the fight. I let him take away the confusion, the fear. I give my shifting Self to him. He is the sun, blotting out the shadows in my soul.

After dinner he draws me a bath, fussing over the temperature, lighting candles along the rim. He leaves, then returns with two glasses of red wine. He reads me James Joyce's *Ulysses*, picking up where we left off before we took the exit to Crazytown.

When the chapter is finished and the wine floats warmly in my veins, I ask him to tell me about growing up in Ireland. Expecting his usual redirection, I'm surprised when he answers readily.

"It was rather dull, believe it or not. My mother and I lived with my grandparents in a cottage along the coast, a bit north of the town-proper. My grandfather was a fisherman all his life. My mother was young when she had me—eighteen. She worked odd jobs, two or three at a time." His eyes twinkle at me. "Reminds me of someone."

I smile wryly. "Then you understand how weird it feels for me to not go to work every day."

"You deserve to relax a bit, Eden," he replies. "You've worked your ass off for years."

I snort. "Are we pretending this is something other than what it is—a total upending of my life? Jesus, Liam, part of me thinks I should be in a padded room. This can't possibly be happening." Resting my head back, I close my eyes. "Maybe I'm already there. I had a psychological break and someone committed me. Right now, I'm strapped to a bed pumped full of drugs. Hallucinating this."

A fingertip traces my nipple. "Does this feel like a hallucination?"

"Yes."

He pinches the tight bud, igniting a frisson of lightning between my legs. I gasp, my eyes snapping open.

"How about that? Still wondering?"

I glare at his smug face. "I think you can do better."

Sliding to his knees beside the tub, he leans forward until his lips graze my ear. "No games right now, dove. Are you ready for me to be inside you again?"

Yes.

No.

"I don't know," I whisper.

He nips my earlobe with his teeth before sitting back on his heels. Mussed auburn hair. Eyes flickering between turquoise and cobalt in the candlelight. I watch him through heavy-lidded eyes, a plea pooling on my tongue, barely held back by my teeth.

"I'd never force you," he says softly. "You know that, don't you? That I only want to give you what you need?"

I remember this morning, being thrown to the bed, and the seconds before. My inner conflict. My defiance and fury.

I recognize the war inside you.

I'm merely proving a point.

And he had.

Even while hating him, I'd wanted him.

I'm terrified that as the world around me continues to remold itself into something new, he'll stay at the center of it. That no matter what I learn, what secrets Liam

Rourke keeps, I will forever be powerless over what he does to me. Powerless over my need for him.

"I'll keep you safe, Eden. I swear it."

I close my eyes and sink beneath the water, remembering the same promise under very different circumstances.

24

AS OUR THIRD date nears its end, I'm plagued by thoughts that Liam isn't as attracted to me as I am to him. Besides goodnight kisses, he has yet to seduce me. Physically, that is —I'm already mentally and emotionally seduced.

Tonight, however, after a light dinner in Brentwood, he doesn't drive me to my apartment as usual. Without bothering to ask, he takes me to his home in the Hollywood Hills.

We don't speak much on the drive there, and I barely notice my surroundings. My panties are soaked by the time he navigates up a winding driveway.

Liam puts the car in park, eyes shadowed as they cut to my face. "Do you want me to take you home?" he asks softly.

My voice comes on the third try. "No."

His lips curve in satisfaction. "Come on, then."

He leads me through the front door, which closes soundly behind us.

"Do you know what I want?" he asks.

I brace myself—body and soul—to be wrong. I'm weightless. Breathless with need and anticipation. *Please, let this be happening. Let me be right.*

Lowering my eyes to the floor, I say the words I haven't spoken in two years. I say them with relief, with an ache that burns so brightly inside me I can feel it. Heat and light.

"Yes, sir."

A soft sigh. "Very good."

He walks toward me, fingertips whispering along the curtain of hair beside my face. I can barely feel the touch, only its aftershocks in my scalp.

"And what should I call you, hmm?"

It's a rhetorical question—he'll call me whatever he wants—but I revel in the dissolution of my identity. My remaking.

Names are given such power over our lives. But they're essentially impotent, a mere collection of letters assigned at birth. How can such a word define me? Does *Eden* mean something in and of itself?

No.

But this one will.

"Dove," he murmurs, a fingertip trailing down my cheek and beneath my chin. With gentle pressure, he guides my face up. "Soft. Innocent. Yielding."

I must betray surprise, because he chuckles. "You're none of those, are you, Eden?" I shake my head. "Voice, please."

"No, sir," I whisper.

He pinches my chin lightly. Staring into his eyes, I see a future that terrifies and enthralls me. He's smiling, the impish grin I've become accustomed to. That I look forward to. Dream about.

But it's the look in his eyes that peels back my layers and finds the dark center of me. The one that craves relief from the pressures of the world. That, if not exactly innocent, is both soft and yielding.

"My dove," he murmurs. "Do you trust me to care for you?"

There's only one answer, and it's true.

"Yes, sir."

"Good. And I will. I promise to keep you safe."

Liam takes me by the hand, leading me through the shadowed house. We ascend an elegant wooden staircase, one side open to the lower floor. Down a hallway, past several closed doors, and through the open one at the end. Large windows overlook the backyard, and in the distance, the glowing band of the city.

"Sit on the bed."

There's enough ambient light for me to see. I cross the room and settle on the foot of the bed, clasping my trembling hands between my knees.

Liam crosses to a dresser. A drawer opens. After a few moments, he turns to observe me. There's a length of red rope in his hands.

"I'm going to go out on a limb and guess that you don't like verbal debasement." As I scramble for a reply, not wanting to disappoint him, Liam cocks his head. "Innocent little dove, aren't you? We'll iron out limits another time. I'll take it easy on you tonight."

He wraps the rope around his hand, the motion distracting me. All thoughts leave my head.

"These are the ground rules. Pay attention." I focus with effort; my breath hitches as he walks toward me. "When I say 'Eden,' I'm checking in. Green means continue, yellow means slow down, red means stop. Got it?"

"Yes."

"Yes, what?"

"Yes, sir."

He strokes my cheek with his knuckles. "That's a good girl. Now I want you to stand up and take off your clothes. Fast, slow, doesn't matter. Then present yourself to me with your wrists together and extended."

Liquid dark eyes pierce me. Unveil me. I sit frozen.

"Now, dove."

Nothing in his voice but calm certainty. He will be obeyed. I will be his. He will take my darkness and replace it with himself.

Oh, sweet relief.

I jerk to my feet. With Liam's gaze sharp and hot on my movements, I step out of my skirt and kick it to the side. My tank top comes off next, then my bra. Cool air skates across my breasts. My nipples tingle and harden under his gaze. Finally, I remove my body's last defense. My thong flutters to the floor.

Before he asks, I offer him my wrists. Smooth nylon coils around them. His hands move surely and swiftly, a blur of skill as the rope draws up around my torso, swings around my neck. Confident fingers sweep my hair up and out of the way. There are knots, a final tug as he finishes, but I hardly notice.

I've never been claustrophobic. Instead I feel like a piece of art. Discovered and brought to life. My breasts are forced high and tight, rope around and between them. The binding isn't uncomfortable, but the pressure on my throat does give me a moment's panic.

"Breathe," he says.

I do. Slowly and evenly until my pulse settles.

"Eden?"

I blink up at him. His tense jaw and furrowed brow. Then I understand. "Green," I whisper.

He pinches my nipples lightly, tugging with increasing aggression until they're distended and red. The pain is distant, soothed the instant it flares by soft flicks of his tongue.

"Spread your legs, dove."

With a whimper of need, I spread my legs. Air touches my most sensitive skin. Anticipation brings a fresh surge of blood. I pulse. I pound. Desperate for his touch. As my hips jerk toward him, Liam smiles. He cups my sex in his hand, spreading me open.

"Drenched," he growls, eyes flashing up. "Get on the bed, dove. I need to fuck you right now."

I scramble onto the bed. It's not easy with my arms bound, but I make do, wiggling until there's space below for him. I finally still as Liam's pants hit the floor.

In the shadows, all I can see is that he's fully erect, long and thick and curving slightly upward. My womb clenches in mingled desire and trepidation. He's big—far bigger than I dared to imagine.

I begin to pant as he strokes himself a few times before rolling a condom on.

"Breathe, dove."

Not until he says the word do I realize I'm hyperventilating. A wave of mortification crashes through me. I must freeze, or stop breathing altogether, because Liam seizes my ankles in his hands. His touch grounds me, calms me. But only for a moment.

I yelp as he yanks me down the bed and throws my legs apart. One finger, then two thrust inside me without warning. A third joins, stretching and priming, pistoning hard until I release a ragged moan.

"Eden?"

"Green, green, green," I chant.

His hand disappears. I gasp at the withdrawal, but then I feel him, blunt and thick, sliding through my wetness and teasing my entrance.

"Please," I beg.

"Again."

"Please, please, sir, please."

Seizing the rope between my wrists and neck, he thrusts inside me. It takes a good minute for my body to accept all of him, for my mind to sort through all the sensations—the constriction on my throat, the incredible fullness, the completion and surrender.

Wetness rolls down my temples; I realize I'm crying.

"Eden," he snaps.

He's called my name several times. He's inside me but unmoving, the rope slack between us.

I sob, drag air into my lungs, and scream, "Green!"

I come on his fifth savage thrust, bucking against him with the rope tight around my neck. My vision washes red, then white. I can't cry out, can't breathe, the pleasure so exquisite it dissolves any remaining sense of self.

With a gentle tug, the rope falls free. I suck air greedily, still pulsing around him. The aftershocks of my orgasm are powerful enough that they feel like separate climaxes.

"You're bloody perfect," he murmurs, hips rolling languidly against me.

When I've calmed enough to open my eyes, Liam covers me. My legs lock around his hips. I open my mouth for his tongue, clench the firm skin of his waist in my fingers.

And slowly, so slowly, his mouth never leaving mine, he drives me once more over the glistening edge.

25

"WHAT ARE YOU THINKING OF, DOVE?"

I turn my gaze from the white tile next to the tub. Memories of our first night together are still vivid in my mind and body. Schooling my expression to disinterest, I reach for a washcloth and bar of soap.

"The first time we fucked."

Liam grunts. I don't look at him, but I know he's wearing an expression that's all too common where I'm concerned. Mingled amusement and surprise.

"Miss the rope, do you?" he murmurs.

"No," I lie. It's my favorite of his toys, and he knows it.

Ignoring his smirk, I build suds on the washcloth and drag it down each of my arms. My movements are economical, artless, but I hear his breathing deepen.

The knowledge that he still wants me doesn't change

anything. I still want him, too, but the once-bright space between us is now twisted and dark.

"Why do you think Maddoc wants to find… Elizabeth?" I'd almost said *my mother,* but she isn't. Not really. I have a mother and she's in Oregon, likely worried out of her head about me.

Liam drops back onto the plush bathroom mat, propping himself on an elbow to watch me. He's hard behind his zipper, pressed tight against the material of his slacks. It must be uncomfortable for him, but from his implacable expression, he's not about to admit it.

"I don't know. Perhaps she took something of his. That's the simplest explanation."

I wash my armpits. "Like what? Money? Drugs? Seems a little greedy when he has more than enough of both."

"Spoken like a woman with no earthly idea of the world she just stepped into."

My hand with the washcloth stills. "And whose fault is that?" I snap.

His eyes narrow. "Not mine. If it were up to me, you'd still be blissfully in the dark."

I scoff and lift a leg onto the side of the tub, scrubbing roughly at my skin. I don't even know why I'm washing —I showered this morning—but can't seem to stop. To avoid psychoanalyzing myself, I think about the woman who birthed me.

Elizabeth Sharpe.

"Do you know anything about her? What she was like?"

"A little. She was gone by the time I came to the city, but people would talk. Especially in front of a boy they didn't think was smart enough to listen. If you take the word of gossipy women for fact, their love story was a fairy tale. She was nineteen, beautiful, from an unremarkable background. He was thirty when he first saw her, with a growing empire, good looks, and Irish charm."

Washcloth forgotten, I stare at him. "Where did they meet?"

"A jazz club. She was a cocktail waitress. Story goes he swept her off her feet, showered her with everything money could buy. They married within six months. You and Alexis came along two years later."

Eyeing the tension in his shoulders, I ask, "What are you not telling me?"

Liam sighs, falling smoothly onto his back with his arms folded behind his head. Candlelight flickers along his tall frame; I notice he's not aroused anymore.

To the ceiling, he says, "Maybe he hit her. Abused her. No one knows. But there was talk about how she changed in the months prior to your birth. She'd withdrawn from her usual social circles. Some thought it was merely a difficult pregnancy. There were other rumors, though, that maybe she could no longer stomach the life her husband led. The payment extracted for all her creature comforts."

"And what kind of payment is that?" I ask, wanting the answer as much as I don't want it.

Instead of answering, he says, "Did you know that until Maddoc came to Los Angeles, the city was known as the Gang Capital of America?"

"What? Isn't it still?"

He gives a short, humorless laugh. "Looking in from the outside, maybe." Sitting up, he meets my questioning gaze. "There's only one way a man becomes what Maddoc now is. He knew his history, knew that the Irish had failed in New York, Chicago, and at home because of lack of organization. He changed things. Took a page from La Cosa Nostra, ruling with order and an iron fist. Maddoc's road to power was paved in the blood of his enemies. Enough of them that his interests are respected —sometimes even protected—by other branches of organized crime in this city."

My heart beats wildly in my chest. "That's what you meant, isn't it? When you said he's not a boss, but The Boss?"

"Yes. Maddoc doesn't give orders to say, the Crips or Bloods, but when he calls meetings, they're not ignored, either."

I stare at the cracked nail polish on my toes, peeking

out of the water. "Holy fucking shit," I breathe. "What am I going to do?"

"You're going to stay with me," he says gently. "I'll never let anything happen to you, Eden."

My gaze jerks to him. "And who the hell *are* you? Why would the so-called most powerful crime boss in Los Angeles give a shit about what you think or say?"

"Politics," he says rigidly.

I frown. "What?"

Liam shakes his head and without another word, rises and leaves the room. The bathroom door closes softly behind him. I sink back into the cooling water, fear and confusion playing ping-pong in my head.

26

THE NEXT TWO days pass in a blur of television sitcoms, sunbathing in the backyard, and ignoring Liam. He's around during the day but keeps to his study and bedroom, with periodic trips to the kitchen. After delivering me dinner each night, he leaves. I have no idea what he does all night long, only that his car is back in the driveway come morning.

When I do see him, I can't speak to him. Gone is the man I first met, with his easy smile and mood-ring eyes. In his place is a brooding stranger. He doesn't shave. He spends hours beating the shit out of a punching bag in the garage. And when our eyes meet, I see nothing I recognize. Not desire, anger, or worry. Just a vast, frigid void.

Friday night, I watch from the living room window as he gets in his car and drives away. Black slacks. Black shoes. Black button-down. I wonder if he has his switch-blade, or if there's a gun in the car. I wonder if he's going to hurt someone.

After all, it's Friday night in Los Angeles.

Heading to my room, I take a quick shower and consider my wardrobe. Most of my clothes are now here, the rest of my belongings from my apartment sitting in a storage container somewhere.

I pull out the silver mini-dress, then put it back. Grab the red dress. Shove it back. After considering and discarding another few options, I finally choose a comfortable cotton dress. Black, with capped sleeves, a low neckline, and a flirty A-line skirt. Dressy enough that I can fit in at a club, casual enough that I can blend into crowds.

I have no idea where Liam goes each night, but tonight, I'm following him.

HIS FIRST MISTAKE was not changing the passcode on his phone. His second was giving me his iTunes password so I could rent movies. And his third mistake was assuming I was too scared to do anything besides hide in his house.

When the app I'm using to track his phone tells me he's been in the same place over an hour, I call a cab.

Twenty minutes later, I see headlights in the driveway and a yellow sedan pulling up.

After a moment's hesitation, I leave my phone on the kitchen island. I don't want to risk him using it to locate me; this way, if he does he'll find me at home. Then I hurry outside and slip into the back seat.

"Where to, miss?"

I rattle off the address, and the driver's eyes widen in the rearview.

"You sure that's the right address?" he asks.

My pulse flutters. Before I ask *why*, or regret not doing more research, I say, "Yes, thanks."

The location isn't residential or industrial, and it's nowhere near what qualifies as a ghetto. I tell myself I'll be perfectly safe, even as the voice of reason reminds me I don't have a phone.

I tell the voice of reason to shove it and concentrate on keeping my panic at bay. I'm still scared. Terrified. But I refuse to be Liam's innocent little dove anymore.

As the cab draws to a stop outside an unmarked black awning in Beverly Hills, I look questioningly toward the driver. "This is it?"

He nods, turning to give me a grandfatherly frown. "Everyone knows this place." He hesitates. "You do know what they do in there, right?"

No.

"Of course," I say with confidence I don't feel.

"Someone's waiting for me. Thanks." I hand him two twenties and jump out.

Liam's fourth mistake—showing me where he keeps rolls of backup cash.

"Be safe!" calls the cabbie, and drives away.

Alone on the curb, I look up and down the sidewalk. I'm on a side street just off Wilshire, and the building before me is sandwiched between a boutique hotel and a modern office building. Beyond its black awning and a stylized C on the black door, there are no distinguishing features telling me what kind of establishment this is.

What the hell is this place?

I'm seconds from bailing and asking the hotel to call me a cab when a car screeches to the curb right behind me. I spin and stumble back a few steps as all four doors open. At the same time, the black door opens, spilling red light onto the sidewalk.

I move back further, toward the hotel's entrance, and watch the car's passengers emerge. Three women and a man. The women are wearing leather corsets or vests, expensive and tailored, none of which do much to disguise their ample breasts and toned, flat stomachs. One wears a mini-skirt and buttery-soft boots; the other two have on tight pants and spiked heels. The man follows behind.

When I see him, I finally understand. He's attractive and young, dressed in jeans and a white t-shirt, his head bowed as he walks behind the women. Around his neck is a thick black collar.

No wonder the cabbie looked at me like I was nuts.

A man—valet, I realize—comes through the red doorway, nods to the women, then gets in the car and drives away. The foursome disappear inside, the door left open behind them.

So many emotions flash through me as I stare at the wash of red light on the sidewalk.

Curiosity.

Dread.

Arousal.

But the last feeling is the most potent, wiping away all others before it.

Rage.

27

"WHOA THERE, where do you think you're going?"

Except for his height—easily six and a half feet—the speaker is the antithesis of a regular doorman. He's so thin I immediately want to take him to Al's for a burger. Long, pale hair falls to either side of a face so angelic I just stare at him with wide eyes.

Behind him is another door, this one covered in padded leather secured by evenly spaced rivets. It looks sumptuous and dangerous, and I want badly to see what's behind it.

"Are you deaf?"

Blinking, I meet the man's eyes. In the crimson lightning, I can't tell what color they are.

"What do I have to do to get in?"

He barks a laugh, eyeing me up and down. "Honey, in that dress you'll be eaten alive in twenty seconds. Run along now and find a sandbox to play in."

My eyes narrow in annoyance. "I'm not leaving."

"Trust me, you're better off. A piece like you will send the Doms into a tizzy."

My mind supplies me with an image of a snarling pack of animals fighting over my carcass. Fear ricochets up my spine even as irritation straightens it.

"I'm not a sub," I snap.

He laughs loudly. "The hell you aren't. Besides, we're invitation only and you're not on the list."

Defeat presses closer, sagging my shoulders. I should have known better. I should have known that where Liam went, I wouldn't be able to follow.

"You actually look kind of familiar. Have you been invited before?"

I have a split second to make the decision. But it's not a hard one.

"Yes. My name is Alexis Sharpe."

I'm pretty sure if there were normal lighting in the room, I'd see the blood drain from his face. As it is, his throat bobs as he swallows hard.

"Alexis, of course," he said breathlessly. "Please forgive me. Your, um, hair is a bit darker and I, uh—"

"Whatever," I say, waving off more stumbling words. "Are you going to let me in or what?"

"Yes, yes, I'm sorry." He moves from the door,

opening it with flourish. "Enjoy your evening at Crossroads."

I step past him, straight into another world.

***

ALL THE TIMES I've envisioned what the inside of a BDSM club looks like, I never imagined what's in front of me. All the stereotypes are turned on their heads. The space is open, modern, and bright, with whitewashed brick walls and discreet pendant lighting.

A gleaming bar takes up the right side, a thick crowd clustered before it. Ahead of me and to the left are various seating areas. Couches and ottomans, rugs and pillows, tables and chairs, all in the same color scheme of white, silver, and muted gold. The only spot in the entire club unoccupied is a sunken circle in the center, just visible through packed tables.

I look up, and up, and see that over the central pit hangs a heavy iron frame, and suspended from it are various leather contraptions. The sight of it makes my neck crawl. The publicness of it. The awareness that it's used and enjoyed before a crowd.

People mill around me, chatting and laughing. They occupy tables and lounge on pillows. If I didn't know what I was looking at, I might not notice the signs. But I do.

Collars. A discreet gag. A few blindfolds. Men kneeling beside the chairs of women. Women at the feet of men. Small gestures, challenging glances. A current of passion and play.

No nakedness. Not yet.

But the night is young.

As I scan the crowds looking for Liam, I'm also relieved to see that I don't stick out in my simple black dress. There's a wide variety of styles present, from jeans and tank tops, to a woman wearing a bodysuit of bright red patent leather, to a man in a tux.

I'm working up the nerve to move when a voice behind me purrs, "My, my, what do we have here?"

A piece like you will send the Doms into a tizzy.

Bracing myself, I turn around. I recognize the speaker as one of the women I saw walking inside. She's tall and curvaceous, her dark skin gleaming. Beside her stands the collared man, his head still bowed. A leash now connects to the metal d-ring at the front. The Domme holds the end, swishing the fringed edge across her cleavage.

Heavy-lidded dark eyes appraise me head to toe. "Whose pet are you?" she asks in a sultry whisper.

My mind stumbles through variables. If I tell her no one, I'm opening myself up to God knows what kind of attention. And I already know she won't bite if I tell her I'm not a sub. For one, I have no control over my expression right now, which is borderline freaked-the-fuck-out.

The man looks up at me, then ducks his head again. There was no fear in his wide blue eyes, but they held a warning nonetheless. *Don't pick the wrong answer.*

Saying a prayer for luck, I tell her, "I'm looking for Liam Rourke."

The Domme's eyes widen. Then she laughs like I told her the joke of the century. "Aren't they all, dollface?" she asks, still chuckling.

The lights around the club dim. The Domme steps close to me, close enough that I can smell the cloying vanilla and cinnamon of her skin.

"If you want Liam Rourke, all you have to do is turn around."

28

I DON'T WANT to turn around. Really don't want to. But my feet move without my permission, spinning me on my heels. The ambient background music fades and a hush moves over the crowd; murmurs rise and fall like a collective heartbeat of anticipation. The overhead lights continue to dim, but a soft spotlight slowly brightens over the sunken pit.

Standing in the middle is Liam. *My Liam.* The easy, carefree version of him. He's relaxed, hands in his pockets as he smiles and chats with the man beside him. Like there's not a thing wrong in the world. Like he knows a secret—a thousand secrets about life and love and death—but he'll never share.

His companion is built like an underwear model, all chiseled muscles and tanned skin above snug leather pants. At their feet kneels a woman. Naked. Head bowed and arms hanging limply at her sides. She has dark-blonde hair and the most perfect, creamy skin I've ever seen.

For a few seconds, I just stare at Liam's smile. A pang of longing hits me as I realize how much I've missed it.

But what the *fuck* does he think he's doing?

The Domme and her sub are gone, swallowed by the crowd as it mobilizes and moves toward the railing around the pit. When my view of Liam is obstructed, I skirt around the throngs and slip through bodies until I'm a few people back from the rail.

I can see his profile but not much else.

"Ladies and gentlemen," says a smooth female voice over the club's speakers. "Welcome to this evening's entertainment!"

A cheer rises, then mellows into polite applause. The voice continues, "Tonight we have a special treat. Master Liam and Master Dominic will be demonstrating proper technique for horizontal suspension…"

As she speaks, the metal latticing begins lowering smoothly toward the pit. White noise fills my ears, and I don't hear the rest of the spiel, only the crowd clapping and whistling at its end. I sway a little, my vision dimming, and a finger taps my shoulder.

"You okay?" asks a woman.

I glance back, finding concerned eyes. "Fine, thanks. Just a little dizzy. Forgot dinner."

She nods sagely. "Is this your first time at Crossroads?"

Since she seems normal enough—no crazy Domme vibe—I nod. "What exactly is going to happen?" I ask, nodding toward the pit.

She smiles. "You came on a great night. Master Liam is awesome. He doesn't come around much anymore. Word is he has a new sub but doesn't want her in the life-style." She shrugs. "Anyway, he's amazing to watch. Get ready for wet panties... if you're wearing any." She winks, then waves at someone nearby. Blowing me a saucy kiss, she moves away.

When I turn back around to face the pit, my palms are clammy and my breathing uneven. I watch Liam and the other man unwinding an apparatus that might as well be medieval torture—horizontal wooden bar, glistening silver chains, black cuffs. Lengths of red rope are removed from another section.

Even at a distance, I recognize the same type of rope Liam uses. Smooth and sturdy. Capable of creating beauty, enhancing pleasure, and causing pain. I shudder in remembered ecstasy, growing damp between my thighs.

I hear a whispered question behind me.

"...doing traditional or shibari?"

Someone answers, "Whatever he feels like tonight."

The hum of the crowd increases, and I sidestep for a

better view. At the same time, the person in front of me leaves and another person shifts. The pit is suddenly right in front of me, the action inside it crystal clear.

The other man—Master Dominic—speaks quietly with the woman. She's on her feet, nodding to whatever he's saying. Liam walks toward them, and her focus shifts. Her eyelashes flutter and her knees bend, like she can't quite support her weight.

I'm very familiar with the look on Liam's face right now. The fact that it's directed at another woman makes me want to burn the world down. Starting with him.

The metal railing is cool beneath my fingers, hard against my pelvis. Liam's broad back is just a few feet away. I don't remember moving.

As he continues speaking softly to the woman, Master Dominic's gaze roams the crowd. He nods to a few people in recognition. Then his gaze lands on me.

Dark, dark eyes sear into mine, full of the same power that Liam possesses. But he's not Liam. Not safe. My knuckles go white on the railing as I fight the urge to bolt.

Dominic continues to stare at me, brows drawing together in a frown. His gaze veers to Liam. He murmurs something.

Liam's head snaps upright.

FUCK!

I turn fast, preparing to dive through the crowd.

"Stop."

Such a small word, spoken gently, but it's pitched to carry. In it is more than the weight of command, though that power alone is crippling. Worse, much worse, is its encapsulation of every kiss, every touch, every perfect moment of intimacy we've shared.

I freeze.

"Turn around."

His voice is closer now, nearer the railing. The people around me titter and whisper, moving away from me like I'm contagious. Maybe I am.

A second passes in which I consider refusal. Consider making a run for it. But I can't. I just fucking can't. Not with so many eyes on me. Not with him waiting behind me. Not with the words from the stranger ringing in my ears.

...doesn't want her in the lifestyle...

A different type of anger builds inside me at the thought that he doesn't want me here. Or maybe I've finally had enough of myself—my constant fear and worry—that I'm giving up and taking a back seat.

Whatever it is, whatever's happening to me, the feeling squares my shoulders. My eyes on the floor, I turn around.

"I don't know whether to whip you or kiss you." His voice is dry and mild, at odds with the severe amount of trouble we both know I'm in.

"I'm sorry, sir," I choke out.

"Are you?" he asks, and those nearest us chuckle. "However shall I punish my disobedient little dove?"

"Suspend her!" someone shouts.

"Paddle!"

"Put her on the cross!"

The crowd goes suddenly quiet; I risk a glance up to see Liam's hand lifted.

"I know just the thing," he murmurs, stepping up to the rail. The difference in floor height puts his face just below mine. A finger lifts my chin until I look into his eyes.

Although I've never seen this exact color in his eyes before—they're dark, almost violet—I know what it represents.

Fury.

"You're going to watch what I do to her. Up close and personal, gagged and bound at my feet."

The words sink in, searing through me. I jerk with the force of the pain they cause. His expression doesn't waver; his anger doesn't dim.

"Say it," he hisses.

My eyes burning with unshed tears, I say it.

My safe word.

"Clover."

29

NOW

I'VE BEEN SLEEPING a lot lately. Not a good sign. My body is weak, my mind fracturing. I have no dreams, at least none that I remember. Unconsciousness is an endless, inky nothing.

Three days ago, I woke to find a blanket draped over my legs and the ropes on my wrists gone. Fresh white bandages covered the raw skin, little dots of blood leaking through the white.

My dawning excitement was momentary—when I tried to move, I discovered my ankles cuffed together and bound with chain to a sturdy pipe. Either I'd been so out of it that I hadn't noticed the change happening, or the little red mark high on my arm is from a syringe.

Since then I've seen no one, heard nothing. No footsteps, no water in the pipes. No cars outside.

I'm going to die here.

Alone and forgotten in the dusty basement of a tiny house in Mexico.

Liam broke his promise.

A car slows outside, kicking up gravel as it comes closer to the house. Shack? Bunker? I have no idea, having spent the trip here in a trunk blindfolded and gagged.

Slam of a car door. Crunch of boots on wood. Keys jingling. The groan of the front door. With so few senses at my disposal, my hearing has become acute. I'm a superhero with an utterly useless power.

At least my hands are free, though I doubt I have the strength to strangle a mouse, much less a person. Especially not this person.

The basement door opens. Footsteps tromp downward. I don't look up, not even when I hear a heavy sigh.

"How are you feeling today, dove?"

30

THEN

AT FOUR IN THE MORNING, the front door slams. From my vantage point at the top of the stairs, I watch Liam stumble and sway drunkenly into the dark kitchen. He's singing softly, mostly humming, but every so often he belts out an accent-heavy verse.

"...so I took her hand, and I gave her a twirl, and I lost my heart to a Galway Girl – Oh!"

He fills a glass with water and chugs it, continuing to hum between swallows. When he's done, he sets the glass on the counter but misses. It shatters on the floor.

"Fecking hell," he mumbles. He stares down at the

mess for a moment, then shakes his head and walks right over it.

Graceless steps carry him to the stairs and up them. His bleary eyes pass right over me, then snap back. I hear a click and see the glisten of a blade in the same moment he sighs heavily.

"Jesus, Mary, and Joseph, I almost stabbed you. What the fuck are you doing?"

My heart drops like a weight from my throat to my gut. "Waiting for you."

He smirks, tucking the switchblade away. "Are you now? I don't suppose you want to suck me off? Always helps me sleep."

"Classy," I snarl, "but no, thanks. I don't suck cock that's been in another woman the same night."

He laughs, loud and astonished. "Oh, you little hoyden. You think I fucked that sub? Trussed her up and fucked her till she screamed?"

Disgust and anger bring me to my feet. "Didn't you? Wasn't that the whole point? The *punishment?*"

He leaps the three stairs between us. I move, but too slowly. Fingers sink into the hair at the back of my neck, and he yanks my face up.

"You do not belong there," he growls, each word enunciated with sharp precision.

"Then where do I belong?" I yell.

"With me," he says furiously. "You belong with *me.*"

I laugh hysterically, shoving him away. He releases my hair before his fingers risk ripping it out. Almost, I wish he hadn't. The pain might have slowed my mental sprint off a cliff. But since there's nothing to stop me, I plummet right into the storm of my emotions.

"But *you* belong there! With them! They worship you at that place. And even you told me I'm the worst sub in the world. I don't know why you keep pretending this will work! I can't be like that, I can't do all the public displays, or scenes, or whatever you call them—God, this is a nightmare! Why won't you just leave me alone? Let Maddoc have me if I'm so... so... *wrong!*"

Liam drags hands through his hair. "Look, Eden, ignoring the absolute horseshit of your last statement, I don't fucking care about the club, about any of it. Sure, it's a part of me—it will always be a part of me—but I don't need it like some of the others do."

He sounds sincere, but he's also drunk.

"Then why have you been there the last three nights?" I demand.

"Why do you even care?" he rasps.

"Because I don't want you sleeping with other women!" I holler. "Or even touching them!"

He matches my volume, yelling, "Why, Eden!"

"Because you're *mine!*" I scream.

Silence descends, swirling around our heavy breaths.

My pronouncement rings in the air. I have no idea which of us is more startled by it, but he recovers first.

"I didn't touch her or anyone else. London belongs to Dominic. I didn't touch her."

My chest deflates. "You lied."

He nods, unrepentant. "Has it ever occurred to you that I don't want you to be anyone other than who you are? The sexiest, smartest, mouthiest woman I've ever met?"

I blink in surprise. "No."

"And apparently the most clueless, as well."

Groaning, I rub my face with my hands. "What the hell is happening to me?"

"I don't know," he says evenly. "But since I'm sloshed and liable to throw my heart at your feet any second, I'm going to spare myself the inevitable splash-back of shit and head to bed."

My heart churns, spinning through fearful shadows and radiant light.

I clear my throat. "Splash-back of shit?"

He grunts and keeps walking.

"Liam?"

"What?" he snaps.

"Did you drive home drunk?"

"No, got a ride."

He's almost at the threshold of his bedroom. "Liam?"

"*What?*"

The cliff before me this time is just as terrifying, but I jump off it willingly, hoping to land on my feet.

"Want some company?"

He stops, glances back. "I'm not fucking you, dove." His lips curl wryly. "Too much whiskey in my veins."

I shake my head. "I just want to sleep. Next to you." After a small hesitation, I admit, "You make me feel safe."

His expression softens. "You really are a pain in my ass. Come on, then." Pivoting, he disappears into the dark bedroom, but I can still hear him muttering. "Madwoman... showing up at the club. Brave little dove... should paddle you till you can't sit for a week. Pigtails. Sitting in the dark for me wearing pigtails. Conniving woman. Jesus H. Christ, I'm drunk."

There's a thump, and he yelps in pain.

"Feck! Stupid fecking bed!"

Swallowing laughter, I follow him into the room.

31

I WAKE up with the sun warm on my back and open my eyes to find Liam's side of the bed empty. Sighing, I pull the sheet over my head.

True to his word, he didn't touch me last night. Not even when I woke up just before dawn sprawled on his chest with his arousal caught between us. Looking up, I found him watching me, his hands locked behind his neck. With rejection stinging in my chest, I maneuvered away and curled around a pillow, finally falling back to sleep.

The house is quiet. Without needing to look, I know he's not here. I can't explain it to myself, but some deep part of me *feels* when he's here. In the same way a planet is bound by gravity to the sun, without Liam, I'm never more aware of being untethered and alone.

Eventually I rouse myself and take a shower, then

nibble halfheartedly on toast. I turn on the TV in the living room for background noise. I reheat yesterday's coffee and scroll through Facebook. Around ten, when I know my parents are both at work, I call the house and leave a message on their ancient answering machine.

"Hey, Mom and Dad, it's me. Just wanted to let you know I'm doing good. Working hard and saving money for school." I almost choke on the lies. "I, uh, miss you. We'll talk soon. Love you. Bye."

I throw my phone on the couch, where it rings a moment later. I see Karina's face on the screen and hesitate—unlike my parents, she has a pretty impressive bullshit meter. The call goes to voicemail, but my phone rings again immediately. Having been down this road with her before, I know she won't stop calling until I pick up.

Sighing, I answer. "Hey, K."

"Where the fuck have you been?" she yells. "Some bimbo answered your door and said she lives there now! I thought you were fucking dead..." She transitions fluidly to Spanish, which she knows I don't speak. But I get the gist easily enough.

"I'm sorry I worried you," I say when she finally winds down. "I haven't called because, honestly, I wasn't sure what to say."

"Tell me what's going on!"

Wincing, I rip off the Band-Aid. "I'm postponing med

school for a year. I moved in with Liam. He said I could quit my jobs, so I did."

She's quiet for two seconds, then explodes. "WHAT! ¿Quién eres y qué has hecho con mi amiga? Has perdido la cabeza!"

Pretty sure she just told me I'm crazy.

"I know it seems… out of character for me, but uh, I've never been happier."

"Bitch, you sound like you're sucking lemons!"

In spite of myself, I laugh. "Because my inner feminist keeps trying to break out of her cage. And I don't want you to think less of me."

Karina sighs. "I don't care if you're shacking up with Mr. Fancy. Shit, besides the choking and spanking he's a regular Prince Charming."

I laugh again, a little wildly. *If only she knew.* My life isn't Disney—it's the Brothers Grimm.

Karina continues, "But you're still going to med school, right?"

"Yes. I just deferred a year. Happens all the time."

Please don't let that, too, be a lie.

"Are you free for lunch?" She pauses. "Or wait, are you allowed to leave the dungeon?"

I really shouldn't have answered the phone.

"I can leave whenever I want, but my car's in the shop."

"I'll pick you up," she says quickly. "Give me the address."

I bite my lip, wracking my brain for a plausible lie, when my excuse strolls in the front door. "Sorry, K. Liam just walked in with lunch. Can I call you later?"

"Put Mr. Fancy on the phone right now," she snaps.

I pull the device away from my ear. Liam stops on the threshold of the kitchen, head cocked in question.

"Karina wants to talk to you."

He holds out his hand for the phone. For the next few minutes, Karina chews him out. Liam gives appropriate responses at the appropriate times, and finally hangs up with a tired smirk.

"She's a good friend," he says, handing me back my phone. He walks to the fridge and pulls out a bottle of water. "Did you really tell her I had a nine-inch dick?"

My face flames. "Uhh—maybe?"

He laughs and takes a swig of water. "Nine and a half, actually."

I roll my eyes. "At a certain point it stops mattering. Besides, most women would rather have an eraser than a pencil."

Liam guffaws. "Good Lord, woman. Where do you come up with this shit?"

I move past him, grabbing a bottle of water for myself. "Whatever. It's not like you're lacking in either department. Where'd you go so early, anyway?"

Walking around the island, he takes a seat on a stool. "Had to get my car and run an errand."

I lower the bottle from my mouth. "What kind of errand?"

"The illegal kind. I'm going to teach you how to shoot a gun."

Definitely not Disney.

32

WHEN WE RETURN from the shooting range, Liam disappears to shower while I drag myself to my room. Facedown on the bed, I float in the echoes of muted gunshots, the tingle in my muscles from repeated recoils, and the lingering smells of oil and gunpowder.

Somewhere within me, behind layers and layers of ice, is the old me. Braids and flannels, her nose always in a book. I'm sure she's screaming down there, past the cold. Screaming and crying at what's become of her.

I liked firing a gun.

No, I *loved* it. The first time I hit the target, I felt like a goddess. Like a Valkyrie of old with a sword in her hands, defending what was rightfully hers. I didn't fully understand just how afraid I was until I wasn't anymore.

Liam was stoic throughout, barely responsive to my ecstatic shouts when I tore the target to shreds.

"You're a natural," he said, unreadable eyes moving from the target to me. "I think we're done for the day."

The drive home was another silent trip, each of us lost in thoughts. The thrill I'd felt soured by the time we arrived home. Now, with my face in a pillow, I acknowledge that the look in his eyes had been disappointment.

Against his own logic, he'd been hoping I wouldn't be able to stomach it.

That I wouldn't be like my father.

LIAM FINDS me some time later. I don't move, just rotate my head on the pillow to watch him walk toward me. He doesn't turn on a light, sitting on the edge of my bed with his back to me.

Elbows on his knees, he bows his head. "Can I tell you a little story, dove?"

"Sure," I whisper.

"For my sixth birthday, my grandparents took me to Dublin for the weekend. They told my mother we were going to Cork because they knew she hated Dublin. She was working that weekend. I remember how glad she was that I was going to have a celebration, even if she couldn't be there.

"I don't remember where we were, somewhere downtown browsing shops, when a man saw me. He looked at me and turned white as a ghost. As we walked back to our hotel, he followed us. My grandparents didn't see him, and I thought I must be imagining things. Why would this man be following me?

"We were almost to the hotel when he confronted my grandparents. He asked them a bunch of questions—my name, who my parents were, where we lived. They gave him nothing. Late that night, three men in ski masks broke into our hotel room. They shot my grandparents and took me."

I jerk upright. "What? Oh my God, Liam—"

"It's okay," he says, "just let me get this out. I lied to you, about coming to the States when I was eight. I was twelve. From age six to twelve, I lived with a man I came to learn was my father. He... he's to Dublin what Maddoc is to Los Angeles.

"My mother, like yours, ran away. But she didn't run far enough. He hadn't known she was pregnant, so she thought we'd be safe with her parents." He makes a harsh sound. "The man who saw me was one of my father's. I looked uncannily like the bastard, even at six years old. For nearly seven years he kept me. Trained me. Tortured me when he had to..."

He trails off, breathing heavily. When I touch his back, he flinches. I pull away, hugging my arms to my chest.

"I'm sorry," I say helplessly.

Liam shakes his head. "I never gave up my mother, and he eventually let it go. He didn't have much to complain about, anyway, as I excelled in every challenge he presented. You asked me once if I killed people. I have, Eden. I killed for my father, and I killed when I escaped him at twelve."

I release the breath I've been holding. "Is that why Maddoc leaves you alone? He's afraid of you?"

Liam snorts. "Hardly. He leaves me alone because I'm a Rourke. A fucking prince of the old world. He's not afraid of me. He's afraid of my father. They're both lunatics."

"You still talk to your father?" I ask hesitantly.

He pivots to face me. "Aye. He found my mother. It's the deal I made to keep her alive. As long as I answer when he calls, she stays unharmed."

I swallow a spike of misplaced horror. "That's terrible. I don't know what to say."

He shrugs. "A consequence of my blood. If Maddoc had his way, I'd already be married to his daughter and pumping out heirs."

My breath dies. "Already?" I whisper.

His eyes meet mine. "The price of your freedom has been set. I'm to marry Alexis."

"*What?* No way! That's—"

"Medieval? Archaic?" He smiles grimly. "Welcome to the underworld, dove."

33

NO, *no, no, no, no.*

I can't formulate any coherent thought beyond that. Beyond a primal litany of denial.

When I press Liam for details, he shakes his head and leaves the room. I don't follow. There's more to the story, more he's not telling me. But I can't even wrap my head around everything he did say.

A mob prince who fled his father, but even an ocean between them wasn't enough. What other sacrifices has he made to keep his mother safe? To keep *me* safe? He was so young… Six years old when he saw his grandparents murdered. I can't fathom it. I just can't.

More than ever before, I want to run away.

I've killed for my father.

"He was a boy," I whisper in the dark. "Just a boy."

I always knew Liam had a past, that he wasn't exactly

innocent. But for the first time, I wonder about his sadism. He's never hurt me—not really—but nothing arouses him more than playing along the boundaries of pleasure and pain.

Is it because of his childhood? The torture he mentioned? *What did they do to him?* His body is perfect, no scars that I've seen. But I know well that the deepest scars are the ones beneath the skin.

The price of your freedom.

Am I willing to pay it? To walk away from Liam, to let him marry my twin, to be sucked back into the life he ran from? Unbidden, a memory rises of the doorman at Crossroads and his words, *"You look familiar."* He thought I was Alexis. Which means Alexis has been to the club at least once.

I've known her a long time.

A sick feeling takes ahold of me. Rolling over, I reach for my phone where it rests on the nightstand, my other hand yanking open the drawer below. My fingers close around a folded piece of paper. By the light of my screen, I reread Alexis's note and the phone number at the bottom.

Then I text her.

are you available to talk?

- Eden

Three little dots undulate at the bottom of the screen.

OMG! Is this my SISTER?!?!
I'm calling right now!
You'd better answer!!!

I'm still wincing at the abundance of exclamation points when my phone starts vibrating. With an aimless prayer, I answer.

"Alexis?"

"OhmyGod, OhmyGod, is it really you? Eden?"

For a pregnant moment, I sit frozen and blank, trying to reconcile the oddest experience of my life. Even with the innate difference in our speech, she sounds exactly like me.

"Eden?"

I clear my throat. "Hi, yes, it's me."

Wherever she is, there's a fair amount of background noise. A car door slams. Men's voices rise and fade.

"I can't believe this," squeals Alexis. "I need to see you! Where are you?"

With your fiancé.

"I'm, uh, staying with a friend in the Hollywood Hills."

"Sweet! We're headed that way in a few, right, Chris?"

I hear a familiar, accented voice. "Aye. Tell her we'll be there in fifteen."

My heart stumbles and trips. "Um, I don't think—"

But Alexis isn't listening. "You know where she is?" she demands. I hear a thud like she just smacked his chest or shoulder. "What's wrong with you! Why didn't you tell me? Whatever, you suck. Eden?"

"Yeah, um, here's the thing—"

"I can't wait to see you! Get ready for the biggest hug of your life!"

She squeals and hangs up.

From the doorway, Liam growls, "What the fuck have you done?"

FIVE MINUTES LATER, I'm sitting mannequin-still on the living room couch while Liam paces before me. He's been alternately cursing me and muttering to himself. Anger rolls off him in waves. The switchblade in his right hand clicks open and closed.

Snick. Open. *Snap.* Closed.

But I won't apologize.

"Did you think I'd just walk away and forget about her?"

The eyes that swing to me are turbulent seas. "You really don't get it, do you?"

I throw up my hands. "Get what? That this whole situation is fucked? Yeah, I get it."

He laughs; it's not a pleasant sound. "Things are a bit more than fucked, dove."

"Does Alexis know?" I ask mutedly. "About the arrangement you made with Maddoc?"

"Yes," he snaps.

Breath leaves my lungs in a whoosh. "And she agreed?"

"She doesn't have a choice. Neither of us do, thanks to you."

I jerk to my feet. "Are you seriously blaming me for this? I suppose you blame me for wanting to go to UCLA, too? For showing up in this city in the first place?"

He rounds on me, pointing at my chest with the closed switchblade. "Horrible fucking luck, it was. And you're welcome, by the way, for making certain Maddoc didn't know you were in his backyard the last four years!"

I swallow my shock, package it for another day. "How long, exactly, have you known about me?" I ask carefully.

His gaze falls from mine and he says gruffly, "Since your picture showed up in an Oregon newspaper after you won a speech competition."

My vision brightens. "That was sophomore year of

high school," I whisper. "You've kept my identity a secret all these years?"

He nods. "And I would have continued doing so, but Maddoc was getting too close. One of his goons spotted you shopping on Melrose shortly before your graduation. My initial plan was to somehow frighten you enough that you ran back to Oregon. But once I had you, I didn't want to let you go."

"Do you regret it? Regret me?"

With a noise of frustration, Liam pockets his knife and closes the distance between us. He takes my face gently in his hands.

"Even though it makes me a complete bastard, no, I don't regret a second. Promise me something, dove. Promise me that when you go, you won't look back. Forget me, forget Alexis, forget it all."

I shake my head, eyes burning with tears. "I can't do that. You know I can't." Grabbing his wrists, I squeeze tightly. "Liam, come with me. Let's run together. Somewhere they'll never find us."

I'm hardly aware of what I'm saying, only that it comes from a fragile, hopeful part of my heart. Liam presses his forehead to mine; his sigh whispers across my lips.

"I can't."

When the cold shock of his words passes, I remember. "Your mother?"

He nods. "She remarried some years ago. I have a half brother and sister back home."

Squeezing my eyes shut, I release his wrists. "I understand."

"Promise me you won't look back."

My heart breaking, I nod. "I promise."

34

ALEXIS AND CHRIS NEVER ARRIVE.

When we've waited forty-five minutes, Liam makes a call. It's brief, and when he hangs up his shoulders are tight with tension.

"What is it?" I ask nervously. "Is she okay?"

"She's fine. Christopher took her home. Maddoc's orders."

"He doesn't want us to meet," I conclude flatly.

"Not while I'm in the mix, I'm afraid." Liam pinches the bridge of his nose. "All right, here's what's going to happen. Pack a bag. Bare essentials. I'll give you money to cover what you're leaving behind. You'll be on the first flight tomorrow to Oregon."

"What—no!"

"Yes," he snaps, hand dropping. "This is over, Eden. Over! I thought... I thought I could protect you, but I can't. Not from your own innocence and curiosity. Maddoc is a mercurial sonofabitch, and you need to be gone before he remembers how badly he wants you."

"My mother, you mean. Elizabeth. Whatever she took from him."

"She took *you*, Eden. But yes," he huffs caustically, "I suppose I'm a larger prize."

My world darkens at the edges, its sun dimming as he moves further and further from reach.

"This isn't right!" I cry, tears finally coming, leaking fast from my eyes. I think of Alexis, but she's mostly a phantom voice. Not real yet. But he is. I walk toward him. Toward the sun.

"You're mine, Liam. Not hers."

He smiles, but his eyes stay shadowed and distant. "You'll find another, little dove. You're young yet."

My hand stings. I stare at it, the pale surface, then at the red mark intensifying on his cheek. He doesn't react, just watches me with his too-knowing eyes.

"I'm sorry," he murmurs, voice thick with regret. "Sorry for everything. Eden, I—" He swallows the words, shaking his head, then turns on a heel and ascends the stairs.

Calm. Graceful. Powerful.

Not mine. But if I'm honest, I always knew he couldn't be. Not for long, anyway.

MY PACKED BAG sits on the end of my bed. A few pairs of underwear. Some jeans, shirts, and a sweatshirt. Toiletries and the laptop I haven't opened in weeks. I've just showered, and my wet hair hangs limp and tangled down my back. My phone is dark in my hand, but lights up when I press the home button.

I read the short text message from an unknown number for the fiftieth time.

Stay away from her.

Is the message from Chris, or another man in the employ of my father? Or is it from the man himself, Maddoc Donnelly? If it did come from him, I now have my answer as to whether he gives a shit about his long-lost daughter.

I don't feel any relief at the thought of escaping. None at all. Beneath a layer of numbness is a maelstrom of emotion. Like a Kraken under calm waters, there's a shifting deep within as chaos rises.

How am I supposed to move forward with my life? What a fucking joke. There's no moving past this. No forgetting this, despite my promise to Liam. Does he really think I can just move to Seattle as planned, go to med school and become a doctor, live a normal life?

There's no life without sunlight.

A cascade of unwanted visions paints my closed

eyelids—Liam and Alexis. Alexis and Liam. Maybe in the dark, she'll feel just like me. Maybe she'll feel better, even. Maybe she's better in the way that he needs. A perfect sub in and out of the bedroom.

I don't want you to be anyone other than who you are.

Maybe he'll forget me.

With that thought, a dark need possesses my limbs. I toss my phone onto the bed and stand. Leaving my hair as it is, I slip out of my robe. Cool air skates across my exposed skin.

The soles of my feet tingle on carpet as I walk from the bedroom, down the shadowed hallway toward the dim outline of his door.

I don't knock. The knob turns silently in my shaking fingers. I take one step, two steps, then drop to my knees and bow my head. No lights are on, but I know he's here. I can feel him.

An eternity passes before he speaks.

"No, Eden."

My breath releases harshly; my fingers clench. "Please, sir."

"Why?" he asks, sounding forlorn, so lost. Just as I am.

"Because I need it, sir."

He laughs, so softly it's little more than huffs of air. "Such a demanding, selfish little dove."

"You like it."

"I suppose I do," he muses. "Did you know there are Doms who specifically want subs who talk back?"

I swallow. "Are you one of them?"

"Until you, no." He pauses; fabric whispers as he stands from the bed. "I won't go outside your limits, but I'll push them. Maybe further than you want. I'm not in a peaceful headspace at the moment."

"I serve to please you, sir."

"What's your safe word?"

"Clover."

He hesitates, the seesaw of power dipping and rising between us. My surrender. And finally, his.

"On all fours, dove. Crawl to the dresser. Bottom drawer. Two lengths of rope. Flogger. Clamps. Black beads. Carry them in your teeth. Don't drop them."

He's the sun, dissolving my darkness and filling me with molten light.

35

IT'S NOT easy carrying the toys in my teeth, my mouth stretched so wide my jaw aches. Liam doesn't speak, not words of approval or any others, as I crawl to him and sit back on my heels.

One at a time, he removes each piece from my mouth. The flogger's smooth, leather-encased handle. Then his birthday gift, the petite clamps hanging from a delicate chain. The two ropes, their ends wet from my saliva. Finally, he takes the string of beads, each one popping as it's freed from my cheek.

"Let's get you ready, dove."

He doesn't have to give me instructions—I know what he wants. I turn on my knees and lower onto my forearms. Deep, even breaths help me relax, help ease the instinctive desire to clench.

A fingertip circles my clitoris, teasing and light and

unexpected. Another finger dips inside me, swirling lazily, building my arousal until I can hear my own wetness. My hips lift instinctively, seeking more, deeper pressure.

"Greedy," he murmurs.

The word is all the warning I have before the flogger comes down hard on my ass. I yelp. He doesn't soothe the sting with his hand like he normally does. Instead, he whacks me again right as he inserts the first bead in my ass.

"Oh, fuck," I groan.

Another blow, harder this time. Hard enough that tears spring to my eyes, that I clench around the bead. The fullness makes me hotter, wetter. Liam dips fingers inside me, dragging the lubrication up to the beads.

"What do you say, dove?"

"Thank you, sir."

Another bead, slightly larger. Fingertips whisper down my spine. Every one of my senses is alive, razor-sharp. He owns them—me.

I press my forehead hard to the floor, breathing through the burning sensation of the final, largest bead.

"Good girl."

He strokes me with both hands, shoulders to hips. Over and over, soothing the beast inside me. The beast in him. It normally takes more than a few slaps to the ass and some beads to push me into a euphoric state. But not tonight. The immense relief I feel at his touch catalyzes my transition.

"Sweet dove. Already floating, are you? I'm not even a little bit done with you yet."

"Yes, sir," I choke out.

His hands retract; seconds later, I feel pressure on my nipples. Hear the sweet tinkling of the silver chain connecting the clamps.

"God, I love you like this," he whispers, giving the chain a little tug. The fiery sensation doesn't hurt—not here, not in the ocean of my calm mind where pain and pleasure coexist.

"Will you fuck me now, sir?"

"No."

"Please," I beg.

"Keep asking and all you'll get is a redder ass. Stand up, dove. Carefully. On the bed."

I am careful, waiting through mild dizziness as the blood rushes away from my head. The hard paleness of his chest gleams through his unbuttoned shirt. I want to touch him so badly my fingers clench, my gaze lowering. He's erect behind his zipper; my mouth waters.

"You want this?" he asks, palming his cock. I nod. "Where do you want it, dove?"

"Everywhere, sir," I whisper.

With a harsh grunt, he undoes his belt and lowers the zipper. "On your knees."

I fall, my mouth already opening, ready to receive him. My jaw in his fingers, he sighs.

"Take a breath."

I do. He works himself down my throat and stills. When I don't immediately gag, I feel a warm swell of satisfaction. Pride at my accomplishment. He strokes my cheek gently as he draws back.

"One more. Longer this time."

I suck air swiftly through my nose, as much as my lungs can take. He plunges back down my throat, this time holding my head firmly against him. His hips rock a few times, forcing him impossibly deep.

"Sweet, sweet dove."

Just when the need for oxygen turns from a knock to a sledgehammer, he pulls out. I cough, gasping. Pain makes a brief appearance—my nipples, my ass. Squeezing my eyes shut, I count to ten. Slowly, my body relaxes.

"Up. On your back."

I need another few moments, but he doesn't give them to me. Fingers clenched in my hair, he drags me to my feet. I scramble up to avoid losing strands.

"Eden."

My eyes flash up to his; the edge of his passion is blunted by concern. It makes me smile.

"Green."

He lifts me by the waist and throws me in one

smooth movement. I land hard on the bed, bouncing a little, the pressure in my ass suddenly intense. I barely have time to process the new feelings before his mouth covers my clit. He suckles me. Then uses his teeth.

I cry out at the sharp pain, then whimper as his tongue relieves it. Then the cycle begins again. Again and again, he bites down, licks. Bite. Lick. When I clutch his head to hold him there, he drags my wrists away from our bodies.

"Grab your ankles."

I don't want to, but I obey.

Here, I always obey.

"Please, sir, make me come."

"Patience, dove," he murmurs as he rises to his feet. His eyes are drunk with desire as they roam my body. I watch him undress, unable to withhold my soft cries. My universe is simple and pure.

I'm empty. He fills me.

I need him.

Once naked, Liam grabs the ropes and binds each of my wrists to its corresponding ankle. When he's done, he sits back on his heels to survey his work.

I tremble uncontrollably. His palms smooth up the taut muscles of my inner thighs. His eyes find mine.

"Please, sir, please—"

He pulls off the nipple clamps, and I scream as circulation returns in a rush, scream again as he thrusts inside me. He's merciless, hands squeezing and pinching my breasts as he slides in and out. Hard. Harder.

The sound our bodies make is music.

Perfect music.

Fingers surround my throat, pressing down. Slowly decreasing my oxygen, so slowly, until I feel every heartbeat in my ears, across every inch of my skin. In my clit, my ass, my cervix as he pounds against it. The pleasure is so acute I almost *want* to pass out. It's too much.

Too fucking much.

"Now, Eden," he snarls, releasing my throat.

I'm more than conditioned to obey him—I *want* to obey with every fiber of my being. I climax so hard, so long, that for an eternity of moments, I lose all sense of time and place. There is only him. I revel in the freedom of it, in giving him all of myself. He's in control so I don't have to be.

As the last pulses of my orgasm fade, he pulls out, then lowers to dip his tongue into my mouth.

Giving my lips a tug with his teeth, he whispers, "Mine. I want all of it tonight."

I nod in acceptance. "Yes, sir," I breathe. "I'm yours."

His eyes close briefly; he draws a shallow breath. Then he rises above me, one hand sliding beneath me to angle my pelvis upward. I feel a tug, and one by one the beads slip out of my ass.

My pulse speeds in mingled fear and anticipation. I

close my eyes, focusing on the press of his hand beneath me, the languor of release still coursing through my limbs.

Cool liquid slides down the crack of my ass. One finger goes in, then another.

"Breathe in and out. Slow and deep."

As the breath fills my lungs, his fingers withdraw. And when I exhale, he slides inside me. I have two seconds to absorb the mind-shattering fullness, the alien but not entirely unpleasant sensation. Then he begins to move.

"Oh God, oh God," I chant.

"Look at me, dove."

Opening my eyes is a battle, but I manage. Ambient light from the windows illuminates his left side while the other is shadowed. Half angel, half devil. But the look on his face tells me all of him is mine.

The light caresses metal as he lifts the clamps from the bed. An animalistic wail rises in my throat. Liam smiles—the devil smiles—and rubber encased steel teases my clitoris.

"No, sir. Please. Oh God."

"Do you serve?" he growls, hips beginning to piston into me. I'm unraveling, my Self fracturing.

"Yes!"

The clamp finds purchase. I shriek, bucking against the pain, against the hands that hold me still. My voice fills the room, pleas and cries torn from me. I have no awareness of what I'm saying, what I'm begging for.

Until he removes the clamp.

I'm gone.

Nothing but pleasure.

Nothing.

Liam thrusts a final time, emptying himself into me with a sigh.

"Easy, dove, easy," he whispers as he slowly pulls out. I keep sobbing, the emotional release just as powerful as the physical one.

Releasing the knots, he gathers me in his arms. He strokes my hair and whispers how much I please him, how proud he is of his little dove.

That no matter how far I fly, he knows I'll always come home to him. For tonight, for the last time, we pretend.

36

NOW

I THINK AT SOME POINT, every person wonders what thoughts they'll have before death. Perhaps they'll regret not living the way they wanted. Being too afraid to go after their dreams.

I don't have that particular regret, though I have others. Many, many others. But not that one. I'm Dr. Eden Sumner, pediatric resident at a well-respected Seattle hospital. There's a motherfucking M.D. after my name.

At least I was—there was. My current accomplishments are probably limited to a missing persons list and weekly prayer vigils in my hometown. Or maybe it's been long enough that I'm presumed dead.

I've never been afraid of death. Not really, and defi-nitely not in the last few years. I thank the many cadavers I sliced and stitched in school. The gunshot and stab wounds I treated during my ER rotation. The ruptured spleens and traumatic amputations. Heart attacks. Anaphylaxis. Drug overdoses.

Bring enough people back from the brink, and the border between life and death blurs a bit. I don't want to die—obviously—but I'm not afraid of it.

Some things are worth dying for.

37

THEN

"HELLO? MOM?"

"In here, honey!"

I follow her voice to the kitchen, where I find her chopping lettuce. She abandons her task and rushes around the island to hug me. The scent of her perfume swirls around me like a second embrace, thick with memories of a different, simpler me.

A crack spreads in my chest, but I hold it closed until the urge to cry passes.

"Oh, sweetheart, I'm so glad you're here." She releases me, leaning back. Teary eyes scan my face and hair. "You look beautiful. But so thin! Are you hungry? Dinner's on the stove."

"Sure, I'm hungry." My words and smile are both lies. "I'll take my bag upstairs and freshen up. Where's Dad?"

"Garage," she says with a chuckle.

"Shocker." I give her a quick kiss, then head back into the hallway for my bag.

Upstairs, my room is exactly as I left it four and a half years ago. A time capsule of a girl who no longer exists.

The twin bed creaks as I sit. I pull my phone from my pocket and stare at it. The case is the same, but the device is new. Not functional yet, as it lacks a service provider. No contacts, no locator apps. No backlog of text messages.

Liam has my old phone. I'd watched him delete all traces of himself from my social media accounts, email, and photos. The only numbers he'd allowed me to write down were Karina and Raul's.

I'd watched him erase us and done nothing to stop him. I don't even know my new phone number.

And neither does he.

All I have left of him is soreness. Light bruising that will fade too fast. An ache when I sit. And an order to close my checking account and open another when I get to Seattle. Since I'm not hiding, I get to keep my name. My parents. Med school and my future.

But I'm allowed no ties to Los Angeles.

To Maddoc Donnelly or my sister.

To him.

Curling into my old, faded quilt, I close my eyes and fall into oblivion.

WHEN I WAKE, the house is dark. Through my partially closed bedroom door, I hear the television downstairs and my parents murmured voices.

My eyes are heavy and swollen, my face and pillow wet. I don't remember what I was dreaming about, but it must have been him.

"Liam," I whisper.

His name on my tongue, I fall asleep again.

I SLEEP THE NIGHT THROUGH, waking up again to sunlight coming through the window above my head. Dawn, or just after.

Dragging myself from bed is a challenge I'm not prepared for. Neither is being awake. There's an ocean of pain inside me that I don't know how to begin dealing with.

The smell of bacon wafts upstairs. It's not hunger that finally gets me on my feet, but the knowledge that my parents are doubtlessly worried. They've been beyond understanding—accepting my bullshit about postponing med school, then welcoming me home with open arms when I called on my way to the airport.

I owe them an explanation, even if it's mostly fabricated. At least part of it will be true—my heart is without a doubt broken.

I change my clothes. Brush my teeth. Throw my hair into a ponytail and pinch my cheeks so I don't look like a dead person. Liam was careful—there are no visible marks on my neck or arms.

I wish there were.

Downstairs, I find them both in the kitchen. Mom's standing at the sink and dad's in his usual spot at the table. He sees me first. He doesn't smile, but his eyes are soft with concern as he stands up and takes me in his arms. It's like being hugged by a bear.

"I'm okay, Dad," I say into his Old Spice-scented flannel.

He draws back, hands cupping my shoulders. "I know you are."

I give him a weak smile—it's more of a grimace.

"Hungry for bacon and eggs?" asks my mother.

I shake my head. "Is there any coffee left?"

She smiles. "I just made a fresh pot. Sit. Still drinking it with cream and no sugar?"

"Yes, thanks."

Dad sits back down, and I drop into the adjacent chair. By the time I'm finished with my first cup of coffee, the tension in the room is palpable.

Out of the corner of my eye, I watch my dad finish his last piece of bacon and push his plate away. Mom takes it to the sink, then pulls out the chair opposite mine.

Here it comes.

They trade a glance. My mom clears her throat. "Eden, sweetheart, we're so glad you're home."

"Very glad," echoes my dad.

He reaches for her hand; their fingers clasp together tightly. As they stare at me, I start to get a bad feeling. Like I'm on the Titanic but don't know it.

"What's going on?" I ask.

Another shared look, this one full of resolve. My mom is the one who speaks, her voice shaking a little.

"Sweetheart, we need to talk to you about your adoption."

Not the iceberg I'd been expecting.

Not even close.

38

Eden,

I don't have much time, so forgive me if I don't waste it. If you're reading this, it's because he found you. Your father, Maddoc Donnelley. It also means you're ready to hear what I need to tell you. I took you—not Alexis—for a reason.

You were born second. Too small, ill. The doctors didn't think you were going to make it. But I knew you would. From the moment I first held you and looked into your eyes, I knew you were a fighter. And you fought. You thrived.

I took you because I knew you'd be strong enough to do what needs to be done. To free your sister as I could not. To save her from a life of guilt, depravity, and blood.

I wish I could be there to help you. Know that wherever I am—dead or alive—I have spent each moment of my life loving you.

I've left further instructions with Margaret and Ben.

Yours,

EGS

WHEN I LOOK up from the letter, my parents are still holding hands tightly. Still watching me with identical expressions of apology and fear.

I say the first thing that comes to mind.

"What the fuck?"

"Eden Elizabeth Sumner," growls my dad.

"It's okay," murmurs my mom. She turns teary eyes on me. "I can only imagine what you must be feeling right now."

I toss the letter down. My heart thrums hard with their betrayal. Almost, it hurts worse than losing Liam. He kept the truth from me for a few months.

They kept the truth hidden for *decades.*

"You knew," I say hoarsely. "All this time, you knew I had a twin sister and that my biological father was a psychopath crime lord? Were you ever going to tell me, if I didn't find out myself?"

My dad winces. "Your moth—Elizabeth... she

wanted us to protect you as long as we could. We agreed to wait until you were twenty-five, but that night at your birthday party, that fellow…"

"Liam," I snap.

"Yes," says my mom. "Liam. He pulled us aside. He… he asked us if we knew who your real parents were. It was so unexpected. We didn't know what to say. He must have known we did from our expressions. Then he told us you were close to the truth, but that he was doing his best to keep you safe."

"He also said we should have never let you move to Los Angeles," grumbles my dad.

"Hold up!" I throw up my hands to stall them. "This is… it's too much. Just let me think."

I stare at the letter, at Elizabeth's hasty scrawl. Nothing makes sense. And it makes too much sense— she took me, saved me, so her other child would have a chance to be saved in turn.

"This woman, my *mother,* is insane if she thinks I can get Alexis away from Maddoc." I shake my head, looking up at my parents. "Were you supposed to enroll me in freaking karate or something? Get me combat training? I'm not Sarah-fucking-Connor with shotguns strapped to my back and a death wish. I'm a fucking student!"

My dad goes a little pale beneath his beard. "If we could protect you from this, we would. Many times over the years, we even considered not telling you." He glances at my mom. "But that didn't sit right with our consciences."

"You can walk away," says my mom suddenly. "That's why you came back, isn't it? Liam sent you away from it? Sweetheart, you don't have to do anything with the information in that letter. Elizabeth... well, she was frantic when she found us. Paranoid. She truly believed that someone was going to kill her. What if your sister— Alexis—is happy with her life? We don't know that she isn't."

"She's right, Eden. You can put this all behind you."

They believe what they're saying. They really do. They think I can click my heels and forget it all. Forget them.

Liam's words filter through my mind: *She doesn't have a choice. Neither of us do.*

And isn't that what freedom is?

Choice?

I pick up the letter, my fingers grazing the words. I'm lost. Alone. No sunlight or gravity. The ground is too far —the fall will kill me.

I make the choice anyway.

"What else did Elizabeth give you?"

My mom's shoulders sag, her face crumpling. My dad frowns, sitting back in his chair with a sigh. He doesn't look surprised.

"You knew what I'd say," I tell him.

He shrugs. "Nothing has ever stopped you from going after what you want. That much, Elizabeth was right about. You're a fighter. So strong."

My eyes well with tears. "I don't feel like I am."

He smiles sadly. "The strong rarely do."

39

I'VE ALWAYS LOVED PORTLAND. When I was a teenager, my friends and I would drive up often on the weekends. We'd spend a day—sometimes two if we found a place to crash—walking around downtown browsing Powell's Books and thrift shops, stuffing our faces with food-truck wares, and relaxing in coffee shops and cafés.

The mid-June weather is beautiful, sunny and warm, and everywhere I look I see the marriage of nature and man. The streets are clean, the sky above a serene, cloudless blue. Sidewalks make space for trees and parks. Even the architecture of the high-rises around me seems purposeful, like each building is art in disguise.

Standing across the street from a massive bank, I double-check the information in my phone. The name of the bank has changed in the nearly twenty-three years since my mother was first here, but the address is the same.

Don't, whispers Liam's voice in my mind.

"Suck a dick," I tell him, and jog across the street during a break in traffic.

The lobby doors are opened by a security officer. I thank him with a smile, then pause to look around. The space is expansive and hushed. White-veined marble floors, glistening dark wood and chrome accents. The building itself is old; there are echoes of the past in heavy marble columns and scrollwork engraved beneath high windows.

"Can I help you?"

I turn to face a woman, mid-fifties, with a sweet smile and intelligent eyes. My pulse jumps in my throat.

"Yes. I, uh, need to access a safety deposit box." I hold up the little key.

Her eyes widen. "Wow, I haven't seen one of those in years."

I offer her the slight, sad smile I've been practicing for days. "It was left to me by my grandmother. She died recently."

"Oh, honey, I'm so sorry," she says, giving my shoulder a gentle pat. "It's not a problem. Right this way, please. My name is Loretta. You have the box number, I'm assuming?"

"Yes."

"Great."

She guides me through a hallway and into another, smaller lobby. At a reinforced steel door, she enters a code for clearance. There's a beep and a thunk, and the door slides open.

"This way." As she leads me further into the room, she glances back with a worried expression. "Now, I hope your grandmother added you as an authorized key-holder."

I nod. "She did. And I have ID."

Loretta smiles. "Excellent."

At a small podium holding a computer, she takes my ID and checks it against the box number I give her. Every second that passes adds another notch to my anxiety. My armpits prickle with nervous sweat.

When she looks up with a smile, I release a breath of unadulterated relief.

"Here we go. Eden Elizabeth Sumner, registered as a key-holder by the box's owner, Elizabeth Grace Sharpe." She smiles again. "It's lovely that you have her name."

I nod, my throat tight. "I miss her terribly," I lie.

With a cluck of sympathy, Loretta motions me once more to follow. Within ten feet or so, she begins to slow, scanning the metal slots just below eye level.

"Here. 8056." She inserts her own key in the top keyhole and gestures to the one below it.

Open, please.

My key turns easily. The panel opens.

Loretta removes the long, steel case from inside and walks to a nearby table. Then she points back the way we came. "I'll be just over there. Come and get me when you're done. I'm so sorry for your loss."

I nod and she leaves. My hands tremble, sweaty fingertips leaving marks on the metal as I lift the lid.

"Holy shit."

Even being somewhat prepared by my parents, nothing on this earth could have softened the shock of seeing what's before me with my own eyes.

Money.

A whole fucking lot of it. Bundles and bundles of mixed denominations: twenties, fifties, and hundreds. Sitting on top of the stacks is a small velvet pouch and an envelope with my name on it. Ignoring the letter for the moment, I pick up the pouch.

I loosen the ties and peek inside.

My breath leaves in a whoosh as I see what Elizabeth stole. What Maddoc wants back. And I know with absolute conviction that regardless of his deal with Liam, I'm not safe.

As long as Maddoc thinks I might know where Elizabeth is—where *this* is—I'll never be safe.

As I leave the bank, my oversized purse crammed full of money, every person I see is a potential threat. I'm sweating in earnest by the time I reach my dad's borrowed truck.

Once inside with the doors locked, I start the car and get out of the city. It takes twenty miles for me to be convinced I'm not being followed. The back of my neck continues to crawl with the fear that someone saw me. Someone who belongs to Maddoc.

This is how my mother must have felt—still feels, if she's alive—every moment of every day since leaving Los Angeles. On edge. Paranoid. Frantic. It makes me feel a twisted kinship with the woman.

"Mother-daughter bonding through fear for our lives," I mutter, then shake my head roughly. "Talking to yourself. You're talking to yourself. In the third person, no less. Get a fucking grip."

I manage to curb the crazy and take an exit about ten miles from home. I find a busy parking lot in a little shopping center with food, gas, and a coffee shop. I park in the last row between two cars under the shade of a massive tree.

Then I open the envelope.

40

—

April 17, 2002

Dear Eden,

I know you have questions. I'll do my best to anticipate and answer them. The first is probably how I got away from Maddoc in the first place. And the answer is a combination of preparation and luck. I told no one about my plans because I trusted no one. Neither should you. There's no such thing as loyalty through affection in your father's world. Loyalty comes at great cost, usually paid for in blood.

Luck must be responsible for the fact we weren't found in the first few days. I was certain we would be. But we made it out. In the following weeks, I switched cars multiple times, colored my hair, and used fake IDs. I paid for everything with cash. If we ever had a tail, we lost it.

You're also wondering if I'm alive. I hope so, but there's always a chance he's found me. I move every few years. Take a new name. I keep to myself. I tell no one about my past. I'm so sorry, Eden, but some day you might have to live this way, too. But I hope not.

As you noticed, there was a lot of money in the safety deposit box. It totals around $600k. But as I'm sure you also noticed, the money wasn't the most valuable thing you found. _That_ is your way out. What can give you and Alexis a future.

Another question I'm sure you have—Why didn't I go to the cops? Because it's too great a risk, then and now. I can say with certainty that at least a few detectives at the LAPD are on Maddoc's payroll. At least one person in the DEA is, as well. No matter how much time has passed, some things don't change. I'll tell you again —trust no one.

I won't suggest where you should go, except to say there are some lovely islands in the world. Between the two of you, I'm sure you'll find a place. That's my hope, my greatest dream. That my girls find a home together somewhere safe.

Don't try to find me. Don't tell Margaret or Ben what you're doing, either. Not because they're not good *people, but because they are, and will do what good people do and call the police.*

Be smart. Be brave. I know you'll figure it out, my strong girl.

I love you,

EGS

"WELL, SHIT," I tell the empty car. I fold the letter and slip it back in its envelope, then pull the velvet pouch from my pocket.

Carefully removing the item inside, I stare at it. Then I get paranoid again, imagining high-powered sniper rifles and zoom cameras, and shove it back inside. It clinks against the other items in the bag. I wince, then logic arrives.

Plastic can't hurt diamonds.

WHEN I GET HOME, my mom is so relieved she starts crying. My dad gives me another bear hug but doesn't speak. After a long look at my mother, he disappears into the garage.

As I nibble on leftovers from their dinner, my mom eventually asks what I found.

"A letter dated fifteen years ago," I tell her, not

meeting her gaze. "A little bit of cash. Two hundred dollars."

She's silent for close to a minute. I force myself to keep chewing until I finish my meal, then take my plate to the sink.

"And did she… tell you what you're supposed to do? How you're supposed to help your sister?"

Turning to lean against the counter, I shake my head. "Just a lot of paranoid rambling about leaving the country." I snort. "Like I'm supposed to do that with two hundred bucks."

I feel bad. I do. But Elizabeth was right—if I tell them there's close to a million dollars, a USB stick, and enough diamonds to buy a small country in my bag, they'll call the police.

They'd probably let me keep the money, though. I could pay off their mortgage, my student loans, and go through med school debt free. It's really too bad none of that is enough incentive to pull me off this runaway train.

The biggest problem with Elizabeth's warning is that even though I don't trust my parents to not call the authorities, there's one person I do trust. Implicitly. With my life. Regardless of whether or not he wants me in his.

But before I go back to L.A., I have to find a safe place for my secret.

41

I WALK into Benny's Feed and Tackle the following morning and head straight to the woman behind the counter.

"Hi there," she says brightly. "What can I help you find?"

"I'm looking for Benny. Is he here today? I'm an old friend."

She gives me a once-over. "You must mean Benny Jr., as Benny Sr. has passed. Can I ask what business you have with him?"

I get out of my head long enough to realize the subtext to her question. My biggest hints are the dangerous gleam in her brown eyes and the diamond on her ring finger. She's a few years older than me, pretty and rosy-cheeked, and noticeably pregnant.

"I'm sorry," I say quickly. "I'm being so rude. My

name is Eden Sumner. Benny was a few years ahead of me in high school. We were good friends." After a pause, I add softly, "But that's all we were."

I've hit the mark with my last statement; the worry leaves her brown eyes. "Eden Sumner?" she asks with a hint of recognition. "Pretty sure Benny told me about you. Were you the one who stuck up for him all those times?"

I shrug. "Kids are assholes. I just did what anyone would do."

This time, her smile is genuine. "As Benny tells it, you did what no one else would do." She picks up a cordless phone. "Let me ring his office. He's back there doing paperwork."

"Thanks."

I wander an aisle nearest the registers, not really seeing much, until the woman calls in my direction, "He'll be right out!"

Less than a minute later, a handsome, bearded man turns into my aisle. Not until he grins do I recognize him. Same dimples. Same eyes.

"Is that you, Eden?" he asks, laughing. "You a movie star yet?"

I gape at him. "Never mind me! Good God, Benny, you look like a different person."

Chuckling, he grabs me in a spine-cracking hug. "Blame my wife, Jenny. You met her up front. She finally convinced me to start taking care of myself so I don't go out the way Dad did." He slaps his flat stomach. "Lost over a hundred and fifty pounds."

"I'll say! You look great. I was sorry to hear about your dad."

"Thanks," he says, old grief clouding his eyes. "Heart attack a few years ago. Business is doing pretty good, though. Hope he's proud."

"I know he is." My warmth is unfeigned; from our many conversations after school, I know he and his father had a close relationship. "Congrats on the beautiful wife. A baby on the way, too?"

His smile is beatific. "Yep. Thanks, Eden. So what brings a big-shot city girl such as yourself back to nowhere?"

I laugh. My desire to get out of Philomath was no secret when we were younger. Even with Corvallis nearby and Portland not too far north, my sights had stayed fixed on bigger, more exotic fish. To my everlasting regret.

"Just a quick trip to see my parents," I tell Benny. "But I wanted to stop by and say hello." *Here goes nothing.* "I have a weird question I wanted to ask you, too."

His brows lift. "Sure, what's up?"

"Does your family still own that land out near Eddyville?"

"Yeah, we still got it. Market's so bad right now it's

cheaper to keep it. Old house has seen better days—needs to be torn down." He frowns. "Why on earth are you asking?"

The chances of anyone connecting Benny and me as friends is slim to none. Not unless someone digs up old detention rosters. In spite of my near-perfect academic record, I'd had a habit of punching bullies. Unfortunately for Benny, he was often caught in the crossfire and punished alongside me.

I take a deep breath. Luck saved Elizabeth and me once upon a time. Maybe it will be on my side again.

"I need a favor."

THAT NIGHT IN BED, I stare at the shadowed ceiling of my childhood bedroom, sleepless despite an afternoon of back-breaking work in the *actual* middle of nowhere.

I've been second-guessing my decision nonstop for the last hour. *I should have looked at what was on the flash drive. I should have made ten copies and sent them all over the country. What if someone finds it? What if they tear the house down?*

What if what if what if?

But for better or worse, it's done. Tomorrow night after dinner, I'm sneaking out of my bedroom window like I've only done once before during a short-lived attempt at rebellion.

I'm catching a bus to Eugene, where I'll follow in my mother's footsteps and find a cheap used car. I don't have a fake ID, but I'm banking on greed to cut the red tape.

Everyone loves cash, right?

42

FOURTEEN HOURS behind a wheel is about eleven hours too long. When I finally enter Los Angeles, it's close to midnight and I'm seeing shadow-people in my rearview. I need food and caffeine badly. Not to mention a toilet. I'm so loopy I don't consider the risk as I drive straight to the one place that has all three.

When I walk in the door of Al's, I'm surprised by the level of nostalgia that hits me. The smell of grease is stronger than I remember, the late-night crowd even more rowdy. Although it's only been weeks since I last wore a frilly apron and a bad attitude, it feels like years.

A shrill whistle briefly drowns out the noise. I look toward the kitchen window, already knowing what I'll see. Sure enough, Raul has his arms propped on the counter as he grins at me.

"Hey, K!" he shouts. "Look what the cat dragged in!"

I follow his gaze across the diner. Karina turns from serving a table, frowning as she looks around. When she sees me, her eyes widen, and she shoves her empty tray at a passing waitress. She jogs toward me, ignoring the angry coworker in her wake.

I eagerly accept her hug. "It's so good to see you," I say, meaning it so much my eyes sting with unshed tears. "I'm sorry I disappeared on you. I want to explain, I really do, but—"

"Say no more," she says gently, releasing me to meet my gaze. "By your face alone, I know you've gone through the wringer. You want to eat?"

I nod. "Yeah. Counter okay?"

She squeezes my shoulder. "I got you, girl."

After a quick stop in the bathroom, I find an empty seat at the counter. There are a few other singles and couples, but the bulk of the diners are larger groups at tables.

Before Karina can get to me, Raul comes out of the kitchen and grabs the coffee pot. I turn over my mug and he fills it.

"Thanks, Raul."

"Sure thing, chica." He leans over the counter to give me a kiss on the cheek, but doesn't pull back. Mouth near my ear, he whispers, "I love you, but you need to leave. People been asking around about you. And I'm not talking about gueros from Publisher's Clearing-house, if you catch my drift."

My body rigid and cold, I sit frozen as he straightens and wipes the counter to my right. He doesn't look at me again—not when he finishes, and not when he turns and disappears into the kitchen.

Karina slips onto the stool beside mine. "Did he tell you?" she murmurs.

I nod. "What do they look like?"

"A few times, white guys in suits. Then others. Bad people. Wearing colors."

Gang members.

I jerk to standing. Reaching into my purse, I pull out an envelope holding stacks of hundred-dollar bills. When I'd counted out thirty thousand dollars, I'd been surprised by how unimpressive it looked in real life. Just paper, thin and without much weight. But at least I could do something good with it.

Giving Karina the envelope, I meet her frightened eyes. "Rent that studio space you always talked about, K," I whisper fiercely. "You're an incredible artist. Get your work out there. Half of it's for Raul. But only on the condition he stops selling drugs."

"What?" She glances inside the envelope. "Holy—"

I hug her hard, cutting off her words. "Thank you for being my friend. I didn't tell you enough how much you mean to me. Be happy, K."

I glance at the kitchen window, where Raul stands watching me. He mouths, *Be safe.* With a brave smile, I nod. Then I let go of Karina and walk out of Al's.

Shit just got real.

———

AFTER A QUICK STOP at the bus depot to rent a locker for the rest of the cash, I go straight to Liam's. Making the detour was an excruciating test of endurance. No matter the color of their skin or style of clothes, every stranger had felt like an enemy.

By the time I pull into Liam's driveway, I'm seconds from a full-blown meltdown. With the last of my sanity, I jump out of the car and race to the door.

It opens as I near it.

"Liam," I gasp, throwing myself at the shadowy figure.

Hard arms come around me, cradling me against a warm chest. I bury my nose in his t-shirt, dragging his scent into my lungs.

Only it's not his scent.

"Ah, lass, sorry to disappoint. But I'm glad to see you."

Horror steals my breath. Locks my muscles. Turns my knees to jelly. In the hallway, a light switches on. Over Chris's shoulder, I see two men walking toward us.

"Gone," says one of them, a thin bald man with tattoos snaking up either side of his neck. "Safe's empty. He's got his passport."

The muscles under my cheek tense. "Maddoc won't be pleased."

The other one, a thickly built blond, smiles when he notices me. "Who do we have here?"

Chris keeps his arms locked around me, but turns to face the men. Feeling like a rag doll, I'm spun until my back is against his chest.

As both men get a good look at me, their expressions slacken with shock.

"This, gentlemen, is the much sought-after Eden Sumner. She not only shares our fair Alexis's looks but her taste in dangerous men." Thick fingers wrap around my throat; he squeezes my airway closed. "You don't happen to know where Liam ran off to, do you, Eden?"

The pressure releases and I suck in a breath. "No," I gasp. "If I knew he was gone, do you think I would have come here?"

My captor chuckles. "Likely not."

The skinny tattooed guy looks at me, beady eyes dragging over my chest and hips. He licks his lips and I shudder.

"What are we going to do with her?"

"Don't fecking think it," snarls Chris. "With Liam on

the run, Eden here is our consolation prize. Would you rather wet your dick or keep your head on your neck?"

Bile burns the back of my throat. Panic washes away my courage. I'm not a fighter. Not strong. Elizabeth and my dad were wrong.

"Please let me go," I whisper.

My flesh crawls as Chris nuzzles the nape of my neck. "Now why on earth would I do that?"

SANDWICHED between Chris and Snake Man in the back seat of a Benz, I can't curb the tears leaking from my eyes or my periodic full-body shuddering. The former is because the zip tie around my wrists is linked to Chris's belt, and the latter is due to an existential freak-out.

I'm ninety percent convinced that I'm being driven to my death.

When Blondie turns off Mulholland Drive and down a small street to the gate at the end, my tears come harder. The men around me are silent, though Snake Man twitches every time I sob.

The heavy wooden gate slides open. We drive through and down a short, curving driveway to the house at the bottom.

As the car pulls to a smooth stop, Chris shifts to face

me and grabs my hands. I yank away, inadvertently falling against Snake Man. At the groping touch of his hands on my hip and the side of one breast, I scream and launch myself right into Chris's arms.

He glares over my head. "Don't touch her."

"Why not?" whines the sleazeball behind me. "It's not like she's actually Alexis. Just the missing sister no one cares about."

"You've got a death wish, Brian," mutters Blondie as he turns off the car.

"Hold still, lass," murmurs Chris.

He reaches for my wrists again, but I don't fight this time. Snake Man—Brian—is still too close, staring at me with an avaricious gleam in his eyes. I don't trust Chris, not by a long shot, but at this moment he's the lesser of two evils.

The knife in Chris's hand slips through the plastic like butter. I sigh at the immediate relief and rub circulation back into my fingers.

"Let's go."

Chris opens the door, grabbing my arm and yanking me out of the car. My shoulder burns as he drags me toward the house. The pain—unasked for, unwanted— triggers white-hot rage.

"Asshole!" I growl at him. "Why fucking bother taking off the zip tie?"

He glances back with a frown. "That mouth, gah. I

don't know how Liam put up with it. You must have a magic pussy."

He hauls me through a smaller, decorative gate toward the mansion's front doors. I trip on uneven stone, and I'm kept from falling by brute force. My shoulder screams.

"Jesus, I can walk, okay? Enough with the manhandling!"

He jerks me to a stop before the front door, then turns stormy eyes on me. "You have one chance—*one*—to save your ass. Tell Maddoc what he wants to know."

"Fuck you."

His jaw clenches. "Let's hope it doesn't come to that."

Fear levels my anger, leaving me cold. "What's that supposed to mean?"

"What do you think?" he snarls back. "How did you think this would go down? With water torture? Besides, it's me or Brian, and I'm pretty fecking sure you'd prefer me."

My stomach jumps into my throat, sending waves of chills down my body. I'm not stupid—he's talking about raping me. I sway with dizziness, my vision dimming.

The front door suddenly opens, bathing us in light. Through my haze of nausea and fear, I see a woman step outside, an unlit cigarette dangling from her lips. She's wearing athletic leggings and a pink t-shirt, and her blonde hair sits in a messy bun atop her head.

I forget to breathe as she looks up from the phone in her hand. Cracked-marble eyes widen on Chris, then swing to me. The cigarette falls as her mouth drops open.

"Eden?"

From Chris's immediate tension, I know this wasn't the plan. He was hoping Alexis would never know I was here.

"What are you doing here, lass?" asks Chris, casually releasing my arm.

Alexis keeps staring at me as she says, "Came for some stuff." Her gaze leaps to him, narrowing. "You promised you'd call me the second you found her!"

He shrugs nonchalantly. My anger makes a comeback. *How dare he pretend he didn't just threaten to rape me!* Holding the words from my lips, barely, is a rising intuition of my own power in this moment. With Alexis in the mix, there's a chance I'm no longer my father's pawn. That I'm now a player in the game.

"I wanted to surprise you," I say, forcing a big smile on my face. I hold my arms out. "Do I get a hug?"

Alexis squeals and leaps forward, crashing into me hard enough to knock me back a few steps. Over her shoulder, I meet Chris's surprised eyes. I arch a brow in return, then focus on the woman in my arms.

My twin.

She smells like bourbon vanilla and cigarettes. Like sunshine and ocean salt and confidence. I breathe her in, and the connection I'd missed when reading her note explodes inside me. In the strength of her arms, the tears that are falling on my shoulder and down my own face, I feel it. Something deeper than love or affection. Deeper than family.

The bond of blood.

44

NOW

THERE'S a rat in the basement with me. Or maybe it's an overfed mouse. Whatever it is, it has a busy social calendar. Squeaking and chittering, scrambling along pipes and the bases of walls.

After two days, I finally let go of the fear of being eaten one nibble at a time. The beastie has paid no attention to me, much more concerned with the scraps of stale food and vomit in my vicinity.

"Hey, little guy," I croak. "What's your name?"

In the ever-present dimness, I see the dark body still.

I hold my breath in anticipation. Eventually, a tail twitch is followed by a squeak.

"I'm naming you Squeaker," I tell my new friend. "Hello, Squeaker. It's so nice of you to visit my humble abode. I've been very lonely."

Squeak.

"Sorry about the mess. I haven't had a chance to clean up in a while. Would you like to hear a story?"

Squeak.

"Once upon a time, there was a bad, bad man. He lied about who he was and tricked people into loving him. No matter how bad he was, there was one girl who believed he could be good..." My voice trails off, even the minimal words taxing my strength.

Squeaksqueak.

I sigh. "That's all for today. Do come back tomorrow for chapter two."

Squeak.

45

THEN

FIFTEEN MINUTES LATER, I'm sitting beside Alexis in the back seat of an Uber because Maddoc recently took away her car. Her *fifth*. Apparently she has a habit of fender benders and forgetting where she parked.

She seems perfectly content to chatter, and I'm perfectly content to listen. As she talks about herself, I experience several odd, dreamlike moments. Moments in which I cannot accept reality. In which I wonder if my life has been an illusion. If I am her. Inside her. Merely a construct of her malformed imagination.

Then I wonder if I'm only having the thought because I saw it in a movie once.

"…and then I said, *Whatever, I'll just Uber around*. I think Uber's gotten a bad rap. I mean, who wants to be in the back of a stinky cab, anyway? They're providing a service I want, so I'm going to use it! It's as simple as that. If their CEO's a dirtbag, who cares?"

"Right," I murmur, glancing at the young man driving us. He's rolling his eyes.

"Exactly!" Alexis squeezes my hand, which has been secured in hers since we got in the car. My fingers feel numb, illusory. *Am I here?*

"I'm so excited, Eden, I can't even tell you. This is kismet. Do you know what kismet is?"

Yes. I'm here.

I nod, meeting her/my eyes. "Destiny, but I—"

"Isn't it amazing? I can't wait to learn everything about you. Do you have a boyfriend? Where did you grow up? What do you *do?*"

When she pauses long enough that I realize she wants me to answer, I clear my throat. "Well, I just graduated from UCLA. During school I worked as a waitress and in retail. I grew up in a small town in Oregon—"

"Oh no, that must have been horrible. How did you stand all the rain?"

I shrug, having heard the same question hundreds of times since moving to Southern California. "It's not that bad. Plus, since I grew up there I never really thought of it as abnormal."

"What was your major at UCLA?"

I'm beginning to get used to her squirrel-like topic hopping. "Biology. I'm going to med school next year." *I hope.*

"Whoa, you must be super smart," she whispers teasingly. "I hated school. So boring."

I make a noncommittal sound. "What do you, um, do?"

She waves her free hand. "A little of this, a little of that. Daddy has a few restaurants and businesses in the city. I'm thinking about taking one of them over. Maybe when I turn thirty." She giggles. "Although I'll probably be married by then."

Before I can consider the wisdom of asking, I blurt, "Who's your fiancé?"

She gives me a confused look. "How should I know? But I'm hoping my future husband is hot, built, and loaded."

What the hell?

My head-to-mouth filter wheezes and dies. "So you're not marrying Liam Rourke?" I snap.

Alexis gapes. "What? No!" She shudders. "That guy is a total freak of nature. He's into some weird shit. Besides, Daddy would never allow it. Liam's father and

Daddy have a huge beef. Like a thirty-year-old hatred of each other. How do you even know Liam?"

I have no idea how to respond. To any of it.

"I, uh, heard a rumor," I hedge, glancing out my window so she can't see my expression.

She squeezes my hand. "Figures. Lies are more prevalent than smog in L.A. Almost everything and everyone in this town is a lie. You can't trust anyone."

My brows jump at the sudden shift in her personality from bubbling to morose. I turn to look at her, but she's staring out the window just like I was a second ago. Gazing at her profile, shadowed and illuminated in turn by passing lights, a vague sense of unease curls through me.

Who are you, Alexis Sharpe?

We don't speak the rest of the drive, which ends outside a luxury condominium complex in Beverly Hills. The second the car stops, Alexis is out the door. I thank the driver and follow her across the sidewalk, past a doorman who does a double take at us, across a sumptuous lobby and into a mirrored elevator.

As the doors slide closed, Alexis looks at our reflections. "Whoa. That's so trippy." She scans my body, a twinkle in her eyes. "If you had a tan and more highlights, we could totally do *The Parent Trap* routine."

Looking at the two of us side by side, I see the proof of

her words. Besides hair color and skin tone, the only distinguishing characteristic between us is my visible freckles. Freckles that would fade beneath a tan. Again, I have that amorphous sense that I've stepped outside reality.

The elevator ascends all the way to the top. Penthouse. *Of course.* With a shy smile, Alexis leads me across a small foyer and unlocks the front door. She flips on some lights, then kicks off her shoes and saunters toward a full kitchen. I deposit my sandals beside hers and follow, pausing to take in the massive, loft-like space.

"...decorator picked everything out. Are you creative? I'm not. The walls would probably still be white if I hadn't hired someone. Do you like it?"

I blink to clear my mental fog, focusing on Alexis pouring red wine into glasses. The fall of liquid mesmerizes me.

"Hey, Eden, you okay?"

I return to the present. "Yes. I, uh... I'm really tired."

Shocked.

Afraid.

Potentially having a schizophrenic break.

I clear my throat. "I drove all the way from Oregon today."

Is it still today?

Alexis frowns in concern. "You poor baby. I'm sure you're overwhelmed. It's probably easier for me, since you're in my world. I'm sure I'd be wigged out if I ran into you in Oregon."

"Yeah," I say weakly, gripping the edge of the kitchen counter as a wave of vertigo overtakes me.

Alexis puts the wine bottle down and hurries to my side. "Hey, you're really pale. Come on, let's get you to bed. We'll have all the time in the world tomorrow to catch up."

I don't argue. Mental and physical exhaustion weigh on me like an anvil. I try to remember the last time I ate and can't. Goose bumps prickle along my body as Alexis guides me down a hallway to a closed door.

"This is the guest bedroom, but it's fully stocked since my girlfriends stay over a lot."

I barely notice the room as I cross toward the beckoning bed. As I fall toward a pillow, I wonder if I'm safe. I must say it aloud, because I feel a soft touch on my hair.

"You're safe, Eden. Rest."

I'm gone.

Empty.

Lost.

46

FOR TEN BLISSFUL DAYS, my sister and I share a home. Meals. Hair products. Makeup. Shopping trips. Massages, mani-pedis, facials. Afternoons on the beach. Evenings on the couch, our feet side by side on the coffee table, a movie muted or paused on the television while we expose our minds to one another. Our inner selves. Our twinned souls.

We're not opposites, like Liam said. Not quite. Instead, we're like two pieces of an incomplete puzzle. Separate, patterned and colored differently, but we still fit seamlessly together even if the rest of the pieces are missing, the bigger picture unknown.

On our first day together—after I slept for fourteen hours, stuffed my face, and rehydrated—I quickly learned that Alexis isn't the woman she shows the world. When we're alone, her mask drops. Her vocabulary expands. She doesn't giggle as much, or flip her hair, or wear makeup. She's not superficial, stupid, or narcissistic.

She's perceptive and cunning. Intelligent and surprisingly philosophical. But also innocently optimistic. She believes in fate. That people are essentially good. That our father lives his life the way he does because of the necessity for darkness to balance the world's light.

On our tenth day together, as we watch the sunset through the penthouse windows, I ask her if she's ever thought of leaving.

She sighs. "I know he isn't a good man, Eden. Even though he was strict and protective of me growing up, I saw things. Heard things." She shrugs a little, turning toward me. "But he's my dad. I love him. And I think you will too, once you get to know him."

The boundaries of my Self blur, shift, then sharpen. So many questions bead on my tongue. So much longing for the truth. *Where's Liam? Where's Elizabeth? Who do I trust?*

I think I trust Alexis. *Do I trust her?* My recent past isn't exactly overflowing with instances of good judgement. I haven't told her about Chris's threat, what I found in our mother's safety deposit box, or the text message telling me to stay away from her.

I'd trusted Liam, but obviously that had been a mistake. *Does he know where I am? Does he care?* At the thought of him, my heart burns. Aches and folds into itself. *Where are you, Liam?*

"You're thinking about him again, aren't you?" asks Alexis softly.

I sigh past the tightness in my chest, briefly wishing I hadn't told her all the dirty details of what went down with Liam. "I just don't know why he lied."

She hums in sympathy. "Maybe he didn't know how to tell you the truth."

I glance sharply at her. "Like what? That he just wanted me gone? Seems a little elaborate."

"Men like Liam feed off control. They don't play the game with us mortals. They create the game board. Sometimes they like to flip it upside down and watch us fall."

Her poetic musings familiar to me by now, I merely nod. "Maybe. Doesn't make it hurt any less."

She turns to stare at the darkening sky. "A few years ago, I had a giant crush on Liam." At my glance, she smiles. "I think it was more about him being so forbidden than anything else. I knew he was a regular at Crossroads, so for about a month, I stalked that place trying to get close to him. This was before Chris's promotion in the... organization. He was mine back then, had to do whatever I said. Oh, he was so pissed when I kept dragging him to the club." She chuckles. "I've never seen him so uncomfortable, before or since."

I hide my flinch by crossing my arms over my chest. The way Alexis talks about Chris… she cares about him. A lot. Maybe even loves him.

I have no idea how to reconcile her adoration of him with the evil asshole who threatened to rape me. So whenever he comes up, I shove the issue down with all the rest of my Think About Later problems.

"Did you find him? Liam?"

Alexis nods, a shadow crossing her expression even as she winks at me. "Let's just say I'm not down for dominance. And before you ask, no, I didn't sleep with him. He taught me a very public lesson about overstepping boundaries. I think that's why Chris hates him so much."

"What did he do?" I make myself ask.

She turns toward me, leaning a shoulder on the glass. "Tell me, Eden, what would *you* have done if Liam walked up to you and told you to get on your knees in front of a crowd of people."

I don't say anything, the answer written on my face.

Alexis nods, smiling softly. "I understand. Intellectually, at least. The freedom of giving up control. But therein lies the problem. I don't have any control to begin with. It's what I want, not what I want to give up."

Adrenaline whispers along my limbs. This is the closest she's come to admitting she's not happy. That she wants a different life.

My sister. My complicated, funny, wise-beyond-her-years sister. If there's even a fraction of a chance I can save her, I have to try.

"I know you love Maddoc—our father," I begin hesitantly. "I know you're loyal to him. But I think you also know that as long as you're here, you won't have control. You'll marry who he tells you to marry. You'll keep seeing and hearing things that darken your spirit." I reach for her, grabbing her hand, and wait for her eyes to meet mine. "I won't lie—freedom can be scary at times. Being responsible for your own life, your own choices and mistakes… But you don't have to stay. I'm telling you, Alexis. Believe me, please. You don't have to stay."

"What are you saying?" she whispers.

I open my mouth to tell her the truth.

The front door crashes open, slamming against the wall. Alexis and I jerk in place, clutching one another, as six armed men in black fatigues spill into the room. They move fluidly, professionally, and wear earpieces and bulletproof vests.

The central figure walks toward us as the others jog down hallways, kicking open doors and shouting, "Clear! Clear!"

"Who the fuck are you?" snarls Alexis.

The unsmiling man reaches up, and we both flinch. Velcro rips to expose a badge on his vest.

FBI

"We have a warrant for the arrest of your father, Maddoc Donnelly." Dark eyes veer to me, but show no sign of surprise. "Eden Sumner, I presume? Have you seen Maddoc recently?"

Alexis's nails dig into my forearm. "Don't answer that," she snaps, then glares at the man. "I want to see the warrant allowing you access to my apartment, and I want to call my lawyer."

47

MY COFFEE IS COLD, the creamer congealed on the top like a pale oil stain. Sitting across the metal table from me is Special Agent David Hernandez, the same stern-faced man who'd given Alexis the warrant paperwork and suggested we voluntarily accompany him to FBI headquarters.

While Alexis shouted about our rights and told him where to shove it, I'd walked across the room to get my purse.

"Eden, what the fuck are you doing?"

The horror and betrayal on Alexis's face is seared into my eyelids. Her expression will haunt me for the rest of my days.

Like he can read my mind, Hernandez says, "You told your sister, 'I'm freeing us.' Are you willing to elaborate?"

I drag my gaze from the table to his face. "Before I say anything, I want protection for my sister. Immunity, whatever. She isn't a part of Maddoc's world—not like that."

He sighs. "Unfortunately, Eden, that's not on the table. Not only do we have hard evidence to the contrary, we have sworn testimony from several witnesses that Alexis is very much involved in Maddoc's business."

My vision sparkles. "You're lying," I rasp.

He glances down at the folder before him. "On November 8, 2016, Alexis Sharpe was an accomplice in the murder of Steven Adams, a businessman with ties to Maddoc Donnelly. Three witnesses watched her stand beside Christopher Daley and give the order to execute Adams with a shot to the back of the head." Closing the folder, he sits back in the chair to give me a level stare. "So, Eden, you were saying?"

That was last year—we were twenty-two years old. I was finishing my degree at UCLA, and Alexis was... was... A scream of incoherent protest claws against my tongue. I swallow it back, closing my eyes until the urge passes. When I open them, Hernandez is still staring at me.

"I know this is a lot to take in. I also know that you just recently met your twin for the first time. Have you met your biological father?"

"No," I whisper.

He nods. "I'm going to be straight with you, Eden, so you'll be straight with me. Two weeks ago, we received an anonymous tip that led us to an abandoned house outside your hometown of Philomath, Oregon. We found a USB drive with enough evidence on it to put Maddoc Donnelly away for a long, long time. Now I need you to be straight with me—do you know anything about that?"

Liam.

With every fiber of my being, I know this is his doing. *How the hell did he figure it out?*

"Meddling motherfucker," I mutter, slumping in my chair.

Hernandez's brows go up. "I'm sorry?"

I shake my head, my mind racing. *What if my mother was right, and I can't trust law enforcement? What if anything I say will end up in Maddoc's ear?*

My inner conflict must be clear on my face, because Hernandez says, "I've been working to bring the Donnellys to justice for over five years, Eden."

My gaze flickers to his face. Lines of fatigue bracket his mouth. His dusky skin is too pale, the collar of his shirt loose. This is a man who's overworked, irrefutably dedicated. Obsessed, even.

I can relate.

"I don't know what's on the drive," I admit. "My mother, Elizabeth Sharpe, left it with my adoptive parents. They never looked at it, just gave it to me a few weeks ago. I hid it."

"Why did you hide it if you didn't know what was on it?"

My already frazzled nerves erupt. "Why do you think? The chances that it held incriminating information were pretty good. I wanted collateral. Protection. Leverage."

He's silent for a moment, dark eyes scanning my face. "To save your sister."

"Yes," I hiss.

Alexis. Oh God, Alexis, what did you do?

I think of the beautiful contradictions of her personality. The jaded woman who's seen too much, who popped little white pills when she thought I wasn't looking, who smokes more pot than Raul, who chugs vodka like water. And the other part of her, a woman with the ability to laugh so hard she cries, to squeal in excitement when her favorite song comes on the radio, to sing and shout and dance in her underwear.

She's had so little control over the course of her life and none over the circumstances of her birth. *Did she do what Hernandez said? Give the order to kill a man?*

I really, really hope she didn't.

But I don't know.

As I float in thoughts that make my stomach churn, there's a cursory knock on the door. It swings open a moment later and a pant-suited woman pokes her head inside.

"What?" barks Hernandez.

"Alexis slipped surveillance sometime in the last hour. Went into her lawyer's office and didn't come out. He's being questioned, but we've got nothing."

"Fuck, fuck, fuck," growls Hernandez. He glares at me. "Do you know where she'd go?"

Fear makes me brash. "I just met her ten days ago," I snap. "What do you think?"

Chair legs scrape on the floor as he stands and looks at his associate. "What about Donnelly? Any word?"

She shakes her head. "We're monitoring the border and airports."

I twitch in my seat. Maddoc is on the run. Alexis has disappeared, much as Liam did. The FBI have my mother's USB stick. If Maddoc finds out that stick came from me… to say I'm fucked would be putting it lightly.

"You're free to go, Eden."

My head whips up. "What?"

Hernandez stalks to the table, leaning forward on his hands until we're face-to-face. "I suggest you forget about your biological father and sister. Move on with your life. Don't look back."

Forget. Don't look back.

Why the fuck do people keep thinking that's an option for me?

Hernandez hands me a small white card, raps his knuckles once on the table, then heads to the door. Pausing on the threshold, he glances back. "If I have any more questions, I'll be in contact. And if you see either of them, you'll call me."

I nod. He leaves, the door staying open. Voices filter down the hallway. Phones ring. The manhunt for criminals continues.

Life goes on.

I LEAVE the massive FBI building and walk aimlessly down Wilshire. It's late afternoon, the sun hazy and orange in the western sky.

I'm finding it difficult to care about whether or not there's a target on my back. Whether Alexis is guilty or not. Whether Maddoc still has people looking for me. What those people will do if they find me.

Tires screech to the curb beside me. There's a mechanical hum of a window rolling down.

"Get in."

On autopilot, I turn and cross to the car. Open the passenger door and slide inside. Close the door. Put my purse between my feet. Fasten my seatbelt.

I don't look at the driver.

"It's over. You're safe."

Words. Words. Words. So many people, so many words. How many lies? All of it. Most of it. Nothing.

A flask tips in front of my mouth. Whiskey spills over my tongue, burns down my throat. I cough, grabbing the flask.

Three heavy swallows bring down my veil of ambivalence enough for me to look at him. I take in his worried expression. His too-blue eyes. Pinched lips. New beard.

And I laugh.

Just laugh.

Because what other option is there?

48

LIAM DOESN'T DRIVE FAR. When he stops the car outside a familiar black awning, I merely sigh and get out. He joins me on the curb and we walk silently to the black door. Three raps of his fist and the door opens.

"Master Liam," greets the same, waifish doorman who let me in last time. "They're waiting for you in back."

"Thank you, Nathan."

The whiskey glows warmly in my empty stomach as I follow Liam's broad back through the padded door. The space is empty of patrons, almost sterile in the harsh glow of overhead lights.

In a distant corner, a vacuum whirs across rugs. It's operated by a woman in sweats and headphones, her head bouncing to whatever music she's listening to. Behind the long white bar, a shirtless man stocks bottles from boxes spread across the counter. As we walk past, he gives us a nod.

Liam strolls to a door in the far corner. White and set flush to the wall, it no doubt escapes notice when the club is open. Three more knocks of Liam's fist and it swings inward.

Not until I see the woman before me do I accept that I'd been harboring hope. Hope that he'd found her, that he was planning to get us out of the country somehow. That everything would work out the way it was supposed to, with Alexis and me together and safe.

A harsh laugh sounds—mine, I belatedly realize.

The woman frowns concernedly at me. "Are you okay?"

London. Belongs to Master Dominic.

"She's fine," answers Liam curtly. "Dominic's here?"

London nods and steps back. Liam's hand touches my back, and I jerk away, into the hallway past the woman who isn't my sister. Doors interrupt the walls to either side of me. Two on each. Liam doesn't look my way as he maneuvers around me and walks to the last door on the left. He disappears inside.

I pause a few steps away and eye the emergency exit at the end of the hallway. *How far can I run before he catches me?*

Not far enough.

Behind me, London says, "I don't know what sort of

trouble you're in, but there's nowhere safer than with these men. Trust me."

I'm not buzzed enough to miss the tone of personal testimony, but I don't have the capacity to care. Whatever her story is, there's no way it compares to the surreal shitshow that is my life.

"Eden," calls Liam. "Come in, please."

"Go on," says London gently.

Sighing, I go.

DOMINIC, I come to find out, is one of Crossroads's owners. He also has some shady habits—if the three handguns resting on a cloth atop his desk are any indication. There are also a selection of knives—none of which are intended for steak—and a few small canisters of what I can only speculate is professional-grade mace.

Sitting on a leather couch opposite the desk, I listen to the men discussing the various weapons. Liam eventually selects one of each. Dominic gives him a small duffle to put them in, as well as a box of ammo.

Then the men turn and look at me for the first time. Two sets of eyes—one blue, one brown—with the same self-awareness in them. They are predators. I am prey.

Only I'm not remotely in the mood.

"What?" I ask sharply.

Dominic's brows lift in surprise; Liam's lower in frustration. "Have you paid any attention at all?"

I make a show of looking around the elegant office. "I'm sorry, was I supposed to?"

"Lord," mutters Dominic.

I roll my eyes. "Yeah, yeah, I know. I've got a brain and a mouth. So unbecoming." I turn my glare on Liam. "Since I don't have a say in what you're planning, Mr. Puppet Master, I figured I'd just wait to be told what to do."

He sighs. "Did you really think I wouldn't come for you? That I wouldn't be aware of every step you've taken in the last weeks?"

My anger is sudden and acidic. "So you just let Chris take me? Were you going to let him rape me, too?"

Hurt flashes in his eyes. "If you'd been in any real danger, I would have intervened."

"Right," I huff. "Like you would have intervened if the FBI had decided to lock me up as some sort of accomplice to my father's many crimes."

His jaw clenches. "It wouldn't have happened."

"Because you know everything, don't you?" I scoff. "You lie, lie, lie because you think everyone is yours to control. It's all a game to you, isn't it? Do you know where Alexis is?"

"No," he answers firmly. "Quite frankly, I don't give a shit. Either she'll make it into Canada or Mexico or she'll get caught. Your sister is not without resources. Tell me, Eden—do you think she would have run if she wasn't guilty?"

"How do you even—" I freeze in sick comprehension.

Liam's gaze narrows. "Yes. I was there. I heard her give the order. In a rare act of civil service, I tracked down three other witnesses and put them in Agent Hernandez's sights."

"No, no, no," I mumble, shaking my head. "She couldn't have... she wouldn't... you're lying!"

"I'm sorry, Eden," murmurs Liam. "I'm sorry."

"Stop saying that!" I yell.

Dominic steps forward, lifting his hands. "Okay, kids, let's cool down."

Liam gazes at me another moment, his eyes soft with apology, then straightens and turns to Dominic. "Your man got the package?"

He nods. "The money has been wired to the offshore account."

Glancing between the men, I demand, "What package?"

Dominic stares at me like I'm certifiable. Liam asks me slowly, "Did you forget what else you hid with that USB stick?"

My jaw drops. Maybe I have lost my mind, because I'd completely forgotten.

"The diamonds," I breathe, lurching forward. "You took the diamonds."

He nods, lips curving gently. "I had them appraised. Dominic found a buyer. You're quite rich, Eden. Would you like to know how much is in your Cook Islands account?"

I lick my lips. *Do I want to know?*

Who am I kidding?

"How much?"

"Roughly thirty-six million."

I laugh.

Liam and Dominic don't.

My mirth fades fast. "That's ridiculous." I glance between them. "Is this a joke?"

The men shake their heads.

My head swims. "Oh no, I think I'm—"

Liam shoves a trash can under my face just in time.

49

LIAM and I are spending the night in the loft above Crossroads. Apparently it used to be Dominic's residence, before he met London. Now it's used exclusively by the club's elite members. Although clean, tastefully decorated, and full of modern conveniences, it's still clearly a fuckpad.

From the discrete hooks on the ceilings and walls of each room, to the bulk of a St. Andrews Cross beneath a cover of red silk and the sumptuous drapes tied with a familiar brand of nylon rope, it's clear the walls have witnessed some serious kink.

Luckily for me, Liam doesn't seem the least bit interested in sex. And though it's the furthest thing from my mind at the moment, I honestly don't know how I'd react if he offered. *Would I surrender? Would I serve?* I'd like to think I wouldn't, but a part of me knows better.

The remains of our takeout dinner sit on the kitchen table between us. Neither of us had much of an appetite. As I picked at my lo mein, Liam discussed the particulars of my offshore account. What it means and what it doesn't mean.

Turns out getting rich off stolen diamonds isn't exactly something you can tell the IRS. I can't access the money all at once or transfer it except in small quantities and with extreme cautionary measures. If I ever do decide to retire on an island, though, I'm all set.

"Who did Maddoc steal them from?" I ask at length.

Liam shrugs. "You give me too much credit, Eden. I didn't know about the diamonds at all until I found them. But if whoever Maddoc took them from knew he did, I doubt he'd still be alive. It's more probable that Maddoc killed whoever owned them. Or even that he acquired them through purchase or trade."

I rub my aching forehead. "Do I even want to know what he'd trade for a cool thirty-six mil worth of diamonds?"

"No, you don't," he says with certainty.

I look up, meeting his stare. "Alexis said… she said I'd like him."

He smiles slightly, but it doesn't reach his eyes. "Irish charm, remember?"

I sit back in my chair. "So what do I do now? Live the rest of my life looking over my shoulder?"

"No. You live the rest of your life knowing that you *don't* have to look over your shoulder. Eden, I know I've broken your trust. I've lied to you. But you have to know —somewhere inside you—that everything I've done was to protect you. I promised to keep you safe, and that promise is still intact. No matter what you do or where you go, you'll be safe."

"You can't promise that. Not when we'll be in different states. Or are you planning to follow me to Seattle?"

Liam shifts in his chair, looking down. "Actually, I'm returning to Ireland."

A spike hammers straight through my chest. "What?" I whisper.

His eyes flash up to mine. In the blue depths I see the last, fragile hope of my heart wither.

"Everything has a price, Eden. Everything. You'll be safe because you're mine. You'll always be mine. An ocean won't change that."

"Liam?" I croak.

He shakes his head. "It's best you don't know, dove."

"Fuck you." I jump to my feet, my chair falling as I round the table. "No. No! You tell me right now what the fuck you're talking about. No more lies!"

Glittering aqua eyes fix on mine. With eerie precision, he says, "I was never engaged to Alexis. That wasn't the price of your freedom. The price was taking my place at my father's side."

After everything I've been through in the last months, I'm surprised I still have the capacity for shock. For horror. For heartbreak. My hand falls, catching the corner of the table. I don't feel the sting.

"No," I gasp. "You can't."

He touches my face, the barest graze of fingertips along my jaw. "Everything has a price. This one is worth it."

I SCREAM. I sob. I pound fists on his chest. I beg him to take it back. I tell him I'm not worth it. I tell him to take the money, that I don't want it. I tell him to disappear— that the man who can find anyone can surely make it so no one can find him. I tell him that *no one* is worth this sacrifice. Not his mother, his half-siblings. And definitely not me.

He takes my abuse. He doesn't subdue me. And when I finally collapse into a weeping puddle, he carries me into a shadowed bedroom. He undresses me, helps me under the covers, and pulls the blankets to my chin.

When I ask him to stay, he removes his shoes and slides in beside me. I burrow into his chest, holding him to me as tightly as I can while my tears slowly dampen his shirt.

He sings to me, stroking my hair until I sleep.

I WAKE up in the morning to an empty bed and a memory of a kiss. On his pillow is a note. Five words, unsigned.

I will always find you.

I cry until I have no tears left, then stare at the words until my tears begin anew.

London finds me sometime later. She helps me shower and dress in borrowed clothes. I'm childlike, numb, and easily manipulated by her gentle yet firm commands. After she's forced me to eat toast and drink coffee, she calls Dominic, who arrives with a plane ticket to Oregon and the money I'd stashed in the bus depot. I don't ask how he knew where the locker was or how he accessed it. Liam must have found the key in my purse.

Liam.

"He's not coming back, is he?" I ask hoarsely.

Dominic's dark eyes shine with sorrow. He knows I'm talking about more than just Liam's physical presence.

"I don't think so," he says softly. "You don't have to forget him, Eden, but you do have to let him go."

My eyes burn with fresh tears. *God, when will they stop?* Wiping my eyes roughly, I swallow back a sob. London squeezes my shoulder, offering comfort I don't feel.

"It's wrong," I whisper.

"Yes, it is, but he made the choice. He did what he thought was right, and he did it to keep you safe. To give you a future. Don't cheapen his gift by resenting it."

I take a deep, shaking breath and square my shoulders. Dominic nods approval and hands me my plane ticket. London gives me my purse, thick with envelopes of cash. Liam already told me that I don't have to declare cash on a domestic flight. Good thing, because I have no idea how I'd explain half a million dollars.

I'm a rich woman.

And a broken one.

Everything has a price.

PART TWO

THE PRICE OF BLOOD

50

SIX YEARS LATER

MOVING ON ISN'T ONLY a choice. It's more than a daily commitment to be present in your life, to turn away from memory and toward the future. It's a feeling, too. And no matter how disciplined the mind, no matter how deeply memory is locked away, feelings aren't so easily smothered.

I have no control over that part of my memory linked to emotion. I cannot anticipate its ebbs and flows, the rate of its dissolution. Those sensory triggers activate without my permission and often at the oddest times—in the middle of my rounds at the hospital, in the shower, while eating sushi.

It's worse when I hear a laugh that sounds like Liam's. When I glimpse a tall, suited man with auburn hair. When I feel a phantom touch on my neck only to realize it's my own hand. And it's worst of all when my boyfriend and I are having sex and his fingers clench hard on my skin—not hard enough to leave bruises, but hard enough that I wish he would.

I've come to accept that I'll never be free of Liam. Nor will I be free of Alexis. She has her own set of triggers: pedicures and massages, blonde hair, the beach. I can't even stand being around women who talk too much, too fast, or with effusive energy.

I'm a haunted woman. Hard to like, a horrible friend. My fellow residents have called me cold, calculating, and self-centered. But I'm an exceptional doctor. No one denies it. Nor can they deny that I'm different with patients—warm, gentle, and almost inhumanly calm.

My chosen specialty of pediatrics gives me brief periods of relief from my ghosts. Neither my patients nor their parents have control over diagnoses and very little over treatment options. They are powerless—a state I understand well—and so as much as I can, I become the power they've lost. I take control because they need me to.

Outside of work, it's harder, my own powerlessness more apparent. Caught between an interrupted past and a future that feels vague and illusory, I feel like a watercolor woman. Diluted and dreamy. But I continue. I move forward.

One step at a time.

51

WHEN I GET HOME from the hospital Thursday night, there's a vase of a dozen red roses on the kitchen counter. Smiling through my exhaustion, I drop my purse on the floor and reach for the little card.

Happy Valentine's Day!

Soft footsteps approach me from behind, and seconds later strong arms wrap around my waist. "Do you like them?"

I nod, still smiling as I turn and lift my face for a kiss. "Thank you, they're beautiful."

Grant grins, dimpling beneath blond scruff. "You're welcome. How was work?"

"The usual chaos. I'm dead on my feet." Slipping

from his embrace, I head for the fridge. "Have you eaten?"

"Yep. There's leftovers in there. Want me to heat them up for you?"

"Nah, I got it." I pull out several Tupperware containers. As I pop lids, I glance over my shoulder and frown. "I thought you weren't working tonight."

He gives me a sheepish look. "Rich begged me to cover. It's his ten-year anniversary with his wife. I'm sorry, honey. Can we do the Valentine's thing Saturday night?"

I sigh. "I work Saturday night. It's on the calendar. You know, the one we swore we'd look at every week?"

Grant blinks his big brown eyes in a highly effective puppy-dog impression. Coming into the kitchen, he tugs the end of my dark ponytail. "I know. I'm an idiot. How about I make it up to you Saturday afternoon? I'll even do that thing you like..." He trails off expectantly, eyebrows wiggling.

I surrender with a laugh. "Fine. Saturday afternoon is officially our Valentine's date." I point at him. "I'm putting it on the calendar. Don't forget."

He kisses the tip of my finger. "I won't." Taking my face in his hands, he presses his lips to mine. "I love you, Eden."

"Love you, too," I mumble against his mouth.

He releases me and grabs his keys from the counter. "See you in the morning."

"Be careful out there."

He winks. "Cops deal with the bad guys. I just save lives."

I smirk. "No, you just keep them alive until the doctors save them."

He laughs, knowing full well that I'm joking. Without paramedics, a good number of people wouldn't even make it to the hospital alive.

"Whatever, *doc*."

The door closes softly behind him.

BEING WITH GRANT IS EASY. We're both dedicated to our careers. Neither of us want children or marriage. He's respectful and kind. Steady and strong. Most days, I can lose myself in the fantasy of this life. I can forget, just like everyone told me to. I can be a committed doctor and girlfriend.

Sometimes, though—especially when my nerves are frayed from a long day—it's harder to pretend. Harder to resist sensory triggers. Today it was an elderly patient singing "Galway Girl." Liam loved that damn song. He sang it in the shower, while cooking, while getting dressed for the day. He sang it softly in my ear as we slow danced around the living room.

"When I woke up I was all alone, with a broken heart and a ticket home…"

The lyrics play through my mind as I do dishes and wipe down the kitchen counters. And I can't help thinking of the day when the song became my life. When I woke up alone, with a broken heart and a plane ticket home.

I pour a little more water in the vase of roses. I don't actually like roses, but Grant does. They remind him of his mother, who passed away last year after a long battle with breast cancer. For him—for the woman I'm trying to be—I pretend.

I pretend elsewhere, too. Out of necessity. For my peace of mind and his. My orgasms are few and far between, but Grant believes what I've told him, that it's always been difficult for me to climax. He'll never know the truth, not if I can help it.

Even if it means I smother a part of myself, I'll never allow another man to become what Liam was to me. My sun. My dom. My master.

Humming the melody of "Galway Girl," I walk into the bedroom Grant and I have shared for a year. I don't bother with the lights. My clothes hit the floor piece by piece. I crawl under the covers, sighing at the sensation of cool sheets on my flushed skin. Rain patters against the bedroom windows, a fitting backdrop for my shifting self.

Against the edges of my tired mind, memories stir and rise. My belly tightens. My thighs clench. My breasts grow heavy and tight. I ignore it all. The arousal. The temptation to touch myself, to tug and pinch and hold my breath. Just as I ignore the echoes of Liam's voice in my ear.

"No matter how far you fly, little dove, you'll always come home to me."

I pray for sleep.

52

I'M NOT QUITE two hours into my rounds Friday morning when the phone rings at the nearby nurses' station. Paused outside a patient's room reviewing a file, I don't notice the ringing stop, the following words. I don't hear rapid footsteps approaching until someone touches my shoulder.

"Dr. Sumner," gasps a nurse, "you're needed in the ER immediately."

I turn, frowning. "What? Why?"

Her eyes are a little wild behind her glasses. "There's someone asking for you. Um... I guess they're being pretty adamant. Psych was called. Security doesn't think she's dangerous, but she's pretty upset."

The back of my scalp tightens. "Does *she* have a name?"

She shakes her head. "They didn't say."

I nod, handing her my current file. "See if Dr. Ling will take this? Patient is stable."

"Yes, of course."

I thank her and walk quickly to the elevator, my white coat fluttering gently against my legs. Figuring it must be a former patient—or more likely, a former patient's mother—I pick up my pace, bypassing the elevator for the stairs. Three floors down, I push through a door and jog toward the ER.

As I round the final corner, I hear an unfamiliar female voice yelling.

"Eden! Dr. Eden Sumner! Get off me—don't fucking touch me—*Eden!*"

I push into a small crowd gathered on the side of the waiting room. "Get out of the way, please," I say tightly. "Move, move."

I finally get through and see the woman.

Shoulder-length brown hair. Mid-forties and petite. Pale skin that showcases bruising on her jaw and temple. Wearing jeans, rain boots, and a winter coat. I don't recognize her. Two security guards flank her, their expressions wary.

Stopping uncertainly, I watch her scan the room. Her head turns in my direction and her eyes find me. They widen.

"Eden," she gasps. She moves like lightning, darting outside the guards' reach and running to me.

I'm so surprised I don't move, just stiffen as she hugs me tightly. She pulls back, her hands moving to cup my face.

"I'm sorry, have we met?" My voice is thin and high. Somewhere in my mind an alarm is sounding. Not a mild beeping, either. A full-blown emergency wail.

"We have to go," says the woman, eyes darting between mine. "You need to come with me right now."

White noise fills my ears.

"Dr. Sumner?" asks a guard tightly. "Psych's on the way."

I glance at him, then look at the crowd surrounding us. "Okay, thanks." My voice sounds weirdly robotic, my limbs tingling as I turn to the woman. "You've come to the right place. We'll get you help."

She steps back, expression falling into determined lines. "I'm sorry, Eden. But I have no choice."

With a smooth movement, she reaches into her coat and pulls something out.

"Gun!" yells a security guard.

There's immediate pandemonium. The formerly curious crowd goes berserk, screaming, shoving, and running toward the exit. A silent alarm goes off, sensors over doors flashing white and red. Hospital personnel shout orders as they frantically follow procedures for lockdown on other floors.

As the space around us clears, the guards—their own guns drawn—order the woman to drop her weapon. They also tell me to get away, to run, but I can't move.

All I can do is stare. Past the dark barrel of the gun aimed at me. Into cracked-marble eyes.

"They found me," she whispers. "I'm sorry, but they'll be coming for you, too."

Four police officers burst through the main doors. More yelling, radios crackling. A tornado of action happens outside the eye of the storm. I glance at the nearby guards, see a decision crystallizing in their eyes. She's not dropping the weapon.

They're going to shoot her.

I don't think. Throwing myself forward, I spread my arms, my back between the guards and her. "No, no!"

"Get out of the way, doctor!" shouts the man on the right.

"No!" I stare down into the woman's eyes. "She won't hurt me. She's not going to hurt me. Are you?"

Her lower lip trembles as she lowers the gun. "I'm sorry. I didn't know what else to do. We have to go. We're not safe."

I shake my head, scrambling for reason in a world gone mad. "Why now? It's been years. There's been no sign of him. I get routine updates from the FBI—Maddoc is gone. Moved on. He's not even in the country."

Distant sirens wail. Real ones, this time.

"My sweet girl, there's no such thing as moving on. Not for Maddoc. He doesn't forget. And he knows about the USB drive." She sighs, shaking her head a little. "I told you not to trust anyone."

The words pull the blood from my head to my belly, where it vortexes into a maelstrom of dread. If he knows where I am, then he knows where I work. Where I live. He knows about Grant. My parents.

Liam, where are you?

"Okay," I whisper, nodding. Turning to face the array of men, I lift my hands. "Officers, I'm going to accompany this woman from the hospital of my own free will. She will not hurt me."

"Doctor! We can't let you do that!"

I find the speaker—the nearest police officer. In my eyes, I see his certainty that I'm going to die.

But I won't. Not right now, at least.

Over my shoulder, I murmur, "Keep me between them and you. Walk backward down the hallway behind you."

She doesn't hesitate, one hand fisting in my white coat and pulling me slowly backward. The line of officers advances. I hear my breath, harsh and loud.

My eyes stay fixed on the officer who fears for me. "I'm going voluntarily," I repeat. "She will not hurt me."

There's a question in his eyes, one with an answer that I can hardly believe.

"She's my mother," I tell him. "My mother."

He pauses, shaking his head. "We can't just let you go, doctor, regardless of who she is. Tell her to surrender her gun. Every exit is covered. There's nowhere to go."

He's right. I know he is. But my rational mind is no longer in control—or maybe the world has turned upside down and I'm finally rational. Either way, I believe Elizabeth. If I don't go with her, people—including us—are going to die. And it's more than the evidence of her split lip and slowly purpling jaw that point to a very real confrontation. I saw the truth in her eyes.

Maddoc found her. She escaped. She came for me.

I hear Liam's voice in my memory. *There's no escape from men like your father.*

"Don't do this," says the officer, correctly reading the intent in my eyes.

"You don't understand," I whisper.

We're halfway down the hallway when three figures move into the space behind the officers. I see them first, then Elizabeth does. She curses. Before I can comprehend why they look wrong—no uniforms, sunglasses—they lift guns.

Motherfucking machine guns.

Elizabeth yanks me bodily down the hall, my feet scrambling to keep up with her sudden sprint. I scream, "Behind you!" but it's too late.

It was always too late.

Gunfire erupts, bullets mowing through police and security guards alike. Blood sprays against the walls, the floor. Several fallen officers manage to get some rounds off.

That's all I see before daylight blinds me.

53

THE OFFICER LIED. No one waits for us outside this particular exit, though we aren't alone. Throngs of frantic people continue streaming out of the hospital. Elizabeth pulls me along until we're lost in the crowds. Sirens blare as police cruisers speed down side streets toward the ER.

My brain is mush from having processed too much in too brief a period. The shock, the terror, the displaced sorrow. *Those men died for us—because of us.*

As chaos continues to reign behind us, Elizabeth pauses to rip off my white coat. She tosses the blood-spattered fabric behind a bush, then grabs my hand again.

Past a parking structure. Across a street. Down an alley. She finally stops at a dark SUV, shoving me into the passenger seat before running around to the other side. The car starts.

She glances at me. "Seatbelt, Eden."

I croak a harsh laugh but do as she says. It's a good thing, too—the tires squeal as she accelerates fast. The alley isn't that narrow, but there are doors lining it. If someone walks out of one...

"Will you slow down?"

Her eyes stay on the alley. "Not until we're safe."

The four-lane cross street approaches. Cars whiz past the alley. She doesn't slow.

"Holy shit! Stop!"

She accelerates even more. When our front tires clear the last building, she cranks the wheel hard. The heavy car slides, screeching in protest. More tires squeal as cars break in a panic, swerving to miss us. Elizabeth's foot stays pressed on the accelerator. Her hands fly with the steering wheel, correcting until we stop fishtailing.

Within minutes we're entering a freeway onramp. The traffic is light; she moves to the carpool lane and matches the speed of the car in front of us.

Then, finally, she glances my way. "Are you okay? You didn't get hit, did you?"

"What? No." I touch my numb face with numb fingers. "I feel like I'm underwater."

"It's the shock," she says matter-of-factly.

"Yes, I know."

"Of course you do," she says softly, with a touch of wistfulness. "You're a doctor."

I stare out the window. Time bends and stretches, slows and speeds. Faces, cars, signs… they freeze for an eternal moment in my mind, then blur as they pass.

"Shouldn't we be going north? Into Canada or something?"

"That's what he'll think we'll do. Besides, do you have a passport on you?"

I have nothing. No phone. No wallet. I don't answer, staring stiffly out the window. Seeing everything. Seeing nothing.

"I'm sorry," says Elizabeth mutedly. "I've lived this life for so long, sometimes I forget what a shock it is initially."

I close my eyes—see blood spraying, a brain exposed—and open them quickly. Thoughts clash in my head, old ones and new ones colliding.

Does Alexis know what's happening? Is she alive? Where's Maddoc? Does Liam know?

I have so many questions. Too many.

"They found me yesterday," begins Elizabeth softly. "I made a mistake. A terrible one. I was here in Seattle because I wanted to see you. Just once. I wasn't going to talk to you, but I just wanted…" She sighs, shaking her head. "I went to the hospital yesterday. Maddoc must have had someone watching you. They ID'd me, followed me back to my hotel."

"Is that how you got the..." I wave at her bruised face.

She nods. "These men, they never expect a woman to know how to defend herself. Even less so to go on the offensive. When I got away this morning, I came straight to the hospital. I was going to try to find you before you went into work, but there's too many parking lots for staff, and I didn't know what kind of car you drive."

Delayed synapses fire in my brain. "I was under surveillance? For how long?"

"I don't know. I didn't know about the FBI leak until yesterday. Men like those who work for your father will think they can say whatever they want in front of you. It makes them feel powerful. Gives them a false sense of control."

I barely hear her as a singular need overtakes my thoughts. "Did the man who took you—did he say anything about Alexis?"

Lips thinning, she shakes her head. "No." She pauses, fingers tightening on the wheel. "After the manhunt four years ago, I lost track of her. She's gone underground. My only hope is that she broke free from the life, that she didn't rejoin Maddoc."

I think of the betrayal on Alexis's face when I went with Special Agent Hernandez, when I'd naively believed I was saving her.

I know he isn't a good man, but he's my dad. I love him.

And even though I don't want to, I remember Liam telling me that he witnessed Alexis ordering an execution. That he saw her stand by while a man lost his life.

There's still a twisted part of me that hopes it's not true. Liam certainly lied to me before, many times. Perhaps he lied again.

Not knowing the difference between lies and truth is a particular type of pain. It scratches at the edges of you. Over time, it digs into the foundation of how you think about the world. It paints everything in watercolors.

"Eden? Are you okay?"

I snort. "Peachy." I glance at her profile, pinched in worry. "Where are we going?"

"I have friends in Mexico."

My eyes narrow. "I don't have a passport, remember?"

"It won't be a problem."

More questions. Too many questions.

I close my eyes and hear a voice.

His.

I will always find you.

And for the first time in nearly six years, I feel the deepest, darkest essence of me stir and stretch. It blooms, obliterating my carefully maintained discipline. Wiping away all traces of denial. My false life. My false self.

What's revealed is *me*. The woman Liam awakened, crafted into existence as surely as a master artist shapes malformed clay. Not his little dove—not soft or yielding.

His little monster.

I am awake.

54

IF ELIZABETH NOTICES a change in me, she doesn't comment on it. My sudden calm, my lack of fear. We drive. And drive. Cross several state lines, change cars twice within two days.

She knows every trick in the book and has four different IDs. When she gives me my own fake ID, I don't even blink. She tells me that she hoped this day would never come, but that hope didn't stop her from preparing for it.

We don't talk about Alexis again. Nor do we talk much at all, at least not about the past, which dwindles rapidly in our rearview. Instead we talk about where we're going in Mexico, how we'll stay for a week with her so-called friends. Just enough time to get new passports and identification. They'll be fake, but mine will bear my real name—the name on the Cooks Island account.

Once the papers come through, we'll go for the money. And then we'll disappear.

I nod. I offer suggestions. Strategies. And when she lists off remote locations for our eventual life, I nod again. *Sounds good.* She sweetens the deal by telling me doctors are always needed. That I can practice medicine —discreetly—wherever we land.

I don't tell her I already know where I'm going, and it's not Morocco, Mongolia, or Papua New Guinea. I plan on flying straight into the sun.

Even if it kills me.

WE DRIVE eight to twelve hours a day, sometimes all night. We stop occasionally to grab food and quick showers at a truck stop or to get some sleep at a seedy motel. When we do sleep, it's in shifts, one of us posted by the window to monitor the parking lot. We request ground level, corner units each time.

On our fourth day of driving, we reach Las Cruces, New Mexico, an hour outside the Mexican border and the city of Juarez. We're going to avoid the major crossing, however, and leave the U.S. through the smaller outpost of Santa Teresa. When I ask again about passports, Elizabeth maintains that we won't have any problems. As she clearly has more experience with border crossings than I do, I let the matter drop.

We find a motel for the night. Shower and eat crappy takeout and watch the news on a tiny television with bad static. Neither of us mention the news clip of the death of twelve men in a Seattle hospital last week or the disappearance of a doctor. Or the search for three shooters, speculated to be members of an extremist terrorist group.

Twelve dead.

Neither of us sleep.

At four thirty in the morning, we get in the car and make the hour-long drive to the border. The sky is still dark, though bleeding to navy as the sun readies its ascent. The line isn't long, maybe ten cars ahead of us.

"Calm down," murmurs Elizabeth. "Unclench your hands."

I take several deep breaths and relax my fingers. We move forward little by little. Before long, we're under the canopy and the kiosk is beside us. A Border Patrol officer peers into the car, his gaze cursory yet piercing. Just as Elizabeth coached me, I don't smile, instead affecting boredom. It works. The officer nods, stepping back, and the light above us turns green.

We drive into Mexico as the sun rises.

A mere four hours later, we enter Chihuahua City. As we near the city's downtown, our surroundings become older and more beautiful. Buildings with incredible colonial architecture sit on nearly every block, and massive cathedrals rise toward the placid blue sky.

It's obvious Elizabeth has been here before; she navigates easily through hectic traffic and thick pedestrian flow. Parking the car in an alley off a busy street, she pulls the keys from the ignition and tosses them down by her feet.

"Don't leave anything behind. We won't be back."

Our duffels slung over our shoulders, we walk to the street and into the light. The air itself is cool, but the sun feels less filtered, searing my eyes and making them water.

We walk three blocks, take a detour through a narrow alley clogged by drying laundry, and finally stop outside an unmarked door, it's cracked wooden surface stained a mottled blue.

Elizabeth knocks.

A tense minute later, the door opens.

A woman's face appears, dark eyes widened with horror. "Corre! Run!" she hisses. She's yanked backward. There's a muffled pop, then a thud as her body hits the floor. Somewhere inside, a child wails.

"No," whispers Elizabeth.

She grabs my arm, nails biting into my skin, and pulls me back. My limbs are leaden with fear. I stumble, tripping over a loose brick. Her grip slips as I fall, my knees biting into the rough ground.

For a second—one eternal second—our eyes lock. I nod. She turns and runs. Time resumes its normal pace, and in moments she's gone, lost in the sun and crowds at the end of the alley.

The man leaning against the doorway watches her go, then turns to me. When I look at him, he smiles slightly. Sunlight shines dully against the dark metal of the gun in his hand.

"How did you know I was going to kill her but not you?" he asks mildly.

I push to my feet, wiping errant gravel from my knees. "I didn't. Not until you just told me."

His sandy eyebrows lift. "You always were a smart one, weren't you, lass? How bout we make this easy—tell me what I want to know, and I'll let you follow your mother."

"What is it you want to know?" I ask carefully.

"Where are they?"

"Who?"

He shakes his head. "Don't play dumb, Eden. Where are the diamonds?"

My blood runs cold. My voice stutters. "W-what? I don't know anything about diamonds."

He steps out of the doorway. Behind him, I see a child —eleven or twelve—crouched over the fallen woman and sobbing quietly. Without even checking her vitals, I know she's dead.

Resolve tightens my shoulders. I look into Chris's eyes. "If I do tell you where these alleged diamonds are, you'll kill me."

He winces. "You're right about that. See, when you turn on the family, you're not liable to be forgiven. And your betrayal was rather extreme, wasn't it? But as you've found, the family isn't without mercy. We let you have a life these six years. I hope you enjoyed them."

"Not particularly, no."

Chris laughs. "I can hardly believe it, but I think I've missed your mouth." He takes another step toward me. "Remember what I told you before? This goes one of two ways. Easy. Or hard."

I take a breath. Swallow past a dry throat.

"I'll take hard."

I don't see his hand with the gun move. There's an explosion of light and sound.

Then nothing.

55

NOW

SQUEAK. *Squeak.*

"Did you hear that?"

"What?"

"That sound? Was that a rat?"

The other man grunts. "Who cares?"

"Rat's carry disease."

"Really? You're worried about one stupid rat in the middle of the desert?"

"Fuck you."

"I prefer fecking your mother, ya maggot."

There's a brief scuffle, ending with the hissed words,

"You'd better get the bitch to talk, otherwise we'll see how much you don't care about rats when Maddoc puts you in a hole with a hungry one."

Footsteps pound up the stairs. The door slams, taking light with it. The second set of feet shuffle around the wall near the stairs.

Squeak.

"Jaysus," he mutters, and finally finds the light switch.

The little hanging bulb in the center of the room flickers on. I watch him approach. He doesn't look happy to be here. Squatting before me, he wrinkles his nose at my stench.

"Lass, time's running out."

"For both of us," I croak.

Chris nods, lips thinned. "Aye. I erred when I let Elizabeth run, thinking you were the greater asset. But I still think you know where the diamonds are. You know why?"

I roll my eyes, pretty much the only protest I'm capable of at this point.

"I think you know exactly where they are, but you've been misled into thinking you're protecting someone. And I don't think that someone is your mother."

His eyes narrow, penetrating and dangerously perceptive. I'm afraid if he keeps digging, he'll hit the mark.

I suck air into my tired lungs. "I've told you a million times, I don't know where these diamonds you keep talking about are. Elizabeth left me the USB stick and some cash. That's it." My voice is barely recognizable, my vocal chords damaged by too much screaming and not enough water.

"You've got to give me something else."

I drop my head to the wall behind me. The shift makes the chains around my ankles clank. My hands are still free, but it doesn't mean anything. Not anymore.

Six of my fingers are broken. I'd had to reset them myself, splinting them as best I could with strips of my ratty t-shirt. Thankfully, no bones broke through the skin, lowering my risk of infection, and the swelling seems to be going down. I have to hand it to him—he definitely knows his way around torture techniques.

I consider his face. The tired eyes, pinched mouth. "Hard working for a psychopath, isn't it?" I rasp.

He closes his eyes briefly. "I don't like hurting you, Eden," he murmurs, a rare note of appeal in his voice. "Please, don't make me."

"Because I look like her," I whisper. "I look just like her. Is she okay? Tell me, please. Is she safe?"

I've asked the question a thousand times, and he's never given me an answer. Now, though, there's a softening in his eyes I haven't seen before. I wonder if it's because he knows I'm going to die soon. Or whether some part of him—willing or not—has come to respect me.

I haven't broken.

Not when he held a flame to the bottom of my feet and inner thighs. Not when my head was forced repeatedly into a bucket of water until I nearly drowned. Not when he didn't let me sleep for four days. When he starved me. Blinded me with a spotlight. When he strung me upside down from the pipes, or used a cattle prod, or broke a few of my ribs and nearly dislocated my shoulder during a particularly memorable beating.

Not when he threatened to rape me.

Not when he actually did.

I don't have Stockholm syndrome. Not even close. If I could watch him being burned alive I'd laugh the entire time and roast marshmallows.

But I can't deny that we have an affinity for each other. A closeness I can't describe or understand. Just as he knows I have the information he wants, I know he hasn't enjoyed what he's done to me. There's a reason I don't have any lasting damage—not externally, at least. Why my hands and feet are still attached. Why I haven't bled or been disfigured. Why he hasn't let anyone else touch me.

We are each doing what we have to do. Neither of us have a choice.

Chris bows his head momentarily. When he looks up,

at long last I see my death in his eyes. Here is where the real pain begins. I'll break—I have no doubt—but first, I want the truth.

"Why did you wait six years?" I whisper hoarsely.

"You were protected by the Rourke name."

The news confirms a suspicion I've harbored for years, but it also means something changed, something that dissolved the Rourke shield. I don't have the courage to ask what happened, but Chris answers anyway.

"There was an internal coup in the organization in Dublin. The Rourkes are no more—the lot of them executed." He shrugs. "They had a good run. Better to go out that way than rotting in cells."

I whisper, "Liam?"

Chris sighs. "He's dead, lass. He's not coming. He never was. If you just tell me where the diamonds are, I swear to you I'll make it swift."

I only stare at him, too tired. Too weak. Too empty. If the sun has set, I want to follow it into the dark.

"Don't, Eden," he says tightly. "She isn't worth this."

Alexis.

I close my eyes.

Chris touches my face gently, a stroke of fingertips. "For whatever it's worth, you've done him proud, dove."

The word doesn't mean what it used to. It's stained now. As broken as I will be soon.

But I know he's right.

Liam would be proud.

WHO NEEDS PERFECT SKIN, anyway? Not me, because my back is missing some and I'm still alive. A fact that will hopefully be remedied as soon as Chris ends his phone call. Apparently the person calling wasn't someone he could ignore—even though we were sort of in the middle of something.

"Pretty rude, if you ask me," I tell Squeaker.

My little friend is perched on a pipe above me, near where my hands are bound in thick rope. Above a twitching nose, beady black eyes are fixed on me. Well, on where the scent of blood is originating. I might find out what it feels like to be nibbled on, after all.

The pain is a burning poison in my mind. A poison with waves. Peaks and troughs. My poor endorphins can't keep up with the shifting tide. For the moment, at least, I feel little beyond the slide of blood down my naked skin.

Brief detours into unconsciousness are a relief. I float between a red haze and searing light. Was there a time when pain was pleasure? I don't remember anymore. There is only pain. Thoughts dance in my mind, their routines truncated.

Rope on my wrists. Liam's voice... Do you serve? *Hot hands on my hips, sliding down my legs... A promise.* I will keep you safe. *What is the truth?* She isn't worth it. *Yes, she is. Isn't she? Or is this the price of my blood?*

Ripples in the sea of pain. A rising wave. I groan, and a voice says, "Hold still." The tone is low, icy with fury. All I feel is relief—he's back. He'll put an end to my suffering.

The pressure in my shoulders and arms releases. Gravity claims me, but when I expect cement floor instead there are hard arms. My back flares in agony. My whimper is a pitiful extension of my inner scream.

I pass out, awaken to movement. Pass out again. Awaken. Open my eyes. Try to. I see nothing. I'm not awake. There's nothing.

Is this death?

56

IT'S the beeping that finally wakes me. The intensely familiar sound painted a false reality in my dreams of scrubs and weeping faces and grateful smiles and children. Strong, brave children in hospital beds. But I'm not waking up from a quick nap during a break at work. There are no patients or parents waiting.

That life is gone, just like me.

Beep. Beep.

My return to consciousness is long. One step at a time taken on shifting ground. Pain, distant. Heartbeat, fast. Breathing, labored. The sole of my right foot itches. My neck is so stiff I'm afraid if I move it will break. Fabric under my cheek. A mattress, too hard against the front of my body. Sterile smells, bleach and antiseptic.

Hospital. I'm in a hospital.

"She's waking up." The voice is feminine and softly

accented. Curt but not unkind. *A nurse.* I hear footsteps, smell light perfume.

Where's the doctor?

"Put her back under," says a low voice.

What? No! I try to say it aloud, but can't find my tongue. *Where's my tongue?*

Movement. Familiar sounds—pop of a syringe, rattle of an IV stand.

Wait—

Gone.

WHEN I HEAR the man singing, I decide I'm finally dead. Only in death would an angel sing me "Galway Girl."

"'We were halfway there when the rain came down— of a day-I-ay-I-ay—And she asked me up to her flat downtown—of a fine soft day-I-ay-I-ay.'"

Liam?

The singing stops.

"I'm here. Can you open your eyes for me?"

Dead.

"You're not dead." A pause; pressure on my bare forearm. "Can you feel that?"

I nod, or think I do.

"Good, now open your eyes."

Blinding brightness. Shapes and shadows. Sunlight on white sheets. My eyes water as I blink rapidly. Blobs resolve into objects. A bed. Small room. Not a hospital—someone's home. There's a pitcher of water on the nightstand, condensation spreading in a circle beneath it. The air is warm, a breeze soft on my back.

My back itches.

"I know it's uncomfortable, but the itch is a good sign. You're healing."

With effort, I lower my chin. My cheek slides on sheets, my eyes following down the line of the mattress. I blink.

My first thought is that it's not Liam who sits in a chair with his fingers wrapped around my emaciated arm. This man's hair is buzzed nearly to his scalp, his face clean-shaven and pale. Beneath the sleeves of a black t-shirt, intricate tattoos line both muscular arms. And this man is visibly scarred—a thin white line interrupts his throat, another one bisects his left eyebrow. Both are long healed.

When I look into his eyes, they, too, are familiar and not. Shadows lurk in their depths, an icy darkness that wasn't there before. But there's also an unmistakable glimmer—a magnetism that triggers six years' worth of longing and heartache.

I have to be dreaming.

"Liam?" My voice is no more than a breath.

A sliver of a smile curves his lips. "Aye, it's me. I daresay the years haven't been kind to either of us."

Laughter. Insane, inappropriate laughter gurgles out of me. Liam's smile widens minutely. My back spasms and I groan, my humor wiped away by pain.

He moves to stand. "I'll get you something."

"No! No, please. Don't go."

After a pregnant moment, he nods and settles back into his chair. I wish he'd touch me again, but he doesn't.

"How?" I ask.

His brows lift. "Care to narrow it down?"

I look for signs of teasing, but there are none. Shifting a little, I wince at the odd tugging sensation on my back. "How did you find me?"

He taps his temple. "Finder, remember?"

"No jokes," I whisper.

"I'm not joking." His expression tells me it's the truth. "It wasn't fucking easy, I can tell you that much."

It's not really an answer, but I leave it be. I don't know if he feels guilty or not—I'm beginning to realize I don't know this man. *Did I ever?*

I stare at the wall beside the bed. "Did you kill Chris?"

"No. He was gone when I found you." A pause. "My approach wasn't exactly subtle. I'm sure he was tipped off."

"He left me to die," I whisper, closing my eyes.

He grunts. "He could have easily killed you before I arrived. Frankly, I'm not sure why he didn't."

I flinch at the lack of concern in his voice. The bland curiosity. Feeling angry, lost, and so, so broken, I drag my eyes to his face.

"Why?" I ask.

"Why, what?"

"Why fucking bother?"

He stills. A predator in repose, no longer wearing the mask of humanity.

"I made a promise."

Tears spill from my eyes; I have the nebulous thought that I'm not thirsty anymore, that my body is hydrated. Odd, to not crave water. So odd.

"How long?" I ask, not bothering to mask my tears. Almost, I wish Chris had finished the job.

Liam looks away, across the bed. There must be a window there, but even the thought of lifting and turning my head is exhausting.

"Nearly six weeks."

Silence. Minutes pass. Or seconds? Time bent its own rules in the dark. *Drip drip.*

I was there forever.

"You get used to it," says the man who used to be Liam. His gaze veers back to me. "And it gets better—the nightmares and flashbacks, the panic attacks and aversions. As with all things, it takes time. But I promise, you'll get through it. You're going to be okay."

Okay. That word is nearly incomprehensible. I blink slowly, then shake my head.

His eyes flare with emotion. "I'm going to kill them all. Every person who knew what was happening to you. Your father, his lieutenants, and your sister."

"No," I gasp.

He laughs; it's a horribly cold sound, like breaking dreams and hearts.

"Time to wake up, little dove." I flinch at the word; his eyes harden. "Alexis is Maddoc's second-in-command. Has been for seven years, since the day she turned twenty-two. She's a ruthless savage and a psychopath." He shakes his head. "I fucking tried, Eden. I tried to keep you safe. Hell, even Christopher tried to warn you away. He loved her once, before she changed. Crazy bastard thought by saving you he could save her. Like there's anything left to save."

She's not worth it.

I stare.

I breathe.

I blink.

"Get out," I rasp. Aqua eyes narrow, glinting danger-ously. I point at the door, ignoring the ricochets of pain in my back. "Get the fuck out, Liam!"

He nods curtly and stands. At the doorway, he pauses. "They'll die for what they did to you."

"Why?" I cry in agony. "It doesn't matter anymore. It was all for nothing. If Alexis—if she really… Goddamnit! I would have told her about the fucking diamonds. She didn't have to—I would have told her…" I trail off, spent.

Something shifts in Liam's eyes. For a moment, he's the man I know. His fingers clench on the doorframe.

"I can't make this right, Eden. I would if I could. I would give anything, everything. Not to ease my guilt or your pain, but for us. For us…" He bows his head. "We'll talk more later."

He's gone before I can formulate a response.

57

THE WOMAN who lives here is Maria Alvarez. I doubt it's her real name, but I don't doubt she has medical experience. She changes my bandages every few hours like clockwork, her movements gentle and precise. On my second day awake in her care, she makes me stand up and start moving.

Even knowing how important it is that I regain muscle as soon as possible, I call her every name in the book. She just laughs, and I keep grumbling until she guides me into a bathroom. I've never been so glad to see a toilet in my life. Or a bathtub. It's not pretty, but together we manage to wash my hair and scrub away the grime that my previous sponge baths couldn't.

Day three and four follow the same pattern. Bland gruel for breakfast, lunch, and dinner. Exercise in the morning and evening. We make it down the hall on day three. On day four, we reach the living room before my legs give out. As she helps me into an ancient wheelchair, Maria tells me I'm pushing too hard.

I tell her she needs to push me harder.

She tries.

By the end of my first week of rehabilitation, I can walk unassisted to the living room and back. I've also had her taper me off painkillers. Whatever was in the pills she routinely gave me, it packed a hefty punch. And I need my wits. I need my mind, splintered as it is.

On the eighth day, I take the new splints off my fingers. I've been putting it off, but I need to ascertain if there's nerve damage or any complex fractures.

Perched on the edge of my narrow bed, sunlight blankets my back. Through the open window I hear the distant roar of surf. I can't see the ocean from my room, but Maria told me it's not far. My goal is that by the end of the week, I can walk far enough to glimpse it.

When I finally take a break, I'm sweating from fatigue and opiate withdrawal, my hands aching badly. Just as I'm debating whether or not to give in to the tears pressing against my eyes, a shadow fills the doorway.

Liam.

This is his first visit since the day I woke up. He looks slightly better; like he's slept, at least. Although I don't want to feel relief, I do. One of my frequent nightmares during the last week was that he wouldn't come back. That he would leave me here, broken and alone.

"How do you feel?"

I shrug, wincing as my back twinges. "Where did Chris learn to break bones? He's pretty good at it. Clean breaks. They should be healed in another few weeks."

Liam leans against the doorjamb, crossing his arms over his chest. "Do you actually expect me to answer that question?"

I glance up, my expression neutral. "Not really. I do have a question, though—who's Maria?"

"She works for a local cartel. Used to be a nurse before her husband got caught up in a bad business deal. Now she's paying off his debt."

"How did you find her?" Even as I ask the question, I know his answer.

"It's what I do."

"Where's her husband?"

"Where do you think, dove?"

I flinch, lifting my hands as if I can block myself from that word. From him.

"What's wrong?" he demands.

Shaking, I lower my hands. "You can't call me that ever again. Never. Ever. Again. Do you understand?"

He's across the room in seconds and kneeling before me. Fingers grip my knees, but lightly, as if he's afraid to break me. *Too late.* I stare at his strong hands, dotted now with small scars, and remember them bruising me. Remember loving it, begging for it. Exulting in it. I long for the ecstasy of surrender like a lost limb—it's never coming back, but it still aches.

"Eden, look at me, please."

No command in the tone, just pleading. I look up. When our gazes clash, it feels like the air is sucked from the room. I want so badly for him to erase the pain. To erase everything. To become the sun again, blotting out my darkness. But there's too much darkness now.

"I can't," I gasp, pushing his hands off my knees. "I can't talk about it."

There's death in his eyes—Chris's death.

"He called you that. How did he—" He stops, shakes his head. "You don't have to tell me."

I press the heels of my hands into my eyes. "It's okay. I told Alexis. When I stayed with her in L.A. I still can't believe…" I shake my head helplessly. "I was so wrong about her. I ignored all the signs. The drug use, the erratic behavior. I wanted so badly for her to be someone she wasn't. God, I'm an idiot. I fell for it. For all of it."

A maelstrom of pain whips against the steel cage around my heart. A little slips free, shortening my breath and misting my eyes. After all that happened in the basement, I'd truly wondered if I'd ever cry again. If my capacity for suffering had been reached.

Wrong.

"I'm sorry, Eden. For the way I told you. You didn't deserve to hear it like that."

My eyes closed, I focus on my breathing and rebuild the barriers around my heart. I straighten my spine, ignoring the immediate burn. When Maria showed me my back for the first time, I could hardly believe what I saw—how such small wounds could cause so much pain. It's no fucking wonder that flaying people is such an old, effective torture.

He'd taken my skin three times. Three strips, roughly an inch wide and three inches long. Parallel to each other, in a neat little row right between my shoulder blades.

I give myself a shake and open my eyes. "Have you ever been flayed alive?"

Liam's brows lift. "As opposed to being flayed dead?"

My lips twitch. Morbid amusement, it seems, is our primary defense mechanism. *At least we have something left in common.*

"It's not pleasant."

"No, I'd imagine it's not. How are the painkillers?"

I snort. "You mean the heroin?"

Liam smirks. "Yes."

"I've been off it for a day now. Hence the sweating and shivering."

His gaze tracks over my damp neck. Deep down, past

the darkness, I feel a frisson of awareness. A feeble flame that gutters and dies from lack of oxygen.

"Why are you here, Liam? What do you want from me?"

Surprise briefly lights his eyes, mellowed the next moment by anguish. "Where else would I be?" he whispers.

58

DAY FIFTEEN. I've seen the ocean—well, the Gulf of California—and I've learned where we are. About twenty minutes north of Los Mochis, a coastal city in northern Sinaloa, Mexico. Granted, I haven't seen a map, so I have no idea where Sinaloa is.

Honestly, I don't care. All I care about is that we're a good five hundred miles from a certain basement. When Liam told me the distance, I believed him. Funny, that. How trust is harder to kill than a person.

But though he's lied to me plenty of times, we aren't the same people. He's not trying to protect my innocence anymore. Nor has he made any efforts to charm me, to draw me in, to touch my barricaded heart. He speaks frankly. No sugarcoating. No teasing banter or secret smiles.

We are changed, both of us.

Maybe someday we'll get drunk and tell each other our stories. Maybe we'll part ways or die first. I don't know how this story ends—for either of us—but I'm sick of reading. I'm restless. I want power back. Control. Freedom.

Choice.

"I can't kill anyone. I won't. But I don't want them to have the money."

Liam looks up from his hand of cards, eyes narrowed beneath lowered brows. "I have plenty of money."

"I don't want your money. I want what belongs to me."

He drops his cards on the table and leans back, crossing arms behind his head. He's still beautiful to me. More beautiful, even. Hardened and refined by the force of his world—smelted and polished to his utmost potential. A killer.

The notion no longer bothers me.

"It doesn't belong to you," he says mildly. "I seem to remember your mother stole its source from Maddoc, who might have stolen it from someone else."

"You know what I mean."

"I don't, actually. Enlighten me."

I toss my cards beside his. I was losing, anyway. "I want what they stole from *me*. I want my life."

"Your old one?"

"Yes—no. I'd like to know that my parents are safe, but I can't go back. I can't be a doctor again."

It's the first time I've mentioned it, but he doesn't look surprised.

Liam's eyes catch the sunset, flaring like flames on water. "Can't?" he asks softly. "Or won't?"

"I'm not looking for psychoanalysis," I snap. "I want to know if you'll help me. I want the money."

The old Liam would have made a graphic suggestion about how I might earn his help.

The new Liam merely nods. "All right."

"That's it? *All right?*"

He looks out the window at the darkening sky. "Yes, Eden. Of course I'll help you."

An aching part of me asks again, "Why?"

He stays absolutely still, a statue of lethal beauty. After a long minute of silence—wherein I watch the sun fade from his face—he turns his head and meets my gaze.

"Until you tell me to stop, I'll follow you. To hell and back if necessary." A ghost of a smile graces his lips. "I serve at your whim, Eden Sumner."

"Out of guilt," I whisper.

He sighs and stands. As he passes me on the way to the door, his fingertips graze my shoulder. For the first time in two weeks, I don't flinch at the casual touch.

"You know it's more than that," he murmurs, and

leaves me to the shadows and at the mercy of my tortured mind and heart.

THERE'S ONLY DARKNESS. No light. *Squeak.* I'm still in the basement. Liam was a dream. He's dead, like Chris told me. I'm alone. A monster defeated, a woman sundered.

Eden.

Without choice, there's no surrender.

There is only defeat.

"Eden."

Memory tempts me. Snatches me in its gossamer clutches, paints me in watercolor. Too many colors together... I am mud.

Sparks of pain in my scalp. Fingers squeezing the column of my throat. He's back... finally.

I will him to finish me.

"Fight, damnit!"

No surrender.

Only defeat.

Cool air on my naked breasts, then weight and heat. Light cocooning darkness. I'm smothered, wrapped tight and aching for release. Freedom. Can there be freedom here? I wonder...

"Come back to me! *Now,* Eden!"

The command jerks me awake with a gasp. A hard male body rests atop mine. Fingers press against my throat. More are clenched in my hair.

"Do you feel the difference?" he growls. "Do you feel the power?"

I do.

But I can't surrender anymore.

With a hoarse cry, I buck and flail my arms, beating his head and back with every ounce of my strength. White-hot rage burns through me, all my weeks of impotence flooding through my limbs like a drug.

My nails find skin, dig and tear. Like a banshee, I wail in an unearthly pitch as I conquer. Somehow, I maneuver atop him. I find his neck with my hands.

I squeeze. Hard. Harder.

Gentle hands cup my face. "Yes," he whispers. "Yes."

The monster is soothed by his touch. Memory swirls and plays across a landscape of bloody red.

"Liam?" I gasp, my fingers unclenching from his neck.

He smiles, moonlight through the window revealing raw tracks on his cheek from my nails, redness on his throat.

His hands keep moving, smoothing down my arms, my hips, until I shudder, fully rooted in my body.

"You were having a nightmare."

I scramble off him, fleeing to the window. Gulping

night air, flavored with the barest touch of salt, I try to make sense of what cannot be understood.

"Why let me hurt you?" I whisper.

Fabric whispers as he shifts. There's a soft thud as his feet hit the floor. "Because I can give you what you need."

I turn, shivering, not in cold but fear, and meet his steady gaze. "And what's that?"

"Control."

I don't pretend to misunderstand, though his offer is numbing. Mind-boggling. A man who thrives on controlling others, on manipulating pawns in games of power…

I shake my head. "I can't."

He nods, standing. "Not yet. Perhaps never." In a surreal mimicking of his earlier exit, he pauses in the doorway. "But should you ask, I will serve."

WHEN LIAM TAKES over my rehabilitation, my progress increases exponentially. Much to both his and Maria's surprise, I was the one to suggest the change. Maria was too gentle, too sympathetic. I need to be hard. To be strong. If I can't put myself back together from the inside out, maybe I can do it from the outside in.

I knew Liam would be merciless and aloof, and I was right. He gives me no quarter. There's no aftercare, no encouraging words. No massages for overworked, underdeveloped muscles. No days off.

This isn't romance—it's war. One army fighting itself. Me against me.

Weeks pass. Our grueling dawn walks evolve into grueling dawn runs. First to the coast, then north along a dusty road with the sea lapping to our left and the sun riding the eastern horizon. One mile. Two. Six.

When I stop passing out from fatigue after our runs, he procures an ancient, sagging punching bag from a storage shed outside. We return to the house, drink water, and keep training. Hard. Harder.

Maria watches us sometimes, when she's not doing house calls for the cartel. She watches with a critical eye as Liam wraps my hands in gauze and tape. She watches in silence as he yells at me, calls me names, curses and spits until I'm angry, so angry, that I punch and kick until my hands feel like they're going to fall off and my legs quiver.

We eat an early dinner together, the three of us. Protein and fat only for me. There's little talk but no awkwardness. We are all soldiers in our own wars. And when I'm strong enough, Liam and I start running in the evenings, too, as the sun sets and light fades from the world.

I run in the dark, Liam behind me. A near-silent shadow. He taunts me, whispers all the things he's going to do to me. Crimes against my body. Ones I would have asked for, once upon a time. The agony of the whip. The pressure of confinement.

I know what he's doing. I don't fight it. I embrace it. He's hacking at my foundation, forcing me to either rebuild or fade away. Forcing me to confront every horror, every degradation, and pushing me deeper. Past the pain. Past the terror. To when I had a choice.

Sometimes I can ignore his words. Sometimes they trigger flashbacks of the basement so vivid that I stumble and fall to my knees, retching against the shadowed earth. And every once in a while, his erotic nightmares make my blood sing with the old, familiar urge. It doesn't last, and more often than not our nightly runs end with me launching myself at him in fury.

Tonight, when he tells me he'll tie me by my wrists to the ceiling and make me climax as he pours hot wax on my breasts, I use his own momentum to trip him fluidly, use my weight to drive him down, land a swinging knee in his stomach, and punch him so hard his head cracks against the ground.

He touches his lip, stares at the shadow of blood. Then he looks up and grins. Proud and unrepentant.

"My little siren."

As my anger fades and my hand starts hurting, Liam laughs. Softly at first, but before long he's howling at the night sky.

"We're seriously deranged," I say, still atop him, glued to his body. His arms stay limp by his sides—we both know if he touches me I'll bolt.

Still smiling, his chest heaving, he murmurs, "*Ní féidir leat a shocrú cad nach bhfuil briste*. You cannot fix what isn't broken. And you are far from broken."

"It doesn't feel that way."

"I know it doesn't. You'll just have to believe me. I've

seen you, Eden. I *see* you. I know what you're made of. You will persevere."

I rise to my feet. Easy, smooth, strong. I'm barely winded. My lungs fill with the cool air, release warm air. For the first time, I can imagine a life beyond tomorrow. I want it. Fiercely.

Freedom from the past.

Liam rises, tall and virile, and brushes dirt from the back of his shorts. Hands on his hips, he stares at the dark water. A titan. A citadel of calm.

"What happened to you?" I ask, surprising both of us.

His head turns slowly, eyes finding mine. "I became my father, and then I killed him."

I stare at his back as he walks away. Before I'm fully aware of my intent, I race after him, then slow to match his brisk pace.

"Liam," I bark.

"Yes, siren?"

I don't comment on the new name. I like it—perhaps more than I should. "Tell me about your throat."

"When my father realized I was stronger than him, that more of his men were loyal to me and his power was draining away, he tried to have me killed. Thing is, you should never bring a garrote to a knife fight."

"And your eyebrow?"

"Courtesy of my dear ol' da." He glares at me. "Do

you want me to tell you about all the men I killed? The children I left without fathers? The women I left without husbands?"

I suck in a shallow breath. "Do you regret it?"

"Does it matter?" he retorts.

Does it?

"No." At his incredulous snort, I roll my eyes. "Oh, am I supposed to be shocked and horrified by the news that bad men died? I can't go back, Liam. I'm not the innocent girl you once knew."

"I know."

I grab his arm, halting him. "Do you?" I ask sharply. "Do you really get it? That she's dead?"

Instead of backing down like I expect, he steps closer, crowding my personal space. His face is shadowed, his shoulders filling my vision. But I'm not afraid.

"I mourned that girl six years ago," he says rigidly, "just as I mourned the man I used to be. But as you said, there's no going back. We are here. We are now. And there is no fate but that we make for ourselves."

My breath comes harshly, his words vibrating in the marrow of my bones. "How did you kill your father?"

He smiles without humor. "What did you call me once? The Puppet Master. I turned his empire against itself and danced in the ruins, all without lifting a finger."

My heart races like a bird in a cage, but I straighten my spine and nod. "Good."

His brows jump. "Good?"

I shrug. "I'm glad he's dead, that you got your revenge. You're free now."

"And will you be glad when Maddoc's dead?" he asks stonily. "Will you be free?"

I look up at the stars. "Honestly, I'm starting to wonder if Maddoc even exists. He's like the tooth fairy or the boogeyman."

The mood broken, Liam chuckles. "Even boogeymen have weaknesses."

"What's his?" I ask curiously.

"His daughter."

I take a breath and let it out slowly, savoring the unexpected gift. The simple acknowledgement that I am not them—not her. They are not my family. Blood has a price, but I don't.

"Come on," he says brusquely. "Let's get back."

We walk side by side on the dusty road, little more than shadows in the night. And in the silence, I feel something I'd thought forever gone.

Safety.

60

EVERY TIME I tell Liam I'm ready, he says I'm not. So we wait and keep training. I heal physically. I become fast and strong. Stronger than I've ever been in my life.

Liam eventually stops holding back in our sparring sessions. It's a rough transition, with more than a few panic attacks and breakdowns. But with each new bruise, I revel in the knowledge that I've chosen this path. Icepacks and ibuprofen are prices I'm willing to pay to learn how to defend, attack, and immobilize a man twice my size. And the times I succeed, landing kicks and punches that bloom angrily on Liam's skin? Icing on the cake.

I still have nightmares, but I don't always remember them in the morning. Other times, Maria or Liam have to rouse me in the dead of night because I'm screaming in my sleep.

On one such night—roughly eight weeks post-basement—Maria wakes me. She sings to me in Spanish until the echoes of my terror fade. After, as she runs a wet cloth over my sweat-soaked face, I ask if she'd be willing to hear what happened to me.

She doesn't hesitate. "Of course I will listen, mi hija."

So I purge my body of memories by voicing them. Once I start, I don't stop. I recount every vile moment, every abuse, every time I wished—begged—to die. I talk until I'm hoarse and dawn begins to brighten the room.

When there's nothing left, Maria bends forward to kiss my forehead. She hasn't spoken or moved or let go of my hand once in the last hours.

Now, she says, "My abuelita told me that the purpose of a storm is to force trees to take deeper roots. Sleep easy now, Eden. Your roots are strong and deep."

It's the last time I wake up screaming.

FINALLY, ninety-four days after our arrival, Liam takes me into Los Mochis to get a passport photo. Then we take the photos to a dumpy stucco building with sagging doors, and in a locked, air-conditioned room with an abundance of computers, a harried man produces my documents. One with my real name for the bank in Cook Islands, another with an alias I'll use to disappear.

I hardly recognize myself.

The woman in the small photo is unsmiling, her eyes too big in a face with sharp, feline angles. Morning runs have given my skin a light golden tone. Freckles mellowed by age and Seattle's weather have reappeared, a sprinkling across my nose and cheeks. My hair, long since I was a teenager, is now trimmed to my shoulders. Though Maria had tried to repair it initially, it'd been so badly matted we'd had no choice but to chop it off.

"I look mean," I tell Liam as I stare at the image on our drive back to Maria's.

He snorts. "You *are* mean."

I roll my eyes, closing the little booklet and holding it in my lap. Staring out the window, I watch the passing scenery without really seeing it.

I'm distracted. Not in the way I should be—with thoughts of leaving tomorrow—but with the man beside me. I blame the dream that woke me in the middle of the night, flushed and panting. I'm used to the nightmares by now, but this wasn't a nightmare. Far from it. Nor was it anything easily dismissed, like a fantasy of our former selves. That, I could understand.

In this dream, it wasn't the old Liam but the new. With arms covered in whorls of what I'd discovered were words. Gaelic script woven into beautiful Celtic designs from shoulder to wrist of both arms.

Those arms were stretched above his head, wrists bound in red rope to a headboard.

"What are you thinking about?"

I blink rapidly and shake my head to clear the disturbing—and arousing—image. Grabbing one of the many disjointed thoughts tumbling through my consciousness, I say, "Elizabeth. It occurred to me that she might be waiting for us."

His hands tighten on the steering wheel. I try not to imagine them straining against a rope. I fail.

"I hope she is—she's got a lot to answer for."

It's an old argument. I sigh. "We had an understanding. I don't blame her."

"She left you to rot!"

I don't say anything. Though I've tried, I can't put into words why I don't resent Elizabeth for leaving me to my fate. She did what she had to do, just as I did. In that last moment of eye contact, I'd seen her belief that I would live. Not for one moment had she doubted me.

Be smart. Be brave. I know you'll figure it out.

"If I see that woman—" Liam begins threateningly.

"You'll do nothing," I snap.

He grunts. "I can't believe you told her about the money."

"You weren't there, Liam! She was. She came for me when you were too busy digging your father's grave to realize you'd put a target on my head."

His knuckles go white and a muscle in his jaw ticks. "I know. Don't you think I know that?"

I huff in disgust. "Yeah, it's no secret you're doing penance."

The car swerves violently off the road and jerks to a stop. Another car honks angrily as it speeds past.

Liam rips off his seatbelt and swivels toward me. I meet his stare defiantly. Inside me, the ugly wound of betrayal seeps into my blood.

"Get it all out, Eden," he growls.

"You want to know? Fine! That first week, Chris told me when he was going to rape me. He said he was giving you ten days to find me and that when the time was up, he'd take what belonged to you. I knew you would come. I *believed*. Right up until he stripped me, hosed me down, blindfolded me, and tied me to the fucking wall. Right until he called me *dove* and told me to pretend it was you. Until he... he..."

Liam reaches for me, but I jerk back, my shoulder hitting the window. I taste salt on my lips but can't feel myself crying.

"Even after, I still waited for you. Through everything, a part of me always thought you'd come. But when it was finally time for me to die, Chris told me you were dead. *I thought you were dead!*"

"I'm sorry," he breathes, tortured eyes tracking my features, the tears that drip from my chin.

"This is your fault," I seethe. "You gave the FBI the USB drive. You took the diamonds."

"Why didn't you tell them it was me?" he demands.

The horrible truth opens like the mouth of a great beast, ready to swallow me whole. My chest convulses on a sob; the jaws of truth snap closed around me.

"I was protecting you. Not Alexis. *You.* I was ready to die for you, to keep you safe from them."

The confession hurts. More than anything I suffered in that basement. More than his abandonment six years ago. More than the revelations about my sister. More than everything, anywhere, anytime.

Tears fill Liam's eyes, turning them a surreal turquoise. He knows what I can't say—that the worst wound of all is his broken promise.

"I didn't protect you, Eden. When you needed me most, I wasn't there. I know it doesn't mean anything, not after all you've suffered, but those six weeks were the worst weeks of my life. I did what I do best, and I failed. They beat me at my own game. However much you hate me, know that I hate myself more."

His words purify my wound, but don't heal it. I don't know if it will ever heal. Calm washes over me, numbs me.

"It's my fault," I say, staring over his shoulder at the brown terrain. "I made you the sun. The center of my universe. But you're a man, not a god. Men aren't meant to be worshipped."

"No, we're not," he agrees mutedly, "but I still failed you. I don't expect you to ever forgive me. And yes, I'm doing penance. But not for the reason you think. I'm here because I belong to you. Because I love you. I have always loved you."

I shift my gaze to his face. See the truth in his eyes. But all I feel is emptiness where the sun used to be.

I shake my head. "I'm broken, Liam."

"No, little siren. You're breaking free."

Then he refastens his seatbelt and puts the car in gear. Another silent drive.

61

WHEN WE ARRIVE at the small, dusty airport, three men are waiting outside the sleek private jet. One look at them and it's obvious they're cartel members. Liam had hoped to avoid a meet-and-greet, but we'd nevertheless prepared for one.

Two of the men are Hispanic, one older and gray-haired and the other middle-aged. They wear crisp linen suits, and Panama hats shade their faces. The third man is white and definitely their bodyguard. Beneath a tight, black t-shirt, his bare arms ripple with overdeveloped muscles, and he's wearing clichéd, wraparound sunglasses. His neck is also the same width as his head. As if those details aren't enough to warn people away, the belt at his waist holds a gun on one side and a wicked-looking knife on the other.

Liam parks the car next to a gleaming silver sedan. He cuts the engine. "Let me do the talking."

"I heard you the first ten times."

He doesn't smile. "I might have to touch you unexpectedly."

I nod. "I'm not deaf, Liam. We already covered this."

He pauses, eyeing me, then nods and exits the car. I follow, discreetly tugging down the hem of the blue bodycon dress Maria picked up for the occasion. The smell of hairspray assaults my nose as a breeze lifts curls from my shoulders. There's so much mascara on my eyelashes that blinking is a delayed affair, and the torture devices on my feet pinch already-abused skin. Despite an hour's worth of practice this morning, I'm still unsteady as I walk carefully toward the back of the car.

"Six inches," I grumble as Liam rounds the trunk with our two duffel bags. "What woman in her right mind—"

"Smile, siren," he hisses through his own fake grin.

I peel my lips back from my teeth and take his outstretched hand. "Better?"

His grin becomes genuine. With a gentle squeeze of my fingers, he guides me toward the welcoming committee. As we approach, the bodyguard lumbers forward and takes our bags. He drops them to the ground and squats to unzip and rummage through the contents.

None of us move or speak until the behemoth rises

and nods to his boss. The elder man steps forward. His deep-set brown eyes linger a little too long on my legs before veering to Liam's face.

"Mr. Rourke, a pleasure to see you again." His voice is crisp, his English perfect.

"And you, Don Solórzano. I appreciate the timely response to my request."

Solórzano chuckles, though his eyes stay weirdly flat. "I don't recall you giving me much of a choice."

Liam laughs as well. If I didn't know him, I'd actually think it was authentic. "A favor done is a favor earned. Now we're square."

Solórzano glances at the younger man. Now that we're close, I can see the family resemblance.

"Did you hear that, Mario? When you do business with the Irish, they always call in their favors. Even a decade later."

Mario nods, then looks our way. "What if the Irishman you do business with loses his name and family? Do we return past favors then?"

My heart picks up nervous speed. I glance at the bodyguard. He hasn't moved, but with the dark sunglasses I can't tell if he's looking at me or Liam. In case it's me, I focus on maintaining my bimbo-blank expression while wondering how far I can run before he shoots me in the back.

Everything's fine, I tell myself. *Just a pissing contest.*

Liam doesn't respond to Mario's veiled threat. He doesn't even look at him, keeping his attention on the elder Solórzano.

Mario doesn't like that but thankfully for us, his father thinks it's hysterical. Solórzano claps his son on the back, still chortling as he walks toward us with his hand outstretched. Liam shakes his hand firmly, the lazy smile on his face not easing my nerves in the least.

"Don, let me introduce my girlfriend, Lizzy."

Solórzano gives me a thorough once-over. My skin crawls like it's covered in ants, but I manage to keep smiling.

"How do you do," I drawl. "Gosh, your plane is just beautiful. So massive and shiny. Thanks a million for letting us borrow it."

Liam gives my fingers a warning squeeze, but Solórzano only laughs again and tells Liam, "Ella es una muchacha magnífica. ¿Cuánto quieres?"

How much? I blink innocently while I imagine stabbing a six-inch heel through Solórzano's neck.

Liam replies smoothly, "No he terminado con ella todavía, pero cuando estoy, te lo haré saber."

Solórzano merely smiles. "Please do." He turns away. "Julio, please take our guests' luggage onboard."

The bodyguard does as he's told, lumbering up the narrow metal stairs to the shadowed portal. Not until he returns, two pilots behind him, do Liam's fingers relax.

"Enjoy, Mr. Rourke," says Solórzano graciously, waving a hand toward the stairs.

"Thank you, Carlos," he murmurs, and shakes Solórzano's hand a final time before tugging me toward the stairs.

I'm so relieved, I blow Solórzano a kiss. "Thanks again!" I say cheerily.

Liam's firm hand on my back saves me from embarrassment as we ascend to the plane. The two smiling pilots step back for us to enter. Liam effortlessly maneuvers me behind him so he enters first. Whatever he sees releases the last strain of tension from his shoulders.

"Welcome señor, señorita," says a pilot warmly. "Our flight duration to Cook Islands is just over twelve hours. Please make yourselves comfortable and enjoy the amenities."

I look past Liam at the luxury jet's interior, which includes fully reclinable seats and a stocked bar, atop which rests platters of fresh fruit, sandwiches, and an ice bucket housing a thick, dark bottle.

The door seals behind me, triggering mellow lighting on the ceiling and floor. The pilots disappear into the cockpit.

Liam crosses the cabin. Ice rustles as he lifts the bottle to read the label. With a smile bordering on smug, he glances my way.

"Champagne?"

I kick off my heels. "Yes, please. Did Solórzano really ask how much I cost?" He nods, peeling the wrapper off the bottle's opening. "What did you say?"

"That I wasn't done with you yet, but that when I was, I'd let him know."

I gape, caught between amusement and annoyance. "What the fuck, Liam?"

His eyes lift to mine, his smile belying the gravity in his eyes. "It's a moot point. I'll never be done with you."

62

I DRINK two glasses of champagne. My body is so unused to alcohol that it's more than enough to get me drunk. Thankfully, it's not an obnoxious, do-something-I'll-regret drunk. An hour into the flight, I pass out in one of the massive leather recliners while in the chair opposite mine, Liam does *whatever* on his fancy tablet.

I have weird, vivid dreams about game pieces and giant hands moving them. Then I wake up in my old apartment in Los Angeles, only my hair is bright blonde and my skin tan. Scrambling from beneath the sheets, I run into the bathroom and see Alexis in the mirror. I'm her. I scream, and the woman in the mirror smiles and waves.

"It's just a dream, Eden. Wake up now."

Humming engine. Recycled air. A cramp in my left calf muscle.

"Ugh." I wipe at my eyes, then stare at my black fingers. Stupid mascara.

Liam is crouched beside my chair, smirking. "Not the best look for you, I'll admit. Though I'm growing fond of the dress."

I glance down to see most of the dress bunched toward my middle. The top hem rides precariously close to my bare nipples. With jerky movements, I tuck the fabric up and down respectively, then focus on him.

"How long was I out?"

"Two hours."

The shades beside my chair are down, but behind Liam I see hazy sunlight through the oval windows.

"Are you hungry?" he asks.

I make a face. "Meh. Head hurts. Thirsty. God, I hate champagne." He hands me a bottle of water. My brows lift as I take it from him. "Are you my genie now?"

Mischief sparkles in his too-blue eyes. "Do you want me to be?"

Yes.

No.

Kind of.

I take a few swigs of water and cap the bottle. Then I clear my throat. "I need to pee."

I scoot off the chair, skirt around Liam, and head for my bag. I do need to pee, and I am a little hungry, but at the top of my priority list is getting out of my bimbo get-up. It makes me feel things I'm not ready to feel, like feminine and sensuous. Nor am I ready to deal with Liam's lingering looks, the desire I'd seen in his eyes.

Not bothering to wait for a response from him, I take my bag toward the back of the plane to the bathroom. Inside, I hurriedly strip off the dress and trade it for soft linen drawstring pants, a sports bra, and a white tank top. Lastly, I make use of the little soap dispenser to wash the caked makeup from my face. My eyes sting as I scrub off mascara, and they're red by the time I'm done.

Staring at my bare face in the mirror, I don't see anyone desirable. I see a tired, jaded woman whose concept of living has been reduced to putting one foot in front of the other.

Will I ever feel joy again?

Will the nightmares ever fade?

Will I ever be able to stand the touch of a man?

The last thought brings an unwanted vision of red rope and tattooed arms. *I will serve.* A flush blooms in my cheeks. Desire flutters in my blood.

Strangely, I feel no revulsion with the arousal. Not like I do when I think of *being* tied. Controlled.

And I wonder.

WHEN I REENTER THE CABIN, Liam is reclining in his chair, the shades beside him closed. His eyes are closed as well, but I know he's not sleeping.

"Liam?"

He grunts.

I sit on the edge of my chair, my knees facing him. "What favor did you do for the Solórzano Cartel?"

He frowns, eyes still closed. "Guess."

"You found someone?"

"Bullseye."

"Who?"

Turning his head toward me, his eyes crack open. "Carlos's second daughter. She'd been kidnapped by a rival cartel."

I clasp my hands between my knees. "And she was okay?"

"Define 'okay.'" He tucks his arms beneath his head and stares at the dimly lit ceiling. "I don't mean to be flippant. No, she wasn't okay. But she was alive. Married with kids now, I hear."

"Did you—do you do a lot of that?" I ask haltingly. "Find missing people and bring them home?"

"Don't make a saint out of me, Eden. I found people for bad reasons, too, and I willingly brought them to their executioners. And before you ask—no, I never asked or cared whether they deserved to be caught."

I mull over the words, recognizing his effort to shock

me. But I'm more interested in his use of the past tense. "You don't, um, *work*, anymore?"

"Not since Dublin. You could say I took early retirement." His head swivels, his sudden stare piercing. "Your turn. How many?"

I frown. "Huh?"

"Six years is a long time for a submissive to go without a dom. How many did you have in Seattle?"

I'm so shocked by the question, for several moments I stare blankly at him. Maybe it's the lack of judgement in his eyes, or the forced intimacy of being locked in a tube hurtling through the sky… but I tell him the truth.

"None."

Liam's expression is so locked down I can't tell if he's surprised.

"You don't believe me?"

He stares and stares until I feel my face warm with embarrassment. Finally, he murmurs, "Forgive me, but I'm trying to decide whether to be horrified or pleased."

I pick at the edge of my tank top. "Why would you be horrified?"

His feet drop to the floor as he swivels and sits up. Elbows on his knees, he gives me a level look. "Because that's a long time to sacrifice what you need. Why did you?"

I shake my head. "I don't want to talk about this."

Those azure eyes narrow appraisingly. "Not even once?"

I shake my head again. "Really, Liam—"

"You're blushing, siren." He drags in an audible breath; it trembles through him. "Was it because of me?"

I stand up fast. "I'm hungry."

I make it halfway to the bar before he grabs my arm and spins me around. I aim an uppercut to his neck, but he blocks it with ease. His hips pivot to avoid my knee smashing his balls, and he seizes my other hand before my nails reach his face.

It takes him a total of ten seconds to immobilize me with my wrists locked behind my back. By his widened eyes, I know he's surprised that I gave up so easily.

I'm surprised, too. By more than my unwillingness to defend myself. I don't know if he can sense it—the wetness between my legs—but it both thrills and terrifies me.

"You want to know if it was because of you?" I seethe to disguise my confusion. "Of course it was. I tried… once. I couldn't do it. You were my dom. My master. And you were irreplaceable."

His gaze dips to my lips. "Ask me."

I bite out the question, "How many subs?"

"None," he breathes.

I can't prevent my jerk of disbelief. Liam releases me,

his fingers stroking up my arms as he guides them to my sides.

"But you've…" I trail off.

A brow lifts. "Yes. As have you."

Something in his eyes tell me he knows I was living with someone. *He knows.* With rising discomfort, I think of Grant—how worried and sad he must be. I've been gone nearly four months. *Does he think I'm dead?*

I turn back toward the bar. Liam doesn't stop me this time.

His voice low with unnamed emotion, he asks, "Will you go back to him, when you have the money?"

Will I?

"I don't know."

I have to, if only to say goodbye. I already know I can't be the woman I was. More walls have arisen between my past and present. Unassailable boundaries between who I used to be and who I am now.

You're not broken. You're breaking free.

I grab a cluster of grapes and turn. "I need you to do something for me."

His gaze lifts from the floor. "What, siren?"

"Teach me to tie knots."

63

IF LIAM ISN'T EXACTLY a patient teacher, he's at least an extremely good one. He has rope in his bag—of course he does—but it's not the usual brand. Not for pleasure. This rope isn't a toy but a weapon.

By the second hour of my training, my fingertips are tender from the abrasive material. But I have four basic knots down. Overhand. Square. Lark's Head. Half-Hitch.

I recognize each of them, but have a new appreciation for how easy he's always made them look. Liam ties rope like it's his instrument and he a virtuoso. I fumble like an infant on piano; more often than not, when I actually succeed, it feels like it's by mistake.

"That's enough for today," he says finally, wincing as he shifts his arms. "You need practice. A lot more practice."

I grimace in sympathy at the red skin beneath the rope on his wrists. "Can you get yourself out of them, or do I have to untie everything?" I'm hoping he has a magician's trick up his sleeve, because my fingers freaking hurt.

He snorts. "With what, my teeth?"

I sigh, dropping onto my seat for a break. We're facing each other, his knees spread. They now rest flush against my outer thighs, my pants and his slacks doing little to block the heat of his body. I stood between his legs for at least thirty minutes as I tested out my new skills on his wrists and forearms. Until this moment, though, I hadn't considered how close we'd been. Or what he might have been thinking as I bound him.

"Any day, Eden."

Tired and sore from using unexpected muscles and concentrating so hard for so long, I don't reply. I keep staring at his bound arms, settled above his groin. It's not my fantasy, but it's close enough. Need slowly unfurls inside me. It's different—I'm different—but it's also the same. There's only one man who can make me wet just by breathing, tied up or not.

"What if I don't want to free you?"

He inhales sharply, muscles bunching. "Don't tease unless you plan to follow through."

Follow through.

Like I've been doused with cold water, I come to my

senses. "I'm sorry. I thought maybe…" I drop my head into my hands. "I shouldn't have said that."

"It's okay," he says gently. "The way you looked at me, even if it was just for a moment… It means more to me than you can possibly know."

I nod helplessly; there's no use denying it.

The familiar sound of rope sliding brings my head up. My eyes widen as Liam unravels the last knot from his wrist.

I gawk. "What the hell?"

He smiles slightly, eyes warm and crinkled at the edges. "Now you'll always know that when the knots are yours, I'm choosing to be bound."

I have no idea how to respond, so I don't.

Liam coils the rope and walks across the cabin to pack it away in his duffel. He then rummages behind the bar and returns with a sandwich and a cold bottle of sparkling water. He hands them both to me.

"Eat, then sleep."

I smirk tiredly. "Sounds familiar." But I take the offering and thank him when he brings me a blanket and pillow.

The window shades are now all pulled, the sky black with night. Our destination, Rarotonga on Cook Islands, is six hours ahead of Los Mochis. We're chasing the future. Strangely apropos.

Despite it being only 5 p.m. in Los Mochis, I'm tired.

So freaking tired. My eyelids are dragging south, my consciousness unraveling. Maybe it's the hours of working knots, or the champagne nap, or the last two months of brutal training finally catching up.

Maybe it's *all* catching up.

I finish my sandwich—which is surprisingly good for airplane food—and head to the bathroom to brush my teeth. When I come out, the cabin is mostly dark, only a reading light on over Liam's head.

I drag my feet to my seat and push the little button until it's fully reclined. Crawling on top takes the last of my strength. I'm out before my head hits the pillow.

"BULLSHIT."

At first, Liam's voice slides at the edges of my dreams. As he continues speaking, however, I shift swiftly from sleep to alertness. His voice is low and tense, his words chilling.

"This isn't a bloody joke. Why would I fucking joke about this? She has to be stopped. If you won't do it, I will." A ten-second pause. "This is a courtesy call, nothing more or less. I'm coming for Christopher and Alexis. If you stand with them, then I'm coming for you, too."

There's a long silence. I think he's hung up, but then

he explodes, *"What!* You motherfucking—" There's another pause, then a violent thud as the phone is thrown to the floor.

I open my eyes and sit up. It takes me a few seconds to find Liam in the darkness. He's standing at the back of the plane, arms braced above him on the wall opposite the bathroom.

"Who was that?" I ask, even though I have a good idea.

"Maddoc. He said he had no knowledge of your capture and captivity. Says he didn't order it. He also doesn't believe it happened."

The last tendrils of sleep clear from my mind. "How did you even—never mind, it doesn't matter. I don't care how or why you called him. Nothing's changed."

"Everything's changed." His tone is soft, almost gentle.

Foreboding tickles my spine. I brace myself. "What is it, Liam?"

"He has Elizabeth."

No. No. No.

I lurch to my feet, adrenaline flooding my limbs. "Oh my God. If she tells them…" I can't even finish, the prospect too horrible.

Liam nods. "Then we're in a race to the money."

I square my shoulders with confidence I don't feel. "She won't break. She won't."

His eyes lift, find mine. "Everyone breaks."

"You didn't. You never told your father where your mother was."

He laughs, low and mirthless. "How do you think he eventually found her? Luck? Oh no, little siren, before I fled Ireland, I broke. It took an axe over my wrists. I saved my hands instead of my mother."

The truth stuns me, but also propels me across the cabin. I curl my fingers around his shoulder. He shudders but I don't let go.

"You still kept her safe all those years. Even if he knew where she was, you kept her safe."

His arms lower, dislodging my touch as he steps back from the wall. Where we stand, there's little light. I can't read his expression.

"You didn't break," he whispers.

My heart flutters in my throat. "No, I didn't. But like you said, I would have."

"You would have confessed where the money is, maybe, but not the other."

Him. Would I have given him up to Chris? Confessed that he found witnesses to incriminate Alexis and Chris, gave the USB stick to the FBI? That he dealt with the diamonds and set up the bank account? Would I have risked putting him at the top of the Donnelly hit-list to save myself pain?

His knuckles graze my jaw. "You don't have to speak.

I know. I feel it," he lifts his other hand to his chest, "here."

I breathe in. I breathe out. *Yes.* Yes, I would have died for him. And God help me, I still would.

"Will this ever be over?" I ask, and my voice is small and lost.

Liam steps forward, wrapping me in his arms. I melt against him, giving myself fully to the strength and safety he offers.

"Yes."

I believe him.

One way or another, this is ending.

64

NEVER HAVE I seen anything as breathtaking and serene as the view now before me. Beyond the wooden railing of the deck, a white-tiled lap pool sparkles, framed by palms and walkways bordered by spongey grass. Past the pool and a low stone wall lies a placid turquoise lagoon, hugged by dense foliage and white-sand beaches until it meets the deep-blue expanse of the open sea.

The air is dense and moist, flavored with tropical flowers. In my ears is a chorus of birdsong and the soft harmonies of wind playing through leaves. Even the sunlight feels different. Liquid. Penetrating and restorative as it seeps into my pores.

Our two-bedroom bungalow is pristine, modern, and secluded. I know it's costing Liam a small fortune to rent, but I've decided not to care. After having the best sleep of my life last night, a run on the beach this morning, and fresh fish and salad for lunch, I'm simply, amazingly content.

"Care for a swim?"

I turn as Liam steps onto the deck. My breath stutters out of me. He's shirtless, in low-slung swim trunks, with a smile teasing his lips and a glimmer in eyes that have the same hue as the lagoon. But that's not what gets me. Of all things, it's his hair, grown over the last months to the length it was when we met.

And almost… almost… I can imagine a different past. One wherein we never parted but grew ever closer. Wherein his only declaration of love hadn't been offered out of pain and guilt for what had happened to me.

"Eden?"

Soft and hesitant. Hopeful.

I clear my throat. "Did you scout the bank?"

Eyes shuttering, he nods. "I also secured a few contacts who will keep an eye out. They have photos of Alexis, Christopher, and Maddoc."

"How much did that cost?"

"A ridiculous amount," he says unconcernedly, then nods at the pool. "I'm going to cool off."

I nod, not moving. I *should* move. I should go inside. Take a nap. Eat some papaya. Prepare for three days from now, Monday morning, when I'll walk into a local bank and transfer a staggering balance into a new, Swiss account. But I can't unglue my eyes from Liam.

Watching him move is one of the things I missed most during those six long years. The grace and power in every step, the song his body sings for me.

He strides down the stairs in the middle of the deck and to the edge of the pool. Brief stretch of his arms above his head, then a fluid dive into the water. Perfect, even strokes carry him to the other side. An effortless flip beneath the surface. Legs kicking, arms slicing and mastering the element.

God, how I want him.

I want his sweat. His heat. The stroke of his tongue. His fingers. The rhythm of his hips. The pressure of his teeth. I don't want to control him or be controlled. I want spontaneity. Chaos. Him. I just want *him*.

I can't wait anymore.

My shirt and shorts are off in moments. My bra and underwear follow. My skin feels two sizes too small, overheated and over-sensitized. As I walk, the pressure between my legs grows, its beat racing to match my thudding heart.

I slip into the cool water as he executes a turn at the other end of the pool. One stroke at a time, he nears. He doesn't see me, sense me.

Then he does.

He stops short, some two feet away, and stands. Water mists from his mouth and nostrils, slides off his shoulders and chest. He blinks, looking beneath the water. Seeing me naked, his head whips up. Predatory instinct and confusion swirl together in his eyes.

I swallow hard, lift my chin. "You promised to serve."

Liam drags a hand down his face. After a pregnant moment, he releases a shuddering breath. "Fuck. Tell me this isn't a dream."

I reach through the water, curling my fingers around him. His cock twitches and swells. My heart beats so fast, so hard that my words come out breathless.

"Does this feel like a dream?"

He nods. "Yes. Very much yes."

I squeeze him. "What about now?"

His eyes flutter closed, then snap open. He takes a step forward, his hand covering mine, guiding it smoothly up and down his shaft.

"What do you need from me, siren?"

Emotion bucks and swirls inside me. The old instinct to submit to him battles the instinct to be in control, to never feel powerless again. But no matter how I wish this was a simple choice—a man and woman unencumbered —it isn't. And it's then I know what I need.

"Vanilla," I whisper.

I don't say more. Nothing else is required. Liam nods, his free hand moving to cup my face as he steps forward and brings our bodies together. The contact lifts a moan to my lips.

His mouth takes mine. So softly. So gently. Warmth

and wetness and slow, deep breaths. He lifts me up, out of the water, and I wrap my arms and legs around him. Our gazes locked, he carries me confidently out of the pool, across the patio and onto the deck. Then into the bungalow and down a hall to a bedroom. My bedroom. The floor-to-ceiling doors are open, allowing warm breezes to dry our wet skin.

He lays me reverently on the white sheets. Looks down at me like I'm a siren in truth—irresistible and otherworldly.

As though we have all the time in the world, Liam leisurely explores my body with his lips and tongue. Every mark of my ordeal receives his attention, from scars to newly earned muscle. I can do little more than gasp, clutching at his shoulders or head, as he tastes and savors my legs, arms, breasts, belly, and hips.

When he hovers at last over the only place he's bypassed, I tense. He stills and looks up. Whatever he sees on my face changes his course. He moves over me, hovers above me. And there he waits, eyes on mine. Accepting. Patient. Dark with need.

Obeying the command of my body, I spread my legs and wrap them around his hips. With a sigh, he lowers against me. His hips rock forward, sliding his cock over my clit and stomach. My breath pants out, not in fear but in anticipation.

"Are you ready?" he whispers.

Swallowing my heartbeat, I nod. "Don't kiss me—not in general, I just… I need to see you when, you know…" I bite my lips, feeling my cheeks warm.

He smiles softly. "I promise. One word and I'll stop, okay?"

Clover.

My eyes burn as I blink back tears. "Yes, okay. Please, Liam. I need you."

"As my lady commands," he murmurs, "so I will obey."

When he's positioned at my entrance, he once more takes his time. Teasing me with penetration, rubbing circles on my clit with the pad of his thumb. He takes so much time, in fact, that I wiggle my hips up in attempt to speed the process.

"Greedy," he whispers, eyes twinkling down at me.

"For you, always."

His eyes close briefly, expression twisting like the words pain him. When he opens them again, a tear drops onto my chest. I gasp, my chest squeezing, my own tears gathering, as he rolls his hips, again and again, until he's fully seated inside me.

And I feel no darkness.

Only light.

I clutch his waist, arching beneath him. "I've missed you inside me. So much."

"And I've missed you," he whispers. "More than you'll ever know."

He pulls out and thrusts again. Slowly, then faster and deeper. But still gentle. So damned gentle. And like he promised, his eyes never leave mine. Not when I cry out and buck beneath him. Not when he finds his own release.

Still joined, he gazes down at me, chest heaving and eyes surreal blue as his tears continue to fall onto my heart. And with every drop, he falls, too.

Back into my heart.

65

SATURDAY AFTERNOON, dark clouds billow on the horizon as Liam and I play gin rummy with a battered deck of cards we found in a closet. I'm about to win for the first time when his phone buzzes. Removing it from his pocket, he frowns at the number, then answers.

"Yes?"

As the person on the other end speaks, Liam rises and walks onto the deck. I absorb the impact of his tall form highlighted against a backdrop of the approaching storm, listening to his half of the conversation.

"When?"

"Where?"

"You're sure?"

"All right. Thank you."

He hangs up, types something on his phone, then turns. The rising darkness at his back reflects in his eyes.

Chills erupt on my arms. The glow of yesterday's lovemaking dims as grim reality surfaces.

"They're here, aren't they?" I ask.

Liam nods and walks back inside. He offers me a hand, and I allow him to draw me from my chair into his arms.

Holding me tightly, his warm breath skates along my earlobe and jaw. "That was my contact at the airport. Six men and two women arrived an hour ago. One of the women was Alexis. The other was described as short, thin, and dark-haired. She was limping, and her face was badly bruised."

Everyone breaks.

I bury my face in his shoulder. "Oh God, what are we going to do?"

Liam draws back, lifting my chin with his fingers. "What do you *want* to do?"

I shake my head helplessly. "There's no way they'll let us get to the bank. Six men?"

He knows what I'm asking. "Maddoc and Christopher are here." I have no time to process that tidbit before he continues, "The other four are soldiers—thugs. And you're right—they won't let us reach the bank alive."

I can't repress a shudder of pure terror. I feel it in my lungs, my gut, my tingling legs. The thought of facing Chris again...

Trembling, I look at Liam. "Should we go? Run? Let them have the money and leave Elizabeth to die? You know as well as I do that whatever piece of information is keeping her alive, they'll get it. And then she'll have outlived her usefulness."

He strokes my jaw. "I think you just answered your own question, love."

I don't want him to be right, but he is. However much Elizabeth is responsible for all that's happened to me, I can't simply walk away. I can't let her die if there's a way to save her. It's not love that motivates me, or obligation as in the case of Alexis, but something much more simple.

I'm the daughter of Margaret and Ben Sumner. Good, loving people who taught me the difference between right and wrong. The importance of standing up to bullies, of courage, and perseverance, and hard work.

But most of all, they taught me that the smallest decisions in life are often the most significant ones. That it's not our thoughts that define us, but the choices we make. How we live each day until the last day.

Taking Liam's face in my hands, I look him in the eye. And I make the choice to live as I would die. Honestly.

"I love you, Liam Rourke. I've never stopped. Whatever happens, I want you to know that."

He covers my hands with his. "I do know. My love for you and yours for me is the only thing that makes sense in this world. I also know that this isn't the end. Our end is being old and gray, spinning tales for our grandchildren."

I laugh. "Grandchildren, huh?"

His eyes twinkle. "And great-grandchildren."

My smile slowly fades. "If you ask me to run with you right now, I will."

"I won't ask you, love."

Surprised, I blurt, "Why not?"

"Because to open a new book, you must first close the old one." His expression hardens, his hands falling. "Even if you ask me not to, if you never forgive me, I still have to close the book. I cannot allow him to live."

Christopher.

The thought of him isn't as visceral as it once was, but the wound still festers, its poison slow to reverse. And the echoes of its devastation will always remain. The nightmares. The flashbacks. And the worst memories of all—the last ones, before my would-be end. When I'd glimpsed the man beneath the monster.

She isn't worth this.

But he'd done all of it anyway.

Maybe someday the miracle of forgiveness will occur. Perhaps when I'm old and gray and telling stories to my children's children. If that day comes.

I gaze out over the deck to see the winds picking up, tossing slender Palms back and forth. Then I turn back to

Liam. My magnificent, powerful, brave, strong, funny, cunning, charismatic love.

"I'll still love you," I tell him, "but I'm still going to ask. Don't kill him."

He's silent for a long minute, then smiles slowly. The devil lives in his eyes. My devil.

"Very well, siren. Seems I've overestimated my ability to resist you. I won't kill him. In fact, that would be too easy. I can think of at least ten different ways to end a man without taking his life."

I grimace, but nod. "So, how are we going to get Elizabeth?"

His brows lift. "Don't you mean, how am *I* going to get Elizabeth?"

My eyes narrow. "Are you seriously pulling the chauvinist card on me? I will break your fucking face."

He laughs.

And laughs.

And then we plan.

66

WHAT'S LEFT of the Donnelly crime family—as far as we know—is ensconced in a home on the other side of the small island. Liam's contacts have been invaluable. When I tell him his new nickname is Spymaster, he scoffs. But it's nevertheless the closest I've come to pinning down what makes him so damned dangerous. People bend over backwards to accommodate him. To obey him.

Maybe it's his blood—the Rourke legacy—but all I know is that Irish charm is a brand of magic in a league of its own.

Saturday night, Liam does reconnaissance of the property in question. I spend the hours he's gone in a knot of worry, powerless over my thoughts. *They caught him. They're coming for me.* An entire hour passes with me hiding in a closet with a knife.

When I finally hear a key in the front door and peek to confirm it's him, I drop the knife and run. The second the door closes, I'm on him, tearing at his shirt and belt in desperation.

Our lovemaking skirts the boundaries of our former proclivities. But we are both savages tonight, claiming each other with violent fervor. I'm above him when my pleasure overflows, my wrists locked by his hands behind my back. My ragged cry is swallowed by a peal of thunder. His body bucks beneath me, riding my pleasure to his own release.

Spent, I collapse on his chest. He gives me aftercare, carrying me to the shower and washing me, then bundling me in a towel and lying next to me on the bed. He strokes my hair until I'm almost asleep, then kisses me until I'm awake again.

"Tell me," I whisper.

"She's being held in plain view in the main living area. No doubt bait. Handcuffed at wrists and feet and blindfolded. The house is single-level, built around the living room. A kitchen and dining room on one side and three bedrooms on the other. Right on the ocean. No pool, but a deck that leads into the house. Both the deck and front entrance are guarded. Windows are all closed and locked in favor of air-conditioning and security."

"Then how do we get in?"

His thumb grazes my lower lip. "The better question

is when. According to my source, a reservation was made for dinner for three tomorrow evening at an ocean-front restaurant."

"It's a trap," I guess.

He nods. "Undoubtedly. But it also means they will all be at the house."

The windows rattle with the force of the wind. A few raindrops hit the glass, then more and more, until water slides in a distorting sheet down the surface.

Liam gives me a soft kiss. "Tomorrow we'll go over a map of the surrounding area and decide entry and exit points. We'll go in together, but out separately."

"What? No!"

"Yes. You're going to get Elizabeth out, and I'm going to deal with everything else. We'll set a rendezvous place and time for the following morning. Then we'll stash Elizabeth somewhere safe, you'll go to the bank and transfer the money, and we'll be on a plane by lunchtime."

I take a shallow breath past my racing heart. "I can't leave you there, Liam. There's seven of them." At his unperturbed expression, I groan. "You're going to blow up the house, aren't you? Like some action-movie hero on a vengeful mission?"

He chuckles. "No. There wasn't room in my duffel for the C4."

"Was there room for a bulletproof vest?" I ask, only half-joking.

"I won't need it."

His preternatural calm is starting to piss me off. I shove at his chest until he scoots back. I need the space to think, to breathe.

"You might die," I whisper. "Don't be so blasé about this. I'm scared for you."

He drags my hand to his mouth for a kiss. "Eden, look at me." I lift my gaze from the sheets between us. "I need you to trust me. And I'm not talking about a little bit of trust, like knowing I'll turn the oven off before I leave the house. I'm asking you to trust me with our lives. Can you do that?"

I think about it long enough that worry blooms in his eyes. When I've weighed the past against the present and future, searched my mind and heart, I find the answer easily.

But I let him sweat a little.

Only after a few, tense minutes do I put him out of his misery. "Of course I trust you."

Liam releases a pent-up breath, then notices the mirth I'm trying to hide. A second later, I'm pinned to the bed and staring at his sharp smile.

"Oh, you little hoyden. You had me for a moment there."

"I *always* have you."

His eyes warm and crinkle. "Aye, you do. I don't know what luck led to you choosing me, but thank fucking God. You own my heart."

"And you own mine."

God, let it be enough.

I DON'T SLEEP much that night. When I do, I dream I'm being chased by a shadowy, malevolent force. I run and run, growing ever more tired and hopeless, and finally turn to confront it—to fight—but what's chasing me is myself.

The final time I jerk awake, I don't bother trying to sleep again. The sky is lightening, washed with pastel-pink clouds. One storm has passed. Another type of storm is beginning.

I don't doubt Liam. I don't. If he says he'll handle the soldiers, my father, Chris, and Alexis, then he will. But I'm terrified that he'll sacrifice everything—including himself—to do so.

Liam's eyes flutter open. He takes in my expression, and the sleep in them clears fast.

"Don't die," I whisper.

He drags me into him with an arm around my waist and kisses my head. "I don't plan to, love. Just going to provide a nice little distraction while you grab Elizabeth."

I haven't asked about specifics for this *distraction*, though from the recent purchase of zip ties, I'm assuming it will involve disarming and restraining. But he also cleaned two guns and sharpened knives yesterday.

I've seen Liam's skill, watched him flow through martial arts routines that looked more like intricate dances than violence. I know he can protect himself, but—

"Promise me. Promise that if things go sideways, you'll get out. We don't need the money. It's not important. I thought it was, but it's not."

"I know," he murmurs. "I promise."

I finally relax in his arms. A hand smooths down my body to my hip. I snuggle forward, pressing a kiss to his warm chest.

For a moment, I feel peace.

"Aww," croons a female voice, "isn't this cozy?"

67

LIAM DRAGS me off the bed toward the windows and yanks me behind him. It happens so fast, I only get a glimpse of the woman in the doorway and the two, unfamiliar men with her.

"Tsk, tsk, Liam," she says chidingly. "Did you really think we'd wait for you like sitting ducks?" As she speaks, her voice moves closer to the bed. She sounds different—so different than I remember. Empty. Cold. *Psychotic.*

My thoughts scatter on the winds of fear. I swallow hard against the urge to vomit. Blocked by Liam's broad back, I glance at the nightstand. There's a gun in the top drawer. Close. Not close enough. As if sensing my thought, Liam's hands tighten on my hips.

Fabric hisses as nails drag over the sheets, likely still warm from our bodies.

"You know, I'm honestly surprised you were this stupid. Did you really think you were the only one capable of gaining contacts on the island? It was a simple matter, really, finding and paying your snitch to report *exactly* what we wanted him to. Oh, and finding someone willing to tell us where you were staying."

Liam growls low in his throat. "What do you want, Alexis? The money? Fine. Give us Elizabeth and it's all yours."

She laughs. Light and airy, and utterly void of actual feeling.

"I think we're past that point, don't you? My sister and I have some unfinished business. Ohhh, Eden," she sings loudly, "where oh where is my Eeeden?"

Chills run down my arms and back. Deep in my belly, a ball of something white and hot forms. It fills me like a tonic, sizzling down my limbs and washing away my fear.

Jerking out of Liam's hands, I move to his side. And there she is, flanked by two hard-faced men. My sister. A woman who played me, betrayed me, tried to have me killed, then changed her mind and opted for torture.

I see nothing of the woman she pretended to be in Los Angeles. That person never existed, a mere figment of my mind and heart.

My hatred of Chris pales in comparison to what I feel now, looking at her.

"Alexis," I snarl in greeting. "I'd say you're looking well, but you actually look like you've been ridden hard and put away wet. Didn't anyone tell you drugs are bad for the complexion?"

Liam whispers, "Shit."

Alexis flushes in fury, lifting the gun at her side. My heart trips in its rhythm as the silencer's little hole comes in line with my chest. Liam throws an arm before me, but I shove it down, stepping forward until my knees hit the bed. Across from me is a warped mirror—I only spoke the truth. For all that we remain identical twins, we look nothing alike.

Her face is puffy from long-term drug use, her skin sallow and dry on a skeletal frame. Despite it all, she's still attractive. Dark hair, nearly black, frames her face in silky strands. Her lips are cherry red and full, currently twisted in a sneer.

"Bold words for a dead woman," she seethes.

"I think if I were a dead woman, there'd already be a bullet in me. Right, *sis?* But there isn't, because you're not in charge, are you?"

Her face turns an alarming shade of purple; the hand with the gun trembles. "You fucking bitch. I'm going to rip out your heart."

My bravado falters. Then Liam's fingers squeeze hard, reminding me who I am. And who I'm not.

"Daddy wants to meet me, doesn't he?" I ask sweetly.

It was the wrong thing to say—Alexis relaxes and smiles. "He does, but he doesn't give a shit about a Rourke." The gun in her hand swings to Liam.

I jump in front of him, hands up. "No!"

Still smiling, Alexis clicks her tongue. "Interesting."

Her hand twitches. There's a muffled pop. Then Liam jerks behind me, his fingers spasming as the window behind us shatters.

I wasn't tall enough to block all of him.

With a strangled cry, I turn, grabbing for him. *Shoulder. Only the shoulder. But too close to a lung.* I staunch the blood with my hand, reaching over his shoulder with my other to find the exit. Small caliber, thank God.

Alexis titters. "Ah, love. I can't wait to take it away from you, just like you took everything from me." Then, to the soldiers, "Bring them both."

I meet Liam's steady gaze. There's no pain in them. Only quiet, contained calm.

The calm before the storm.

Cruel hands grab my arms, yanking me up. A zip tie wraps around my wrists, locking them before me. The other man drags Liam to his feet and likewise binds his hands. He winces but doesn't fight.

His eyes stay trained on my face as his lips shape one word. A word that makes no sense.

Clover.

As punishing hands pull me across the bedroom, my

mind spins in confusion. What the hell does my safe word have to do with anything? No word is going to get us out of this.

It isn't until my gaze lands on Alexis's smug smile that I remember the conversation we had six years ago. She told me she didn't understand submission because she lived without freedom to choose her own path. She wanted control because she *lacked* control.

Clover.

Alexis has no power.

But I do.

68

I'M NOT AFRAID ANYMORE. Sometime between being blindfolded and being thrown in the flatbed of a truck, I let go or reached my fucking threshold and just stopped caring.

Or maybe I've merely regressed into the version of myself that survived six weeks of captivity and torture. Not the abducted, battered version, or even the animal who only cared about living another day... but a clear, cold version—a woman detached from expectation and consequence.

And that woman gives zero fucks about playing by the rules. In fact, I'm thinking of changing the whole damn game.

The truck starts, jerking backward and turning onto the road. As we pick up speed, I realize I have a new superpower. This time, it's my sense of smell. Still utterly useless. My nostrils wrinkle with the coppery tang of Liam's blood, and the musky body odor of one of Alexis's henchmen. My sinuses sting with the metal of a gun and diesel gas fumes. But I can also smell the earth, moist from the recent storm, and the salt of the nearby sea.

Every time the truck hits a pothole, my head cracks against the divots beneath me. On a particularly bad jolt, Liam murmurs, "Are you all right?"

"Shut the fuck up, Rourke," snaps our armed companion.

"I'm fine," I say, not bothering to whisper. "How's the shoulder?"

"Hey! No talking!"

"Just a flesh wound," replies Liam, and I can hear the smile in his voice.

"I don't think I've ever asked you—what's your favorite movie?"

Our guard mutters angrily, but we both ignore him.

"*Gangs of New York*," replies Liam.

I snort. "That's original."

"What's yours?"

"Hmm… probably *The Usual Suspects*."

"Really?" he asks in surprise.

"Yeah. Nothing is as it seems. No one knows who the Puppet Master is until the end."

A foot stamps close to my head. "I said *shut up!*"

I tilt my face toward the voice. "Or what?" I ask blandly. "You'll put a bullet in me? Throw me over the side? I don't think so. I think you'll do exactly what you've been told to do, which is deliver me unharmed to my father."

Silence—and Liam's quiet laughter.

A few minutes later, the truck veers off cement onto gravel and stops. As Alexis and the other man exit the cab, our guard—no doubt relieved—throws down the tailgate. Another man's weight joins us. I hear Liam curse; a third set of scuffling feet tell me he's now standing. Seconds later, I'm yanked upright. My blindfold is ripped off, pulling a dozen hairs from my scalp.

My eyes have barely adjusted to sunlight when I'm shoved forward so hard I slide, trip, and fall to the ground at Alexis's feet.

My hip and shoulder scream on impact. I clench my teeth against the pain and breathe slowly through my mouth. Alexis smiles down at me, looking entirely too pleased with herself.

So I smile back at her. "Daylight is a good look on you, sis. Really brings out the circles under your eyes and the scabs from picking your face—"

She kicks me in the stomach. Hard. White light explodes behind my eyes as the air whooshes from my lungs. I double over, coughing for oxygen.

"Goddamnit," hisses Liam. "You bitch."

Coughing, my eyes streaming, I stare up at Alexis. "By the way, why send men to kill Elizabeth and me in Seattle? Without us, you had no chance of finding out what happened to the diamonds." I grin. "Ah, I forgot—only one of us got the brains in the family."

"Shut your whore mouth," she snarls.

She tries to kick me again, this time aiming for my face. Instinct takes over and I whip my bound wrists up, splaying my fingers to catch her boot a few inches from my nose.

Surprise flickers in her eyes before it's masked by rage. She shifts her weight, ready to use my grip against me and stomp on my head.

"That's enough, Lexi," says a deep, musical voice. She hesitates for a moment—the hate in her eyes vivid—then wrenches her boot from my fingers.

Blinking to clear my eyes of dust, I see a pair of powerful legs in navy slacks walking toward us from the house. My gaze drags up, over a tucked-in white dress shirt, a broad torso and shoulders, and finally to the handsome face of a man in his late-fifties. Light-brown hair peppered with gray. Short beard. Pale eyes somewhere between blue and green.

Maddoc Donnelly doesn't *look* like the lunatic Liam told me he is, but there's no denying his air of absolute command. The silence around us is so acute I can hear the crash of individual waves on the shore behind the house.

Maddoc frowns at me. "Are you hurt?" he asks, not sounding concerned so much as annoyed. I shake my head, gingerly maneuvering into a sitting position.

Here goes nothing.

I suck in a breath and smile.

"Hi, Dad. I heard there was a family reunion?"

THE FEAR'S BACK. Little, teasing tendrils ever since Liam and I were separated after being brought inside. Maddoc gave me his word that Liam wouldn't be killed, but as I know well, there's an entire spectrum of suffering that doesn't lead to death. The thought of Chris or Alexis hurting him is an itchy bastard—it won't leave me alone and is slowly undoing my devil-may-care attitude.

I'm going to need a lot of therapy after this.

If there *is* an after.

There's a tumbler of single malt scotch in my hand, now freed from the zip tie. It's not even nine in the morning, but Maddoc offered the drink like it was orange juice instead of booze.

I haven't taken one sip, but I don't think he's noticed—he's on his third glass. Or fifth, sixth… however many he needed to get moving this morning. From the slight yellow tint in the whites of his eyes, I'm guessing he's been drinking heavily for the last twenty or thirty years.

We're alone in a small, island-themed office just off the living room. Liam was dragged further down the hallway, presumably to one of the bedrooms. Elizabeth was nowhere to be seen, and I haven't asked Maddoc where she is because she might very well be dead already. I'm not sure my bravado can withstand the news.

Maddoc sits behind a small desk with palm trees carved into the legs, while I'm in an uncomfortable wicker chair opposite him. If I ever had any doubts that the man facing me is my father only in blood, they've been reduced to ash over the course of our conversation.

"To put it bluntly, Eden, I don't know whether to believe you or not."

I shrug. "You asked. Not my problem if you don't like the answer."

He has the stone-faced-mobster look down, so I might be imagining the amusement in his eyes. In the following silence, I hear muffled voices from the living room, and purposely don't think about Liam or Elizabeth.

Maddoc finishes his current drink and sets the tumbler on a coaster. "Do you have any proof?" he asks carefully.

My brows lift. "You want *proof* that I was tortured?" He nods. "How about the strips of skin missing from my back? Would you like to see them?"

The color drains from Maddoc's face, then floods back in a crimson wave. "What?" he hisses, leaning forward with a fist on the desk. "How many and where?"

My voice flutters out of me, "Th-three. Between my shoulder blades."

As fast as it came, his rage fades. He sags back into his chair like the information aged him a few decades. With unfocused eyes, he stares at the office door.

"Oh, Christopher," he whispers, "what have you done?"

69

WHEN MADDOC BLINKS and looks at me again, I realize the shit is about to hit the proverbial fan. I finally cracked the mobster mask, and now I can clearly see the man Liam described. *Mercurial. A lunatic. Slippery as an eel and smart as a fox.* And from the look in his eyes, I add another: *cold-blooded killer.*

I really hope this is what Liam intended—it's not like we got a chance to hash out a plan. I'm banking on knowing him well enough to understand what he meant by *Clover,* along with the faith that he knows what it means to me.

Power in surrender. The power to stop, control, and alter my circumstances. We're probably fucked either way, but I trust Liam. So I surrendered. When Maddoc asked, I told him everything. Every detail. He didn't believe me, not until now. Apparently Chris has a long-standing calling card for torture. If I'd known, I would have opened with that little gem.

Since I'm still surrendering, I take it one step further. I beg.

"Please, let us go. Please. We won't ever bother you again. The money is yours. We'll disappear. Please."

Maddoc regards me for a long moment, then shakes his head. "I'm sorry, Eden. It doesn't work that way. Elizabeth stole from me, and Rourke is a loose cannon."

My stomach freefalls. I look wildly around the room, as if I can squeeze an idea from dust motes dancing in shafts of sunlight. Maybe I can, because an idea comes. It makes me want to scream, but it's all I've got. Everything. My final play to get Liam and Elizabeth to safety.

"If you let them go, I'll stay with you. I'm a doctor. I can work for you. For free. I'll swear fealty, or whatever you want. The jaundice in your eyes and the spider angiomas on your nose are indicative of liver problems. You might have cirrhosis. It can't be cured, but it can be halted. I'll help you get healthy again…"

I trail off, panting from my tirade, when I realize Maddoc isn't remotely swayed. Pain signals break through my hysteria, and I look down to see blood welling on my thighs where my fingernails broke the skin.

"I admire your loyalty, I do," says Maddoc flatly, "but you'll be staying regardless of what happens to the others." He stands up, opening the desk drawer and removing a huge revolver. "Stay here."

Liam.

I lurch to my feet as he stalks toward the door. "Wait, no!"

I grab his arm as he's reaching for the doorknob. He shakes me off, slanting me a venomous glare. "Calm down. Rourke is safe for the time being. It's Christopher I have business with."

I stumble gracelessly backward until my hip connects with the corner of the desk. The pain is a distant buzz. I'm frozen to the spot, my mind blank of everything but the knowledge that I just signed Chris's death warrant.

Maddoc tears open the door and disappears. I hear his muffled voice, tight with anger and Alexis's name. Her response is indistinct, but her vicious tone matches his.

Then Maddoc roars, "Fucking tell me! Is it true? My own flesh and blood betrayed me? Went behind my back with *my* men? Shot up a goddamn hospital and killed twelve people on orders from my fucking *daughter?*"

Ah, I think dimly, *so that's what he's pissed about.* Liam was right, after all. Maddoc's only weakness is his daughter.

Chris pleads, "Maddoc, listen, please—"

Alexis screams, "Yes! It's true! You're nothing—a

worthless, impotent has-been. It needed to be done, so I did it!"

More voices. Some raised in agreement, some in disbelief.

Chris yells, "No, Alexis! What are you thinking? Put down the fecking gun."

Ohfuckohfuckohfuck

A set of footsteps pound down the hallway. A man flies past the open office door toward the living room.

"Alexis!" yells Chris. "Please, this isn't the way!"

Maddoc hollers, "Drop that gun, you stupid cun—"

A gunshot splits the world. Momentarily shatters the voices in the living room. Two more shots follow. So unbelievably loud. Copper fills my mouth as I bite through my lip.

Then, as the buzz in my ears fades, I hear screaming. Everyone is yelling and screaming.

My brain restarts, adrenaline flooding my limbs with purpose.

Liam.

I run for the door. When I reach the threshold, I grab the doorframe and swing my body to the right. Away from the living room. *Don't notice me. Don't notice me.*

I run smack into a thick body. Hard fingers grip my shoulders. "What the fuck?" snarls the guard from the truck.

My training takes over. I don't think or feel—just move. Jab to the eyes. Punch to the nose. Duck and block. Kick to the groin. Elbow to exposed neck. It takes seconds to put him on the ground. Another to disarm him, another to clock him in the temple with the butt of his own handgun.

A shrill note fills my ears, my vision pulsing in time with my heart. Behind me, the yelling continues.

Scrambling to my feet, I see two doors ahead of me. One of them is slightly ajar. I leap over the unconscious man and dive into the room, shutting the door behind me and locking it. Small bed, window, single nightstand, narrow closet. Empty.

"Fuck," I hiss.

As I turn back to the door, I hear a thump behind me. Then another. My gaze veers to the closet. I lurch forward, yanking it open.

Liam grins around his gag, showing no sign of pain despite the angry, seeping wound in his shoulder. Crammed into the space beside him is Elizabeth. She blinks up at me, tears falling across her cheeks.

I make quick work of their gags. Elizabeth gasps, "Eden, thank God."

The first words from Liam are an order. "Get my phone. Drawer in nightstand."

"What?" I bark, yanking ineffectually at the zip ties on his ankles. *Motherfucking zip ties.*

No more gunshots have sounded, and to my growing panic, the noise from the living room is tapering off.

"Do you still trust me?" murmurs Liam.

I make a sound—somewhere between a whine and a sob—then I jump to my feet and race to the nightstand. Yanking out his phone, I turn around.

"Now what?" I whisper.

"Dial this number." He rattles off an international phone number and makes me repeat it back as I type.

I hold the phone to my ear, my hand shaking as I listen to the ringing and imagine armed men bursting into the room any second.

Then the line picks up. Through crackling static, a man says, "Hernandez. Are we a go?"

I blink dumbly. "Uh—"

Liam hisses, "*Green.*"

My numb lips obey the command my brain doesn't really register. "Green."

There's a pause. "Copy that."

The line goes dead. I lower the phone and stare at Liam. "Now what?"

He smiles slightly. "Now we wait. Come here. Nice and cozy already, but there's room for one more."

Liam shifts around, stretching his legs over Elizabeth's feet to make room for me on his lap. I walk forward and gingerly find my footing to lower myself. When I'm inside the closet, braced against his uninjured shoulder and my legs tucked into the space between their bodies, Liam nods to the sliding door.

Before I pull it closed, I glance at Elizabeth. She looks as stunned as I feel.

"Who was that?" she whispers.

"A friend," replies Liam.

The lines between my mental dots are fuzzy, but growing more distinct each moment. Hernandez. *Hernandez*. There's only one man by that name who comes to mind.

But I can't fathom what it means. How it's possible.

Liam's breath teases my ear. "I'm sorry I didn't tell you, love. I couldn't risk the information."

The thought lines grow taut and clear. But I only have one question. "How?"

"You left his card at my house. I hung on to it on the off-chance I'd need it someday."

"Tell me what's going on," pleads Elizabeth.

Neither of us answer, because at that moment we hear a heavy crack of splitting wood and new, loud voices shouting.

"Police!"

"Drop your weapons!"

"Get on the floor!"

"Hands behind your heads!"

The walls are thin. There are muttered expletives

from the living room. Thuds as guns and knees hit the floor. Grunts and more cursing.

"Alexis Sharpe, drop the fucking gun. You're under arrest for drug trafficking, money laundering, and murder."

I recognize the final man's voice. Not that I actually needed confirmation that FBI Special Agent David Hernandez is here to save the day.

There's a beat of silence before I hear my sister's voice. Like she's sitting beside me instead of several rooms away, her words ricochet in my ears and down my body.

"Not a fucking chance, pig."

—BANG—

The solitary gunshot convulses every muscle in my body. I jerk against Liam and hold my breath, listening, listening…

…but there's only silence.

70

AS WE'RE GUIDED down the hallway by Hernandez, Liam tells me not to look into the living room. But I stop. And I look at the end of the Donnellys.

It's not pretty.

Alexis shot Maddoc in the chest. He's propped against a wall, eyes glassy with death, blood pooled on the tile beneath him. On his lap, loosely clutched in lifeless fingers, is a gun. And lying several feet away is his last victim, dead from a gunshot wound to the throat.

One of Chris's hands is extended toward Maddoc, like he was trying to help his boss or seek forgiveness. His eyes are closed, his face relaxed and surprisingly peaceful.

I hope that wherever he's gone, he finds absolution for his sins. But I'm also grimly satisfied at the prospect of him burning in hell for eternity.

Another man lies beyond Chris. From the angle of his body and the gunshot to the head, I surmise that Maddoc fired his gun twice, missing Chris the first time and killing the other man.

The final three men are gone, having been shackled and hauled to the police van parked outside. Hernandez told us two of them were ID'd as shooters from the hospital. The third is the one with his brains leaking onto the floor.

I should be relieved I didn't kill that man in the hallway, but I'm not.

I stare at Alexis the longest. Unlike Chris, her face is locked in a rictus of her last moment's emotion. Rage and defiance. I imagine there was satisfaction in her, too, at the end. She exercised the ultimate power of the individual—the choice to live or die.

In her death, at least, we finally have something in common. I made the same choice in a basement not long ago. I'd been ready to die.

I don't feel anything but apathy. Not yet, anyway. Not even when Elizabeth's cold fingers grip my own and she begins weeping softly over the death of her daughter. Perhaps out of guilt for not taking her instead, or not taking us both, or both of our failures to save her...

"Eden," murmurs Liam.

I turn away, my fingers slipping from Elizabeth's. Someone dressed Liam's wound with gauze and tape.

"Do you need to go to the hospital?" I ask mutedly.

He shakes his head and offers me his hand. I stare at it long enough that I finally feel something. An unpleasant something. Like a swarm of bees has taken residence beneath my skin.

"You lied to me. All this time, you've been working with Agent Hernandez. You didn't trust me."

His eyes remain beseeching, but his hand falls. "Let's get out of here, love. I'll explain everything to you later."

"No. Explain it to me *now*."

His gaze flickers to where Agent Hernandez stands near the front door and back to me. "I was trying to uphold your wishes that no one die unnecessarily. Eden, there was no way on this earth that Maddoc or Alexis would have let us go. You have to know that."

I take a step toward him, feeling Elizabeth's focus behind me. "You didn't look surprised this morning. Did you know they were coming for us? Is that why you insisted I wear pajamas to bed?"

Liam flinches, either at the look in my eyes or my tone of voice. "Yes," he admits softly. "My contact—the same one Alexis made—was the undercover police. I received a text when she left here this morning. You were still asleep."

A deep tremor runs through my body, leaving a poisonous fissure in its wake. I take two more steps until I'm right before him.

"You set me up," I whisper. "You couldn't help it, could you? The need for secrets. To create the game and control the players. It's who you are."

Hernandez turns toward us. "Coroner's on his way," he says, not unkindly. "Time to get going."

We both ignore him.

"Eden," Liam says calmly. *So fucking calmly.* "We can talk about this later. I did what I had to do to keep you safe. You said you trusted me with our lives. Did I fail you? Are we not alive?"

"You *used* me. How did you know I'd find you? Be able to get your phone? What if that guard had overpowered me?"

He shakes his head. "He didn't, and he wouldn't have. I heard every blow. You were perfect."

I shake my head; the movement feels like slow-motion. Like I'm underwater. Suffocating.

"That's what you meant by 'Clover,'" I say, more to myself than him. "I thought you were telling me that I had power. But you were telling me that *you* did. No matter how much I want to be your equal, you'll never allow it. I will always be your dove, your *submissive* to control."

I see his moment of comprehension—the moment he realizes he's lost me. The blood drains from his face, and his eyes take on a vivid, grief-stricken hue.

"Eden, please," he whispers.

The chaos inside me detonates, but I'm too numb, too far gone to scream. Instead, I grow calm and still. Utterly contained.

I become him.

"Goodbye, Liam."

I glance a question at Elizabeth, who nods, then I walk past him, past Agent Hernandez, and into the brilliant light of day. Squinting, I walk toward the closest uniformed man.

"Any chance my mother and I can get a ride home?"

He looks over my head—at Hernandez, no doubt—then nods and waves a hand. "This way."

The drive back to the bungalow is brief. I thank the officer and lead Elizabeth inside. She helps me pack my duffel before I remember I have nowhere to go, no money, and the bank doesn't open until tomorrow.

I sit listlessly on the bed Liam and I slept in. Made love in. Misery rushes toward me, a tornado I'm in no way, shape, or form prepared for.

Then Elizabeth turns from the dresser. "How does room service sound?" she asks, holding up a banded roll of hundred-dollar bills.

The tornado passes by without touching down.

Elizabeth tosses me the roll. I stand up, tuck the money in the front pocket of my jeans, and grab my duffel from the floor.

With a final look around at my happily-never-after, I head for the door. "Room service sounds fantastic."

71

ELIZABETH and I stay in Rarotonga another four days. Without the threat of imminent death hanging over our heads, we actually talk. Slowly and tentatively, we get to know each other. And I learn what it took to make her break.

Me.

"I should have known Maddoc wouldn't risk Alexis turning on him. He brought her in so young. It warped her." Tears fill her eyes. "It was always too late to save her. I didn't know. I'm so sorry, Eden."

I shrug off her apology. We're about six parallel dimensions past *I'm sorry* for all the shit that's gone down.

"I didn't know, either," I reply muted. "She was a great actress."

Elizabeth shudders, staring sightlessly toward the sea

visible from our balcony. Giving no indication that she heard me, she continues, "She wanted you dead. I heard her talking to Maddoc, trying to convince him you weren't worth the risk of keeping alive. So I made a deal with him. Your life for the details you gave me about the bank and money. Maddoc was many things, but always stood on his word. He overruled Alexis."

"Why did they keep you alive?"

"I gave them enough to confirm the account existed— your social security number and information so Alexis could call. But I only told them one of the account numbers every day."

"Huh. Wish I'd thought of that." I take a deep breath of the moist, tropical air. "I wonder if Maddoc was surprised when the monster he made killed him."

"I'm sure he was. A parental failing, perhaps—seeing our children as who we want them to be rather than who they are."

The similarities to Liam and his own father don't escape me. Or surprise me. Creations killing creators isn't new to mythos, literature, or psychology. Freud especially would have a blast analyzing the Donnellys and Rourkes.

"At least in your case, I was right," continues Elizabeth. "You are exactly as strong as I knew you were from the moment you were born."

I'm not strong. Beneath my diamond shell, I'm shattered.

A million flecks of blackest dust. But I don't say it. Keeping my mouth shut so she can find a measure of peace with her choices is a small price to pay.

"You didn't break," I muse aloud. "Just made a deal."

Elizabeth glances at me, one brow raised. The sunset glows in her cracked-marble eyes.

"Sharpe women don't break."

My smile is grim. "No, we don't."

At least on the outside.

ELIZABETH ASKS a billion questions about my childhood, high-school years, med school, and my brief career as a doctor. Neither of us mention the gaps in my timeline—meeting Liam and Alexis post-graduation, the six weeks in the basement, and the months with Maria in Los Mochis. Elizabeth drinks my words like water, smiling wistfully and tearing-up in intervals.

I learn, too, about her life since escaping Maddoc. What it was like after she left me with my adoptive parents. Various careers and cities she lived in for long stretches before paranoia set in and she moved on. She really loved Tucson, Arizona, and is considering a permanent home there.

When she asks me where I want to go, I know she means where I want to make a home. Since I don't have an answer, I tell her Philomath. It's my first stop, anyway, so not entirely a lie.

On Thursday morning, we take a cab to the airport to meet Hernandez. Since neither Elizabeth nor I have valid passports, he arranged for private transportation back to the U.S. courtesy not of the FBI, but of the CIA. Disenchanted after the leak of my involvement with bringing down the Donnelly family in Los Angeles, Hernandez found greener pastures.

As we board the private plane, I ask him why he kept his old FBI phone number. And when he looks at me in confusion, I shake my head and say, "Never mind."

Just another lie.

MORE HOURS ARE LOST on the flight to Los Angeles, but only three this time. When we finally land and taxi to our gate, it's nearing 10 p.m. Elizabeth is fast asleep in her seat beside mine, while across from me, Hernandez bends to pack away his laptop. When he's done, he gives me a solemn look.

"I want to apologize for the leak that put your life in danger."

I nod. "Thanks, but my life was in danger anyway. Liam was right about one thing—once Maddoc found me, he wasn't planning on letting me go."

"Did you…" he clears his throat, "talk to him before you left?"

My brows lift. "You were there for our last conversation. Pretty sure it was self-explanatory."

Hernandez shifts in his seat, looking decidedly uncomfortable. "You're certainly entitled to make the best choice for yourself, and I know as well as anyone that Rourke is a criminal, but… well… there are certain things you haven't been told."

I snort. "No shit, Sherlock. Care to enlighten me?"

He shakes his head, grimacing. "Against my better judgement, I swore I wouldn't say anything more. Except… he told me to tell you that if you want to find him, he'll be waiting."

My shriveled heart thumps with momentary life, then goes numb again. "Thanks for the cryptic message."

He shrugs, clearly relieved to have gotten it over with. "Do what you want with it, Eden." He pauses, gazing out the window at the approaching terminal. "There's only one thing about this case that still bothers me."

"What's that?"

"A long time ago, before you were born, Donnelly was suspected of stealing diamonds from a Chinese diplomat. But when we seized all his assets and account records, there was no sign of anywhere near the type of wealth we expected. Nor did we find the diamonds at any of his properties."

"Maybe he took them with him," I say, shrugging.

Hernandez shakes his head. "If he had, he would have had no problem rebuilding his organization outside the U.S. But the three men arrested are all that's left of the Donnelly crime syndicate." His dark eyes pierce mine. "Do you know what I think?"

My heart races. My palms itch with panic.

"What?" I make myself ask.

"I think that whoever has the diamonds, they probably deserve them."

THE FIRST THING I do after disembarking is lead Elizabeth as far away from Hernandez as I can, as fast as I can. Then I find a payphone. When Liam took my phone away six years ago, I developed the habit of memorizing numbers. One of the first ones I memorized is what I dial now.

Karina and I have kept in close contact over the years. She did what I asked and rented an art studio with the money I gave her. Nowadays, she's a minor celebrity with a dedicated following of A-listers. A fact neither myself nor Raul let her forget.

She doesn't answer the first time, so I fish out another quarter and dial again.

On the fifth ring, she answers groggily, "What?"

"Hey, K. It's me." There's a long silence. "Sorry, it's Eden. Hello?"

"Is this some kind of sick joke?" she asks stonily. "Who the fuck are you? How did you get this number?"

I start laughing. Then I start crying. "It's really me, I swear. Remember when we decided that drunk roller-skating should be a thing, then spent twenty-four hours with ice on our asses?"

Karina swears loudly, then sobs. "Eden? Eden! Holy shit, girl. Where are you? What happened?"

"It's a long fucking story, but right now I'm at LAX. I'm with my biological mom, believe it or not, and we need a place to crash for the night."

There's a thump and a curse, then Karina's familiar, beloved laughter and more crying. "Crap, I just fell out of bed. Can you wait for twenty? I'll come get you right now."

I wipe at my eyes, my heart filled with the first true joy it's felt in what seems like years. "Yes, we'll wait. Thank you."

Keys jingle and a door slams. "Oh my God, Eden, I can't believe it. I'm so glad you're okay." She breaks down into deep, shuddering sobs. "Fuck, I need to pull my shit together before I get in the car. You swear you'll wait for me?"

"Yes, I swear. We'll wait on the curb at the end of the arrival terminal. I'll be the bitch sobbing and waving."

She laughs. "Okay, honey. Hang tight."

I slowly hang up the receiver and turn to Elizabeth. Tears in her own eyes, she embraces me tightly. And when we part, she smiles and hands me another quarter.

"Call your parents."

So I do.

72

How many tears
does the body hold?
Infinite.

How many hours
can the body sleep?
Forever.

Drip. Drip.

73

I DON'T LEAVE my childhood bed for three weeks except to pee, eat, and run. I run and run and run, going nowhere as fast as I can. Sometimes, too, I sit in the bathtub—with or without water—and stare at the white tiles until my vision distorts and they turn the color of blood.

IN ANOTHER LIFE, Liam must have been a reporter. Those bastards are sneaky as fuck and world-class liars.

I was sold to a sex-slavery ring.

I was undercover for Interpol.

Eden is dead and I'm actually Alexis.

I single-handedly brought down a crime syndicate.

I'm a hero.

A hero!

After my tenth hysterical meltdown, my parents unplug the desktop computer and hide their smartphones.

I WAKE up one day to a commotion outside. Twitching back the curtains in my room, I see news vans lined up against the curb and reporters milling around like so many hungry ants.

My first and strongest emotion is rage for whoever told the press where I live. Then disappointment, because it means I can't run today.

Later, my mom comes in with breakfast and tells me it was our elderly neighbor, Henrietta, who spilled the beans. Ninety years old and mostly deaf, she's known me since I was a baby.

Robbed of my anger, I cry instead.

THE DAY after the news vans finally give up and leave, I accidentally answer the house phone. We changed the number early on because of all the unwanted calls, so it doesn't occur to me it might be a reporter.

Within an hour, I field tens of calls. It becomes a

game, and I keep a running tally of how many seconds it takes them to deliver their pitch.

"No interviews."

Click.

"No movies or books."

Click.

"I don't want your money."

Click.

Then there are the calls from people who've known me for years but who suddenly think I'm a winning horse to bet on. They sour my mood fast and ruin the game.

"No, I don't need a ghostwriter, Mr. Lin."

Click.

"A green bean casserole for my story isn't a fair trade, Mrs. Cole."

Click.

"No, Marge, I don't want a homecoming party."

I unplug the phone again, and we get another new number.

SOME DAYS, I really miss Maria.

EVERY DAY, I miss him.

74

THE FIRST DAY I feel remotely human, my mom and I drive to Seattle. For my first stop, she stays in the car.

Grant and I have spoken on the phone since my return, but seeing him face-to-face in our old apartment is surreal. He hugs me so tightly and for so long that I battle the urge to introduce his nuts to my knee. Thankfully, the feeling passes.

I relax in his arms. We cry together, then hold each other for a while. I tell him I loved him, that I'm sorry he suffered when I went missing, and that I want him to be happy. That it's not his fault everything's different. That I'm different.

He says he understands, and all he wants is the same —for me to be happy.

We both know there's no going back.

AT MY OLD HOSPITAL, I'm treated like a celebrity. Begged to come back. Offered higher pay and better benefits. My mom heads off the mob. We stay only long enough for me to retrieve my personal belongings and tell an administrator I won't be returning to work.

How can I help people when I'm broken?

ONE MORNING near the end of August, my dad finds me sitting on the front lawn watching the sunrise, his not-well-enough-hidden bottle of whiskey cradled in my hands and a blanket over my shoulders.

He goes back inside without saying anything and reappears a few minutes later with fresh coffee. The whiskey bottle is pulled from my fingers and replaced with a warm mug.

He sits beside me with his own coffee. We sip in silence as the sun breaches the horizon.

Eventually, he stands and brushes dew and grass off his pants. "Guess what we're doing today?" he asks.

"What?"

"Buying you a car."

I squint blearily at him. "Why?"

"Do you remember when you were a teenager and

you read *On the Road* by Kerouac, and you decided that driving across the country was the only way you'd find your true artistic self?"

"I also thought blue eyeliner was awesome," I grumble.

"You're taking that trip, Eden."

Still half-drunk, it's a few seconds before his words sink in. Then I gape. "You're kicking me out?"

He nods perfunctorily. "It's time for you to hit the road."

75

TWO MONTHS LATER

MY DAD SAVED my life that day. I don't pretend to know how he figured out what I needed. Maybe it was just a guess, or he was sick of my moping. But I think he knew that the only way to find something that was lost was to search for it. It was obvious that I was lost, so he decided I needed to get off my ass and go searching for myself.

With no other plans that day or for my future, I thought *fuck it* and agreed to go car shopping. Thus, my first large purchase post-Rarotonga was a new car. Sturdy. Reliable. Unremarkable.

My dad didn't bat an eye when I paid for it with a

thick envelope of cash. Nor did my mom comment when, on the morning I set out, I handed her a small duffel full of money. After hugging them both, I drove away on my pilgrimage to nowhere, hoping to find what had been lost.

I've been on the road for the last eight weeks with no one but myself for company. I won't lie—it was a rough start.

But then a funny thing happened.

The hum of tires, the drifting sky, the rest stops, national parks, mountains and lakes, every roadside motel and diner… every lonely meal, every song belted out over the radio, every photo taken on my phone, the tourist traps and monuments… like pieces of a puzzle I didn't know was forming, all came together.

And about a week ago, as I was driving into Tucson to visit Elizabeth, I looked through a dirty windshield at the dusky evening sky, and I saw the finished puzzle of me.

Not the innocent dove. Not the little monster or the fierce siren. Not the doctor, daughter, sister, friend, or lover. Not my fear or anger. Not my love or hope.

Just… *me*. Every mismatched, inexplicable, contradictory part of me. Every good memory. Every traumatic one. Everything. All of it.

Liam was right, the bastard. I was never broken—I was breaking free.

I STILL HATE LOS ANGELES, but when Karina invited me to the opening night of her newest gallery show, I couldn't think of an honest excuse to miss it. I was already in Tucson, a mere seven-hour car trip away.

Early this morning, I said goodbye to Elizabeth, leaving her grinning in the driveway of her modest, recently-purchased home on the outskirts of the city.

As I drove west, nostalgia crept over me. For what, I wasn't exactly sure. But I knew what it meant.

My pilgrimage was nearing its end.

Now, as I wander through a glamorous crowd at a downtown gallery, I feel remarkably serene. I'm no longer affected by the glances of strangers. I no longer care that in my slinky, burgundy silk gown, I'm the definition of overdressed.

When I called my parents today, I told my dad what I was feeling. The stillness in my mind, the fading of my generalized anxiety, the sense of being a part of the world rather than on the outside looking in.

He was quiet for long moments, then told me that he was glad my insides finally matched my outsides. Oddly, I knew exactly what he meant.

"Dang, girl, look at that dress! Your ass looks positively delish."

At the familiar, flamboyant voice, I turn away from a

painting to find Raul grinning at me. He's wearing a black suit with tiny rhinestones sewn onto the lapels, a top hat, and glittery white sneakers. Miraculously, with his dramatic makeup and whip-thin frame, he pulls it off.

Raul gives me a spine-cracking hug and kisses my cheek, then leans back to study my face. His eyes, I notice, are clear. According to Karina, they've been clear since I went missing. Only when he'd been clean for a month had she given him his portion of the money. He'd bought a car, quit selling drugs, and started taking classes at a local school for fashion design.

"You look better," he says gravely. "You find a new dick to suck?"

Nearby, there are murmurs of shock. I just roll my eyes. "No, thanks for asking. And thanks, I feel better."

Raul glances over his shoulder, then steps closer to me and lowers his voice. "I've got intel that's been eating at me, and I have to tell you. You know I can't keep secrets."

I laugh. "True. What's going on?"

"A month or so ago, your dude came into Al's. He didn't order food, just sat at the counter for three hours. I finally came out of the kitchen to tell him to piss off, but man, he had some sad fuckin' eyes."

My heart is now somewhere in the vicinity of my stomach. I open my mouth, but no sound comes out.

Raul clucks his tongue. "Just like your eyes right now. All sad and lovesick and shit. He finally manned up and asked how you were. I wasn't gonna tell him shit, but," he shrugs, "I'm a sucker for blue eyes. Told him you were good. Staying with your parents as you figured stuff out."

"Okay," I finally wheeze.

He squeezes my arm in sympathy. "He told me not to tell you he came in, but you're my girl and he's just a dick with a pretty package. And I can't keep secrets."

In spite of myself, I laugh. "Thanks, Raul."

He winks. "Did you see Karina yet?"

"Nope. Just got here a little bit ago."

Linking his arm through mine, he throws me a saucy grin. "She's probably hiding somewhere crying into her champagne. Let's go slap some sense into her."

I nod sagely. "That's what friends are for, right?"

"Amen."

AROUND ELEVEN, I run out of steam. Whether it's the long drive catching up, or the high heels on my aching feet, I just want pajamas and a bed. The opening was a success—Karina sold six of her eight paintings. She, Raul, and a crew of friends decide to continue the celebration at a nearby club, and I take advantage of the transition to tell Karina I'm toast.

Armed with her spare house key and permission to eat the fudge ice-cream in her freezer, I retreat to my car and immediately take off my shoes. *Sweet relief.* Wiggling my toes in pleasure, I start the car and head toward Echo Park.

Before I know it, I'm in the driveway of the cozy, three-bedroom house Karina and Raul share. My headlights illuminate a modest front yard and windows with drawn curtains. Despite my body's demand for sleep, I can't seem to make myself turn off the car.

Nostalgia returns tenfold, this time for a city I've loved and loathed in turns. Used to traveling on a whim, I don't think much about it as I back down the driveway and head for Santa Monica.

When I get there, I don't park, but I do stare overlong at the lights of Pacific Park. And when thoughts of Liam inevitably come, they're free of resentment. I know everything he did, every lie and misdirection, was for the purpose of keeping me safe.

Now all I feel is sadness for what we've endured and longing for a future we might have had.

You'll always come home to me.

His words and the conviction they'd carried float through my mind. And I realize it's the final question—one half of the reason I've been wandering, lost and searching, for months. Years, even. Since a broken heart and a plane ticket home.

I fulfilled my part, finding all my pieces and fitting them together. But for better or worse, I still don't know if the reason I'm wandering to begin with is because home isn't a place, but a person.

My mind and body in perfect agreement, I drive toward the Hollywood Hills.

Straight into the sun.

When I arrive at the familiar house, there's no car in the driveway and no lights on inside. But the lawn is manicured, the hedges trimmed. Possessed by instinct—or insanity—I park and jog to the front door.

The handle turns easily, the door opening without sound. My heart hammering, I step inside, tiptoeing only far enough to peer into the shadowed kitchen.

A coffee mug sits on the island about six inches from the sink. Beside it rests a folded paper towel, a spoon lying perfectly in the center. *Liam.* There's no freaking way a new owner or renter would leave their empty mug in the exact same spot in the exact same way.

My heart calms. I retrace my steps, closing the front door behind me and getting back in my car. For a few minutes, I stare sightlessly ahead. Excitement mingles with apprehension as I consider going back into the house to wait for him. Then I remember the message he gave Agent Hernandez.

If you want to find me, I'll be waiting.

And I suddenly know that I can't go inside. Can't wait for *him* to find *me*. It's not what he's asking, and it's not what I'm willing to do.

"You want me to find you, Liam?" I ask as I put the car in reverse. "Game on."

76

WHEN I WALK under the familiar black awning into a wash of crimson light, I don't wait for the angelic doorman—*Nick? Nathan?*—to speak.

"Open the door, please." Polite but firm.

Instead of chewing me out or threatening me, his mouth drops open before resolving into a wide grin. "Sugarplum, you're here!"

I frown. "What? And what did you call me?"

He shakes his head quickly. "Nothing—never mind." Jumping off his stool, he opens the padded door and gestures with flourish. "Crossroads awaits, madam."

As I pass him, I pause and take in his ecstatic expression. Wry humor tilts my lips. "I'm on the list, aren't I?"

He winks. "Every day of every week."

I don't know whether to laugh or sigh. I settle for thanking him and walking into the club. The first thing I notice is the spotlight over the pit. An amplified moan confirms that a scene is being played out for the delight of the crowd.

The communal focus is a blessing, as no one really notices as I walk toward the bar. I muse that the lack of interest could also very well be a side-effect of my dress —vivid red with a near-scandalous cut. A smile tugs my mouth as I wonder if the few people who glance my way think I'm a Domme.

Despite the action going on, the bar is packed two-deep with patrons. I wait and finally find an opening, squeezing through bodies until I reach the counter. My only plan right now is a shot of something strong.

He's here. I can feel him.

What I don't expect is to recognize the bartender who rises from a squat directly opposite me. Seeing me, London of the perfect-skin does a fair impression of the doorman, her mouth dropping open with surprise.

"Eden! Wow, you look so different, I almost didn't recognize you. Are you looking for Liam?"

"Yes, I am. Is he here?"

She nods. "He's in Dominic's office. Go on back." When I hesitate, she grabs a bottle and a shot glass, which she fills to the brim. With a grin, she hands it to me. "Down the hatch."

I throw back the shot, then cough. "Christ, what was that?"

London chuckles. "Liquid courage."

"Thanks," I say dryly.

She tosses her head toward the door at the end of the bar. "Now go on. But take it easy on him, will ya? He's… well, you'll see. Good luck." Then she turns to another customer, taking away my last excuse to stall.

Once again fighting the equal urge to laugh and sigh, I skirt around the bar to the white door. *Deep breath.* I open the door, revealing the familiar, empty hallway.

The first step is the hardest, but I take it. The door swings shut behind me, and the noise from the club is instantly muted.

Another step. Then another and another, until there's only one more door between us. There I stop. My breathing has reverted to erratic and shallow. I can taste my pounding heartbeat at the back of my throat.

My goddamn panties are damp.

"You're a fucking mess," I mutter.

From the other side of the door, an amused voice says, "You're right. I'm an absolute mess without you."

The door opens inward, pulling the breath out of me. Turquoise, bloodshot eyes. Messy hair gone too long without a trim. Days-old scruff. Worn t-shirt and faded jeans.

Home.

Home.

I clear my throat. "Can I come in?"

Liam steps back from the doorway. "Yes—absolutely, come in."

My body humming with his nearness, I barely resist reaching out to touch him as I walk to the couch and sit.

Liam closes the door and takes a step toward me, then stops. Whatever expression I'm wearing causes him to change direction. He leans against the desk instead. Hands braced tightly on the surface to either side of him, he watches me expectantly.

I lift my chin. "Will you tell me now?"

He nods. "Anything you want to know."

The question that comes out of my mouth first surprises both of us. "How did you find where I hid the diamonds?" Until asking, I hadn't realized how curious I was.

A brow arches. "Burying a lockbox under a porch wasn't exactly original."

Chagrined, I demand, "But how did you figure out my connection with Benny? I never told you about him."

"Trade secrets," he says, smirking.

"Liam!" I bark.

The familiar, joyful rumble of his laughter makes my heart pound hard. I want badly to smile, but maintain my stern expression.

He finally lifts his hands in surrender, laughter lingering in his eyes. "The new phone I gave you before you left L.A. was bugged. I tracked you to Benny's. Wasn't hard to figure out the rest."

My eyes widen. "I knew it!" Feeling vindicated, I lean forward and cross my legs. "Okay, now tell me about Hernandez."

Liam sobers, chest expanding on a sigh. I study him carefully for signs that he's preparing to lie, but I don't find any. For better or worse, whatever's coming is the truth.

"Hernandez tracked me down in Dublin last year. I don't know how, but he put together what happened to the diamonds. He gave me an ultimatum. When the time came, either I did whatever he asked me to, or he would freeze the account and arrest you for the theft. I called bullshit—until he told me about his move to the CIA and named the bank on Cook Islands. And I knew he wasn't bluffing."

I release a slow breath. "And then?"

"He called me when you went missing. Same day as the shooting in your hospital. We improbably found ourselves on the same side—trying to find you and the Donnellys."

"Why didn't he want me to know?"

His eyes soften with apology. "Because six weeks... it's a long time for a person to be victimized. Even after I found you, when you were rehabilitating, he wasn't convinced he could trust you. I told him he could, Eden. I swear it."

I snort in disbelief. "He thought what—that I'd been brainwashed into a bloodthirsty Donnelly?"

"Or had Stockholm syndrome, yes." He says it without judgement.

Though we've never talked explicitly about Chris and the complex feelings he evokes—hatred and sympathy— from the compassion in Liam's eyes, it's clear he can relate. Knowing he has similarly conflicting feelings about his father is both tragic and cathartic.

I'm not alone.

"It's a psychological mindfuck, isn't it?" he murmurs.

I nod, sighing. "I guess I can see where Hernandez was coming from. But why didn't you tell me that day? Was it because he was in the room?"

"No, love," he says softly. "Blame it on the blood loss. I do, sometimes. I couldn't get my head straight. All I knew was that you were walking away from me, and that if I tried, I could stop you. Instead, I pushed you away. A large part of it was I didn't believe I deserved you. I still don't—not really. But I also knew you needed something I couldn't give you."

His gaze flickers over my body, cataloguing every-thing from my relaxed posture to my long, unbound hair and the bold, sultry dress. I hear his words, even if he doesn't speak them—*whatever it was, you found it.*

I drag in a shuddering breath. "Then you came here and waited to see if I'd come back to you."

"Aye," he whispers. "And have you?"

I want more than anything to fall to my knees before him, to surrender in a way I never have before. A way I didn't *understand* before. Resisting the instinct takes every ounce of willpower I possess. Or nearly every ounce, because with the last drops I have left, I stand and square my shoulders.

"It depends."

"On what?" he breathes.

"Whether or not you're still willing to serve."

His eyes widen with surprise, swiftly overtaken by relief. That's all I glimpse before he steps toward me, bows his head, and lowers gracefully to his knees.

"I serve at your pleasure."

The next breath I take crosses the boundary of flesh into spirit. *Does the soul sleep, only to awaken?* Because that's what it feels like is happening—my soul's first breath of life after a long sleep. An expansion of unparalleled warmth and *rightness*.

Tears prick my eyes as I take his face in my hands and guide it upward. In his brilliant eyes, I see us together. Not as we might have hoped, but as we are. And we are perfect.

I stroke my thumbs across his cheekbones. "I wouldn't know the first thing about topping you. Can you imagine me with a whip? I'd probably hurt myself. And you know I can't tie knots to save my life."

I lower to my knees, shifting forward until we're chest to chest. "I like this better, anyway."

Liam's confusion shifts to something infinitely more transparent and precious. His warm, strong hands cover mine. Mirth and love shimmer in his eyes.

"Eden Elizabeth Sumner, did you just make your Dom kneel as a *test?*"

I nod. "Yes, definitely. In case you were wondering, you passed."

His lips twist comically before he releases laughter. "Thank God. I'm not very good at following orders."

My laugh is light—as light as I am.

"Neither am I."

EPILOGUE

LIAM

WHEN I WAS A LAD, my nanna used to tell me about the man she hoped I'd become. Loyal and kind like my grandad. Brave and strong like my great-uncle Cornelius. Intelligent and ambitious like the sons of our neighbor who left home to earn college degrees. Generous and passionate like my mother, though Nanna was adamant that I not listen to the latter instinct until I was much older and wiser.

I've always known the past cannot be changed, but for many years I didn't know I could find peace with it. Nor did I imagine I could ever see myself as the man my nanna wanted me to be.

Not until I met her.

"What are you thinking about?" she asks, her hands sliding over my shoulders to my chest.

"You," I answer, tilting my face to see her upside-down smile. "Come here."

Bare feet round my chair, angled to face the cliffs and the aqua waters beyond. I don't notice the view—not right now—but watch her instead, waiting to see what she'll do. How she will present. It doesn't matter to me which path she chooses, only that the decision is hers.

I love her submission, of course, but not for the reason she thinks. With her, it's always been less about control than how free she allows herself to be in my care. Her trust is the greatest gift I've ever received, one I strive daily to prove myself worthy of.

Eden pauses beside my chair to gaze for a moment at the ocean. She takes a deep breath, then another. I study her profile, noting the faint lines of weariness.

"Tough day, love?"

She glances back at me with a shrug. "Not especially. Some days just hit harder than others. The lack of basic healthcare of so many of the island's residents..." She shakes her head. "It's appalling and frightening. My work here will never be done. But I'm also homesick. I feel guilty, I guess."

"Miss the boys, do you?"

She nods, finally turning to face me. "Don't you?" she asks wistfully.

"At the moment, no. While your parents were running errands today, the heathens decided to take apart the engine of Ben's beloved '64 Mustang."

She gasps in horror. "Oh God. Where was Maria?"

"Out back in the garden. The boys told her they were going to watch a movie." I bite my lip against a smile; to tell the truth, I'm rather proud of my savvy little deviants.

Eden groans. "That poor woman probably wishes she'd never left Los Mochis."

"Unlikely."

Her eyes soften. Getting Maria away from the Solórzano cartel wasn't easy—the best undertakings rarely are. Six years later, though, neither of us regret the dent the transaction left in our joint wealth. Maria is family, as much a grandmother to our boys as Margaret, Elizabeth, and my mother. They're lucky to be so loved. As I am.

Eden's voice brings me back to the present. "Are the boys still alive?"

I chuckle. "Quite. As punishment, Ben is making them put the car back together. Under supervision, of course."

She laughs softly, eyes warm with mingled affection and exasperation. The remains of her troubling day fade from her expression as she focuses on me.

"And how was your day, Mr. Rourke?"

"Productive. Found the missing boy. Turns out he forgot to tell his parents he was taking a fishing trip with some friends."

She smiles in the small, private way that belongs only to me. In that smile, I see the best version of myself.

"Come here, Dr. Rourke," I say firmly.

Her shoulders relax at my tone even as her breath hitches. I wait, not anticipating one behavior or another. She will tell me what she needs, and I'll give it to her. In the meantime, I revel in her indecision.

Two steps to my side. A pointed glance from those magnetic, mystifying eyes of hers. Then a graceful descent to her knees.

"Sir?"

I've been silent too long, lost in the beauty before me. "What do you want, siren? Name it and it's yours."

"You, sir. Only you."

I cup the back of her head, the weight of her hair sliding against my fingers. She wants me to clench and pull the strands, so I don't. It's much more rewarding to watch her squirm.

"In that case, dear wife, I serve at your pleasure. You have exactly thirty seconds to take off your clothes."

THE END

ACKNOWLEDGMENTS

To everyone I pitched this idea to who said, "That sounds horrific and awesome," thanks for the (wincing) support. I hope Eden and Liam won you over as they did me.

My endless gratitude goes to all the amazing bloggers and readers who've supported this release, and special thanks to the incredible M. Robinson for her cheerleading and invaluable guidance. Ena and Amanda at Enticing Journey, you ladies rock my world! To the fabulous Alessandra Torre Inkers group and the wealth of knowledge and camaraderie so freely given by its members.

To my fabulous beta readers, especially Beta Boss Extraordinaire, Steph Poe, and to my fellow writers who walk on the dark side. Thanks for being as twisted as I am!

To my Grammy O'Halloran, who lived and loved like she meant it—with dignity and grace—and gave me my first books on Irish history.

Also, in no particular order:

- Horror movies
- Gardening
- Michael Fassbender (not kidding)
- Coffee
- Galway antics with KG
- Cartoons
- My crews on Insta and Facebook
- Rainy weather
- Google (#realtalk)
- Did I mention caffeine yet?
- All the husbands who do dishes
- Heating pads
- Ewoks
- D + S (more than cake)

STAY CONNECTED

www.lmhalloran.com
lm@lmhalloran.com

ALSO BY L.M. HALLORAN

FORBIDDEN ROMANCE

The Dark Before Light

The Fall Before Flight

The Muse

ROCKSTAR ROMANCE

Breaking Giants

Breaking Silence

Loving Wild (2025)

SMALL TOWN

Room for Us

Time for Us

DARK ROMANTIC SUSPENSE

Double Vision

Perfect Vision

The Golden Hour

Art of Sin *(Illusions Duet #1)*

Sin of Love *(Illusions Duet #2)*

ABOUT THE AUTHOR

When not writing or reading, the author can be found chasing her daughter. Some of her favorite things are puzzles, podcasts, and small dogs that resemble Ewoks.

Home is the Pacific Northwest.

lmhalloran.com

facebook.com/lmhalloran

instagram.com/lm.halloran

tiktok.com/@lmhalloran

pinterest.com/lmhalloranauthor

bookbub.com/authors/l-m-halloran

amazon.com/author/lmhalloran